CRIES IN THE NIGHT

"Valérien!"

It was a thin scream, the cry of a bird, a young voice, frightened.

"Valérien!"

A voice from the yard but from very far away, moving, echoing, almost too high to hear.

Josie was wide awake, her heart thudding. Simon. She ran to his room, switching on lights. He was there, awake, sleepy, puzzled.

Step was up, too, padding along the passage in her slippers.

"Did you hear it?"

"Just outside our window," said Step.

"What did you hear?" asked Josie

"A name," Step said. "Something like Parapet."

"A frightened voice," said Josie. "Terrified."

"Yes. Two terrified children," agreed Step.

"Children from the village," Josie said. "Coming for a dare, then getting lost and frightened."

"Children from the village," Step repeated. "Lost and frightened, indeed. Lost and frightened for a long, long time. What a terrible thing to hear."

SIEGE

DOMINI TAYLOR

HarperPaperbacks
A Division of HarperCollins*Publishers*

HarperPaperbacks *A Division of* HarperCollins*Publishers*
10 East 53rd Street, New York, N.Y. 10022

A hardcover edition of this book was published in 1989 by Harper & Row, Publishers, Inc.

Cover illustration by Earl Keleny

First HarperPaperbacks printing: October 1991

Printed in the United States of America

HarperPaperbacks and colophon are trademarks of HarperCollins*Publishers*

10 9 8 7 6 5 4 3 2 1

ONE

The old lady looked up from the roadside, tilting her head to see the steep yellow grass, the rocks touched to silver by the sun, the irregular profile of the ruined castle. She was wearing a floppy cotton hat, once prettily floral, now stained by decades of gardening, travels, and her husband's watercolor painting (he wiped his brushes on it, if it happened to come to hand). Her arms were freckled from the sun. She wore sensible sandals. Her name was Marjorie Schofield, but from the moment of her second marriage, being a stepmother and step-grandmother, she had been known as Step. Nobody could remember how this started, but once established it was a part of life. Even her husband Giles always called her Step. She was happy with this undignified nickname. Dignity was not important to her. Being given a nickname was being made welcome. She had always disliked the name Marjorie.

Two of her three step-grandchildren stood beside her, looking up at the castle because that was why they were there. Step was keen on castles, these ruins in this part of the South of France. Not Carcassonne—theatrical, overrestored, commercialized—but these little isolated monuments to ancient faith and cruelty. That was what Step said they were. She had a shelf of books about them; but she was careful, as a rule, not to be a bore on the subject.

The children could hear the voices of the rest of the family from the car out of sight round a corner, and the tinkle and bustle of the picnic being spread. There was no other sound—no wind, bird, cowbell, water, or radio. Nothing moved. There was no movement of clouds in the sky, because there were no clouds in that sky. The sun was very hot. Step, fair-skinned and thin-haired, was wise to wear that hat.

Step said, in the special, important voice that people use for quotations: "The grass in the fields was dyed as red as roses."

"What made it red? Flowers?" said Peter Christie, who was used to swaths of poppies in English cornfields. "There are no flowers now."

"There were no flowers then."

"Rust? Minerals?" said Tanja Kemp. "I saw a whole red hillside in Arizona."

"It was blood."

She was going to say more. She was inviting questions.

The children exchanged glances behind her back. Neither made a face at the other. They did not know one another well enough for that; they did not trust one another enough. To each, the other was not only a stranger but a foreigner, of peculiar habits and language, of doubtful neutrality. They did not know if they were on the same side. They were both just twelve years old, almost exactly twins, sharing a sign of the horoscope and nothing else at all. They lived 3,000 miles apart and the distance seemed greater.

"Whose blood, Step?" said Peter at last, because one of them had to say something.

"Old men and young, grandmothers, children, little babies."

"The people who lived here?"

"They sheltered here from the butchers. They were peaceful and honorable."

"Why were they killed?" asked Tanja.

"They called it a Crusade."

"The crusaders went to Palestine," said Peter.

"They went to Palestine, and some of them came back, and some of them came here."

Peter's mother called them to lunch, bought two hours before in the market in Castelnaudary. They sat in the shade of an awning stretched from the back of the minibus. There was a kind of liver sausage, cheese, crispy bread, salad, melons and grapes, mineral water and local rosé from the cold-box. There was much licking of fingers. Tanja's father took some pictures. Step pulled the brim of her hat down over her face, so as not to be photographed, but Simon Kemp tricked her into raising it by pretending to be stung by a wasp.

Simon was seven, half-brother of both Peter and Tanja. They could not agree on the way to eat a melon or pronounce "tomato," but they could agree that Simon was spoiled.

"Gotcha," said Robert Kemp, winding on the film.

"I wish you wouldn't do it," said Step. "Photographs make me look like a shrunken head in a museum. The anthropological section. I always think it's not only boring but discourteous—spreading out people's private lives for inspection by a gawping public. Gawp. What a curious word that is. I wonder what the lepidoptera can be."

"How did we get on to butterflies?" said Giles, her husband.

"I mean etymology."

"Do you remember advertisements for a thing called Pelmanism?" said Giles. "In magazines, before the war?"

Step did. Their frail old cousin Gwen Woodhouse did, though in all her years in West Africa she could have seen few magazines. To the others the subject was as antique as Step's crusaders.

"Do you suffer from a grasshopper mind?" quoted Giles from the advertisements, much in the tone his wife used when quoting the medieval chronicler of Languedoc.

"I do," said Gwen. "Always did."

"I don't," said Step, "and never did, except after too much wine at lunch. Another thing I don't, and never did, is have a nap after lunch, but I'm tempted today."

"I never did either," said Gwen, "because I couldn't, but now I shall."

"I did when I was young," said Giles, "but now daylight's too precious."

"They told me I should," said Robert Kemp, "but I wake up feeling like hell."

Tanja Kemp was helping her stepmother pack away the picnic things.

"We don't need to take these melon skins home, Josie," said Tanja. "They're biodegradable."

"You can't just litter the countryside with them."

"Of course not. Tuck them away out of sight. In a year they'll rot right down. They'll enrich the soil."

"No, we must take them with us."

"Truly, Josie, that's silly. All we get is a smell and a lot of bugs."

It was a battle of wills, a tiny demonstration of the difficulty of being a stepmother, the difficulty compounded by being the English stepmother of an American stepdaughter; by being the gentle and reasonable stepmother of a child with a character already defined, angular, and made of titanium steel.

It was a stupid little thing to make an issue of, but it was doing the child no favor in the long run to be limply acquiescent. Rule: people having picnics must not leave a mess. Rule: twelve-year-olds obey, although they have a right to explanations.

Tanja looked mulish. She was sure that on this point she knew best. She had seen ants teeming over watermelon skins, right there in the trunk of the car.

Josie glanced at her husband, Tanja's father. Rob was a biologist. He ought to know how long it took for melon rind to break down into compost. But he was not going to back her up. He was not going to back anybody up. Since his breakdown he had not taken sides in any argument about anything, because if he did he felt a cold blackness coming at him from the corners of rooms.

Rob sat in the shade of the awning beside old Gwen, whose eyelids were drooping. Rob's eyelids were not drooping. He looked a little less haggard, here in this empty and beautiful place, 3,000 miles away from laboratory, colleagues, stress, overwork, betrayal: but his face still showed tension, muscles too visible, a twitch that came and went, as though there were a continual possibility that he might suddenly scream.

Peter did not intervene either in the disputation about melon skins. A fraught family life and an English boarding school had made him careful about jumping in. He thought his stepsister should have done what she was told, and that his mother should have stood no nonsense, but he was not going to stick his neck out by saying so.

Tan was turning out to be a pain, much as expected, but you had to admit she was a good-looking pain. She was tall for her age, like Peter himself, with short straight hair so blond it was almost white, a golden tan, small nose, curving mouth a little like Twiggy's, blue-gray eyes. It was a pleasure to be seen with her, but not to talk to her. He had nothing in the world to talk to her about; but, since his mother had married her father, he couldn't always walk out of a room when she came into it.

Step Schofield did not intervene in the argument because she did not give a button what they did with bits of melon. There were important things in life, for which energy and concentration must be reserved, and melon skins were not among them. She was not aware of witnessing a diagram of the difficulty of being a stepmother, because for her there was no such difficulty. She, widowed, had married Giles Schofield, a widower, in 1975. She found she had a stepdaughter called Josephine, decorative and talented, herself just married, and she immediately and permanently adored her. She was aware that her love was returned, and that she made Josie laugh. She went off to climb the goat track to the castle. She would illuminate what she had read by what she saw, and she would see with eyes widened by her reading. The steep climb was no problem. She was a tough old thing, active as a spider, made of wire and leather bootlaces.

She knew she was a figure of fun, in her stained and ancient hat and her sensible sandals; but she was nearly seventy, and being a figure of fun was itself more fun than being the sort of old lady she associated with the food halls at Harrods.

Giles himself did not join the argument, although he was prone to joining arguments, because he was entirely preoccupied. He had taken his folding chair and his easel twenty yards up the road, and he was blissfully painting the castle. Cops and robbers could have raced past him, a three-headed monster gibbered, bombs dropped: Giles was busy painting the castle.

Giles was happier with Josie's second husband than with her first. It was a pity Rob had had a crack-up. Giles did not know what that meant or what it felt like or how a fellow got one—he himself had gone through the whole of the war in Africa, Italy, and France, then served in Malaya and Korea and Kenya, and he had been excited often and frightened sometimes, and never the slightest bit loony. Rob of course was a cleverer man than himself, a scientist, an intellectual. No doubt he subjected his brain to much more pressure. He was a *grand prix* car. They were always breaking down. Giles was a battered old Land Rover, a bit hard to start in the morning but good for a few years yet.

Peace and quiet were supposed to be necessary for Rob. They were things Languedoc was full of. That was one reason they were here, the son-in-law's convalescence. Another reason was this new historical bee in Step's bonnet—she was mad to see all these places where the people had a Persian religion. The two came together very nicely when the farm was offered to them. It also meant that Peter could spend the summer with his mother, instead of with his father and the new bitch, and Tanja could spend the summer with her father, instead of her mother and the gigolo, and poor old Gwen could have a treat which would probably be her last.

The place had one serious drawback—the midday sun was so hot that your wash dried the moment you laid it down, and you could never do a sky wet-on-wet.

Josie gestured silence to Tanja: old Gwen Woodhouse was asleep. Tanja nodded and grinned. The stepmother—stepdaughter relationship was perfectly all right when carried on in dumb-show. Josie felt sleepy herself.

She looked round for her sons. Neither was to be seen. It could be assumed that Peter was looking after little Simon—he was very responsible for his age. He was a prefect at his prep school. He was all that his father was not. He might verge on priggishness—Tanja might think so, Step might even think so—but it was a fault on the right side. Meanwhile he was a very good-looking boy. Josie could think that with objectivity, as she really saw him so seldom. She could think so with honesty also because Peter looked so much like his father. Did he have his father's charm? It was not obvious. He was almost painfully typical of his age and background. He was shy and prickly. With luck he would be neither charming nor charmless. Charm worked for a few years, making other effort unnecessary. It was the most destructive of all the gifts of the fairies. A charming man past a certain age became a dog wanting its head stroked. Harry Christie had reached that stage. It was sickening to see. Peter saw it all the time. Perhaps his straightness, his correctness, his priggishness, were a reaction against his father. Presumably Harry lived on handouts with the terrible Angelika von Stumm. Charm in youth had disqualified him from any other career.

Old Gwen Woodhouse, come to think of it, had charm. It was even visible as she slept under the awning, on cushions from the minibus, her face composed of crumpled rose petals. She lived on handouts, too. Of course she did. How else could she live? Probably she had never been aware of her charm. She had used it, unconsciously, in the service of God, and her missionary husband, and their greedy Congolese congregations.

Muzzily meditating on the chemistry of charm, Josie dozed under the awning. Gwen was fast asleep beside her, knocked out by unaccustomed wine. Rob sat motionless but wide awake, alert for black animals in the margins of his skull. Giles, twenty yards away, squeezed raw umber into his sketching palette. Ants arrived in hundreds in the baskets where the melon rinds were. Josie thought she had won that argument, but really the ants had won it.

* * *

Step paused, halfway up the precipitous track to the castle. She was not tired. She wanted to savor the moment. She took off her hat and fanned herself with it, and turned to look out from the hillside, out to the south.

The country was completely new to her, and completely strange. It was not like any country she had ever seen. She had imagined it, in her Somerset armchair, and she had imagined it wrong. The view was breathtaking yet comforting. The valley teemed with ghosts, and they were friends.

Step stood on a southern-jutting spur of the Montagne Noire, which is not one mountain but a range running forty miles east and west. Fifty miles almost due west lay Toulouse, fifty miles almost due east Montpellier. Southeast, not so very far away but hidden by hills, was the Mediterranean, the Golfe du Lion, where Tyrians and Romans and Saracens and Normans had creased the sea with their ships. Thirty miles due south Step could see the gray flanks of the Corbières, the hills which gave their name to millions of bottles of cheap, honest red wine. Between the two ranges of hills lay the enormous valley of the Aude, with the Canal du Midi often close to the river, flanked by ancient plane trees like an avenue in a city with music in its cafés. In all the flat ground at Step's feet the wine was grown, the vineyards stretching south from the hills to the river, south from the river to the hills. Among the vineyards were fields of melons, the plants flat to the ground as though exhausted by the heat. Did the people worry about the skins? Step thought not.

In all the big landscape which Step from her eminence

could see, there were no isolated houses, farms, barns, mills, buildings of any kind. In England and New England and other parts of France, cultivators lived over the shop. Here they lived in villages, packed together for comfort, and went out in the morning to their vines and melons and came back in the evening to the television. One village was partly visible, to the southwest, over the shoulder of a bluff. The colour of the huddle of houses was difficult to define. Old rose? Dusty pink? Like most of the lowland places of Languedoc it was built entirely of brick. The bricks were astonishingly large, so that strangers thought they were quarried stone, and wondered what strange stone it could be and where it had been dug out of the ground. But it was all mud from the river, slapped into cubes, baked by the sun, and dragged by oxen to the places where the people were.

They built castles and cathedrals of the big pink bricks. When, eight and nine hundred years ago they traded with the East, with the Balkans, their aromatic warehouses were made of bricks. Greeks came, Turks, Bulgarians. It was those last who brought the message of Mani from Babylonia, the message which gave this countryside its special magic, its glory and its agony.

Step saw things in strong colors, and described them in strong words. She thought Mani would have done the same.

There was not much known about Mani, but what there was Step knew. Mani, Manus, Manichaeus was born two hundred years after the birth of Christ, of whom he probably never heard. In that time the established Zoroastrian priesthood was probably luxurious and corrupt; it certainly claimed the function of intervening between the individual and God. Mani dreamed a dream and saw a vision: an angel commanded him to preach a new and purified religion. He made many converts. Presently, of course, the priests had him put in prison, and, of course, after twenty-six days he died there.

One might be contemplating events at any period of history, including yesterday.

Mani taught of the simple struggle between good and evil, light and darkness. His teaching spread westward, into the Balkans. It was carried by Balkan merchants into France, at just about the time Duke William the Norman conquered England. The region about the city of Albi became one of the centers, so the Manichaeans were called also the Albigenses. For some reason they were called Cathars, too, but Step had no idea why. They were always called Cathars in Languedoc. It complicated things for Step, when she tried to explain this blazing and amazing triumph of truth to the others—those ancient people that she knew, whose religion she shared, had so many different names meaning exactly the same thing.

Step had not started her studies intending to become a Cathar. It had happened. She believed in the struggle against darkness, and the ultimate responsibility of the individual. That was the teaching that had made the Cathars the most excellent people of Europe, esteemed and trusted by their Christian neighbors; and it had been too clean and clear for Rome, for the corrupt and avaricious Church of the thirteenth century, so by and by they sent their mailed men and their inquisitors and slaughtered the women and children.

It had been real and shocking to Step, even before she

had seen the place, reading her books in Somerset. Now the ghosts of the Cathars shouted from the scorching vineyards and from the stones of the little castle.

Step raised her eyes from the huge vine-planted graveyard to the horizon. Far to the south and to the west was the great chain of the Pyrenees. There were different ghosts there, the vivid memory of Roland at Roncevaux, the echo of his horn calling to Charlemagne . . .

Step heard a horn unlike Roland's, the impertinent soprano of a French car, the toot of a little man going too fast because it was his only glimpse of manhood. The road was a long way off and she would not see the car. The driver would have a limp mustache, and a jacket of synthetic fiber on a hanger in the back of his car. No. Step reproved herself. She put on her hat, turned, and climbed toward the castle.

Peter Christie was not looking after his tiresome little American half-brother. He was looking for him. He had realized that the kid had slipped away. It was when Tan was squabbling about melon skins, Mum was trying to keep her temper, Gwen was more or less zonked, Step was zonked in another way on her medieval carry-ons, Grandpa was painting, and Rob was looking inward or sideway but not outward. Nobody saw Simon go. He had been told not to scramble over the ruins on his own, but that was obviously what he was doing. Peter felt a small shadow of apathy. It was very hot and he was sleepy after a big lunch and he didn't care much about Simon, who seemed more important to Mum than he should have been. Then he heard a referee's whistle of shocked conscience, of concern for his mother's feelings. He dragged himself off the rug on the ground and went to look for Simon. He didn't say anything. He didn't want anybody fussing.

Unlike the single visible village, the castle was built of stone. In the blazing sun it was a kind of tawny silver, with shadows of blue and brown. Step thought: they might have brought this rock down into the valley for their houses, or they might have brought bricks up to the hilltop for the castle, but they had more sense.

Thinking about it, Step was impressed by the sense of the men of ancient Languedoc. They had religion without ritual, faith without flummery, and they built with materials that were to hand.

It had been a pretty small castle, even at its biggest and best. Its best had probably been about AD 1215. Then the yard-thick walls had been irregularly tumbled. Any trace of roof had completely disappeared. The interior was carpeted with a wisp of dry grass, silvery, which crackled underfoot like tissue paper. No water. The people had taken refuge here, the people of the village she had seen and other villages of the neighborhood—had come for safety from the "crusaders," other Frenchmen, levies of the nobles of the north jealous of the gaiety and grace of the princes of Provence, greedy for conquest, who had convinced themselves that they were fighting the battles of Christ. Christ was an angel of light. Mani knew that. All the Manichaeans knew it, the Albigenses, the Cathars. The destruction of these people was the work of Satan, butchery, genocide, neither more nor less so than the gas chambers of Buchenwald.

The "crusaders" did not storm a castle like this. It was solid, it crowned a hilltop, it was defended by men of passionate conviction; it was impregnable to direct assault before the days of gunpowder. The invaders sat round it. The people at last went mad from thirst, and the children began to die. The people came out, down the hillside, surrendering, trusting to the mercy of men who fought under the cross. And then the grass in the fields was dyed as red as roses.

Step pictured the siege, the mothers of babies, growing despair under the implacable sun, the glare of the sun on the breastplates and swords at the foot of the hill, on the red-cross banners of the "crusaders." And the crime of the people was to lead simple and honorable lives, to battle with the forces of darkness each in his own soul, to reject the spiritual authority of a fat, corrupt bishop in a distant palace.

All about Step, on the silvery grass within the castle, mothers and babies waited, hollow-eyed, dust in their hair, waited until their blood dyed the grass in the fields below.

Simon Kemp knew he was being disobedient. He knew also that Dad was too sick and Mom too gentle to punish him. Tan might give him a belt, maybe Peter. The thing was to stay clear of them. It was a stupid rule they made anyway. He could walk along the top of a wall. It made no difference if the wall was a foot high or a hundred feet high, your feet went one in front of the other just the same. What was he supposed to do, sit like a dummy with a lot of grown-ups asleep? What was the point of coming all the way to Europe if you just sat around in the shade? What was the point of coming to this castle if you didn't take a look at it?

Feeling only slightly wicked, Simon climbed the hill toward the castle.

Tanja Kemp saw from the corner of her eye that Peter had slipped away. She saw that Simon was not there either. They had gone off to climb around in the castle. Tanja tried to feel indifferent, superior. She failed. The boys had gone off, having fun, while she did the chores, cleaning up after them. That was how it had always been, a sexist racket, a conspiracy. She didn't *mind* helping Josie, but it was not fair that she always did and the boys never did.

Anyway the stuff was packed away, melon rinds and all.

Where was Step? It was funny that she herself had a stepmother and her stepmother had a stepmother. They all got along pretty well. You couldn't fail to get along with Step, even though she tried to force-feed you with information. There were a lot of tangles in the families of a lot of the kids Tanja knew, and she thought her own tangles were pretty easy to handle, except maybe for Peter, who was already the kind of Limey they made jokes about. Step-Grandpa Giles was, too, but they were different jokes. Giles was nice, but his paintings were terrible. Josie was a much better artist. Josie should make time to paint. Josie gave herself to Simon and Dad, and on this trip to Grandpa Giles and Step and Gwen and Peter, and the farm and keeping house and all, and really she should keep some of herself back, realize her potential. She needed to be a little more feminist. Not a militant, a butch, a bra-burner, but not a doormat either. Men had it too easy with women like Josie around. No way was Tanja going to live that kind of a life. She put a value on herself, even if Peter didn't.

She wondered again what the boys were doing. She was jealous of the fun they were having together.

She looked round at the others to see if she was wanted, needed, if anything was expected of her. They were fine, except Dad, who was fighting enemies in his head that none of the rest of them could see. She felt a surge of concern and love, like a flatiron turning over in her belly. There was nothing she could do. Anything that needed to be done Josie did. That was best. It was no good feeling excluded.

Feeling excluded, curious about what the boys were doing, Tanja walked away from the minibus to the sudden steep slope of the hill.

As to what happened next, they all had different accounts.

Step admitted that she had been preoccupied. She ought to have been bearing in mind that there were young children in the group, that children scramble, that the walls of the castle were dangerous, that parts of the hillside were virtually cliff. Because of all these things she should have been keeping an eye out. But they knew her—an old crank with a new hobby. This was the very first Cathar castle she had actually set foot inside, of all the little strongholds, all over Languedoc, reduced in the Albigensian Crusade. She was more excited than the rest of them could understand. Oh, they could understand? Yes, she had talked a bit about it. Well, even so, she was full of contrition. She should have been alert and she was indulging her fancy. The first she knew that anything was wrong was a commotion halfway down the hill, out of her sight, fifty feet below the walls of the castle, screams, stones falling, awful. She climbed a bit of the tumbled wall to see what was going on. She couldn't really see. There were rocks in the way, and the glare of the sun was dazzling. She saw there were people in a heap on the hillside, by the goattrack. They seemed to be children; they seemed not to be dead. By the time she got down there, they were at the bottom. And everybody seemed to be in one piece. Really the whole thing had passed her by. Guilty as she felt, it was probably just as well. Silly old ladies with historical hobbies should be kept well away from accidents.

Peter's story was that he was halfway up the track, on a steep part, looking for Simon, hoping that Simon was not already risking his neck on the ruins above. There was a rattle of loose stones above him, and he was frightened for a moment of a landslip, rockfall, avalanche. The ground was steep enough for that. A few little stones came down harmlessly, and then a body, over a spur and skidding down the cliff. It was Simon, screaming, helpless, falling. Simon had lost his footing, taken a stupid risk, done exactly what he had been told not to do. Peter managed to catch him, grab him as he rushed by, but in doing so he lost his own footing and they skidded a few yards downhill together. Did they know how slippery the grass was, so dry, on the steep part of the hill? It was hard to stop once you started. Peter was angry because he had been frightened. The whole thing was Simon's fault, for being cocky, for thinking that he knew better, for risking other people's necks as well as his own. No, Peter wanted no particular credit for saving Simon's life. He just grabbed at him without thinking. Anybody would have done the same. Simon might not have been killed anyway, just mashed up, a few bones broken. When they did manage to stop sliding, they ran into Tan, or she into them. Probably she helped stop them. The important thing now was not what he did, it was that Simon should learn his lesson.

Tanja's account was confused, reluctant, surprisingly so from a child so strong-viewed, decisive, communicative. She had been quite a long way below, climbing the track, unable to see anything above because of overhanging rocks. There was a noise. Screams, and stones falling. She climbed up in a hurry, guessing the boys were on the hill, guessing Step might be there and in trouble. They were sliding. She stopped them. Maybe they were stopping anyway, as the slope flattened. No harm was done.

There was more to Tanja's story. She said that was it, that was all that she could tell. But there was more. This was obvious to Josie and to Rob, who knew her: perhaps not to the others, who hardly knew her at all. She would not come right out with it, even in private, even to her father. But she gave, to him, enough of a hint. She thought Peter was trying to push Simon down the cliff.

Why would he do that? It didn't take a psychologist to guess. There was no corroboration whatsoever for Peter's story.

There was no corroboration for Tanja's story. She might have been much farther up the hillside.

Simon himself said he knew exactly what had happened. He was passionately certain. He had *not* been taking any stupid risks. He had *not* been doing anything dangerous. He was being *very* careful. He was a pretty good climber anyway. He was going slow and careful and paying attention to what he did. There was no need to scream at him. It wasn't his fault. *It wasn't his fault.* He was pushed.

Impossible. A stupid lie, to get out of trouble. Who could have pushed him? There wasn't anybody there to push him. People don't push little boys down cliffs. Tell the truth, Simon.

It's true, it's true, cross my heart. *I was pushed.*

Simon got himself into this corner and he wouldn't come out of it. All the grown-ups knew it happened with children—adults too, sometimes. They got themselves into positions they could not retreat from without admitting lying, without looking fools, so they repeated and repeated the lie, and insisted and insisted it was true, and probably started to believe it.

Simon could show them the exact place where he was pushed. But none of them was going to climb all that way to have a stupid lie repeated to them.

Simon cried gustily all the way back to the farm, which was irritating and upsetting for the rest of them. It was because he had been frightened; because his knees and elbows and back had been grazed, not very terribly but enough to be sore; because they all kept saying he was telling lies. He insisted between sobs that he was telling the truth.

They said he was lying because he knew he had been naughty and silly, that he was going on lying so as not to admit he had been lying. *Pushed?* Of course he hadn't been pushed. He was betrayed and unsafe, because he was disbelieved. He was a rebel. Crying was his only demo.

Rob Kemp drove back the twenty-five miles to the farm. He was safe to do that. He was probably not ready for heavy traffic in a city, for that kind of pressure, the decisions, the impatience of other drivers; but these roads were empty.

The farm was called Montferaude. The nearest village, not very near, was Montferaude-St-Antonin. Step had discovered the place back in the spring; it was advertised in the classified section of a travel supplement of one of the Sunday papers. Giles remembered the whole process with horrid clarity, as they hummed back in the minibus. The farm belonged to an English family who were usually there all summer but were spending that summer in Australia. Step went to London to meet the people, coming back exhausted off the train with all kinds of typed details, references, photographs and a large-scale sketch-map. She was excited.

Step had always been hooked on corners of history. Not for her the grand sweep of Macaulay or Toynbee, but funny old books with marbled endpapers, by Victorian parsons about their parishes. *The History and Antiquities of Lesser Sleepycote*—that had been her line, by all accounts, long before Giles had met her. She became expert on aspects of history that nobody else was interested in, that nobody else had heard of. This was, perhaps, their charm. Nobody could put her right.

Step was an enthusiast.

She enthused about gardens, flower arrangement, earthenware, folk art. Report said that she had, at one stage of her first marriage, a spinning wheel and a loom and a sinister shelf of homemade vegetable dyes. It was surprising that she did not still have these things. Then somebody dangled in front of her the juicy bait of comparative religion. She became a student of heresies. She saw them as heroisms, the bucking of establishments. She became a student of isms without number, sects little and large, the stuff of footnotes. It was all fine by Giles. It sometimes made dinner late, but his painting often made him late for dinner anyway.

The Cathars were Step's latest and greatest hobby. It had all happened in the most ordinary way. Somerset neighbors had been asked to join a couple who had chartered a barge on the Canal du Midi: a superior barge, skipper and cook, no self-catering nonsense. A great deal of photography went on. Step sat through the results more patiently than Giles. The barge's cook was a middle-aged woman from Cumbria who had lived in Languedoc for ten years. She had absorbed the local tradition of the Cathars. Like many others before, she had become hooked on the Cathars, through whose country the barge majestically swam. The Cathar story was, indeed, of commercial merit, being part of the tourist interest of the area. Hearing the story was part of the package the passengers had bought. The passengers, on return, told their friends, even as they passed round the photographs. The seeds fell mostly on stony ground, but not with Step. The Cathars were just what she liked. That was years ago. She was still as hipped as ever on the Cathars. No other intellectual interest of hers had lasted half so long. She knew this and explained it. She said this was more than a study, a hobby. She was a convert. She was a Manichaean. She still went to church in Somerset, but she no longer took communion. She said that the doctrine of transubstantiation was superstitious gobbledygook. She said so even to the vicar. She said that bread was bread, and it was fine to eat a chunk of it as part of a ritual of fellowship and thanksgiving, but that bread should magically become the actual body of Christ . . . What Mani had brought to the subject was simple common sense, Step said, and Giles admitted that she made it damned convincing.

Reading all she could lay her hands on, Step naturally wanted to go to the country of the Cathars, Albi, Toulouse, Narbonne, ancient Languedoc between Provence and Gascony. The barge would have done, but it was too expensive. A hotel and a hired car would have done, but for more than a very few days they were too expensive, too. Josie's new husband was rich, though an academic and a scientist, but they lived in America. There was nobody else Giles and Step could sponge off. Giles had his Major-General's pension, but their life in Somerset took every penny of that.

Then came, in the same week, Step's discovery of the farmhouse to let at a nominal rent, and news of Rob Kemp's breakdown. The telephone bills for the following weeks were awful—Giles and Step to Josie and Rob, Josie to Peter, Josie to her first husband, Peter's father, Josie to Rob's first wife, Tanja's mother, Step to Peter's housemaster at boarding school, Peter to his father and stepmother, Tan to her mother and stepfather, what were all their plans for the summer, who'd bring whom where, what dates, what clothes, how much French currency, how do we hire a big enough car, is the water safe to drink . . . ?

Giles distanced himself from the appalling logistics. He had always had a talent for delegation (one reason for his success as a soldier; one reason, perhaps, why he had not had greater success) and he spent all spring at his easel.

Step brought to the whole hassle the enthusiasm she brought to everything. It was a great awful jigsaw of timetables and feelings and hurt pride, and Step battled with it without counting the cost in telephone calls.

The inclusion of old Gwen Woodhouse had been a last-minute idea and a good one. They gave her six months to live. She was no longer in pain, thanks to a faith healer in Wimbledon. As the widow of a missionary, she was completely penniless. Giles was her only living relative of her own generation, except his sister, who had lived abroad ever since the war, and her husband had had no family at all. In a quiet way Gwen was pretty good company. She was useful, too. After a lifetime in West Africa she spoke fluent French, while the rest of them struggled at a schoolroom level. There was plenty of room for her at the farm and in the minibus. She took up less room than Simon, and made less noise.

Peter and Tanja could agree about Simon, and they could agree about Gwen. You could not disagree about Gwen. She was the most completely admirable, completely lovable person either of them had ever met. You could not imagine her being mean, small-minded, jealous, spiteful, even for a second, under any provocation. She had given her life to other people not because she had decided to, but because that was the sort of person she was. She was pretty frail. She was built like a small bird, like a figure made of twigs and wisps of grass, light as thistledown. Probably in all those years on the equator she had had every kind of fever, drunk polluted water, eaten miserable food. Looking at Gwen made you ashamed of yourself and of the whole human race.

Though a firm, practicing, middle-of-the-road member of the Church of England, Gwen was not shocked by Step's antique heresy. She had lived for forty years among darker faiths, animism and devil worship, and in the midst of unthinkable cruelty. She smiled tolerantly when Step denied the doctrine of the Redemption, when she said that Moses and John the Baptist were false prophets, when she talked about light and darkness as though God had made the one and not the other. Gwen's smile said: What a surprise you're going to get! She never laughed at Step, but she made Step laugh at herself.

They bypassed the village, then turned up the track to the farm. It was a steep climb, the track corkscrewing, banks hiding the view. Then they pulled into the paved yard with buildings on three sides.

The origins of the place were immemorial. A building had stood there long before the Romans came. Generations had taken stone from stone, and put them back a little differently, so that the buildings grew, shrank, changed, to meet the different needs of fathers and sons, and greedy widows, and vulnerable heiresses. Of any bit of wall or paving it was impossible to say, "That is a thousand years old, that only a hundred." Some old parts looked new because they had been restored and repointed, like the citadel of Carcassonne or the Palace of the Popes at Avignon; some new parts looked old because fires had been lit in front of them.

It was on a hilltop so that it could be defended. It had been defended, perhaps, by the Cathars against the crusaders, perhaps part of it then knocked down and afterwards built up differently. Even Step could only guess about that. It was all built of stone, because it was on a hill where there were plenty of stones.

One end of the main house was a dovecote, a stone tower of a height and massiveness ridiculously disproportionate to the housing of a handful of birds. Below the dovecote itself were storerooms, the walls slotted for beams from which all manner of produce would have hung. There had been smoked hams, great cheeses, strings of onions and garlic, firewood stacked, crocks of olives and sacks of dried beans on shelves long crumbled, and in the cellars skins of wine before the world ever invented barrels.

The house itself had a big stone-flagged kitchen and one other big ground-floor room. They could all sit comfortably round the kitchen table. They could all sit in the other room, but not comfortably. Beyond the kitchen were extensive larders, pantries, sculleries, and little stone-flagged cells for brooms and boots. There were bedrooms above, and an attic which was a warren of little rooms. It was a place for a tribe rather than a family.

The owners had furnished it locally. There was nothing from Peter Jones. Most of the tables and chairs and overpowering dressers looked as though they had come with the house when it changed hands in 1960.

Other tribes, or the vassals of the tribe, could have

been piled in their scores in the barns. There had once been sheep and goats and a few cows, perhaps oxen, buffalo, horses. Now there were a broken-down tractor, two carts with no means of pulling them, a ping-pong table and improvised badminton, many cobwebs.

Electricity came up the hill on the west side; it went into a shed with a locked door and a warning sign, and out of the shed on wires all over the farm. There was a telephone. Water was pumped up the hill electrically, and stored in a tank behind the barn. Another pump took it up to a cistern in the attic. The owners had warned them about the water: "You don't need to ration it, exactly, but don't leave taps running."

There was no air-conditioning, pool, tennis court, Jacuzzi, fitted bar. There was a television set which produced only snowstorms and a sound of tearing paper.

There was no view from the downstairs windows—only the yard, the farm buildings, and a solid windbreak of cypresses. But from the attics the views were gigantic—the thirty miles of vines and melons, and the distant humps of the Corbières.

There was no garden, no attempt at a garden. It was possible and pleasant to sit on the stones of the yard, and there was rudimentary furniture for doing so. There were geraniums in terracotta tubs. Scanty grazing and vineyards long abandoned surrounding the buildings, flat for a little to the north, then falling away, falling away immediately on all the other sides. The people who lived here had gone downhill to make their livings.

The flat piece to the north was an irregular wedge of about an acre. The thin grass was punctuated by rocks which had the appearance of alienated masonry. Some of it might have been a ruin. The rock itself could have been dated by a geologist, but as to any use it had been put to, the whens and hows were unguessable.

Simon's very first words, the very first time he set foot in the house, were, "This place is spooky." Before Josie had time to disagree, or Step to agree, he said, "What am I gonna *do* all day?"

There turned out to be no easy answer to that one.

Simon was meeting Step for the first time, though Tanja had met her on an earlier trip. It was obvious that he found her very strange indeed. Gwen Woodhouse was normal, even in Simon's experience, a little old lady like lots of others in any New England town. There was nothing normal about Step. Her hats were crazy, her shoes, what they all called her. Even her religion was crazy.

He said so. It was not rude. The others said so, too. He had learned at once that you could say anything to Step, though not to Grandpa and certainly not Peter or Tan.

But this time, when he said Mani-whosis was crazy, Step told him not to say that too loud, too often, in this place. She said that would be a foolish thing to do, a risky thing.

He could not tell if she was joking or not.

TWO

Simon's unimportant injuries were bathed with disinfectant. Band-Aids were put on one knee and one elbow, although he thought he should have had more and larger dressing owing to the gravity of his wounds.

When it was time for his supper, he was still insisting that he had been pushed. Repetition had made him word-perfect in his story. Somebody he never saw reached out from behind a rock and pushed him. There was now no chance of his admitting that he had slipped and fallen. He might do so when he was thirty. Josie was cross that he persisted in a blatant lie. She was on the point of sending him to bed without supper. Surprisingly, Step intervened. By making faces at Josie, she indicated that Simon was a very young and energetic child, and must have food. Josie relented.

In her annoyance and embarrassment, and in her relenting, Josie was reliving the past, previous motherhood, the experience of looking after a young boy. That had been more difficult, because her first marriage was then long dead. It did not survive the arrival of Peter. Harry Christie had refused to be a father, although it seemed he liked being one now.

Floodgates of memory were opened by Band-Aid, the smell of disinfectant, the sound of a young boy lapping soup, the dry white wine on the table between her elbows.

Josie Schofield was born in 1953, her father then a major commanding a company of his regiment in Germany. All during her childhood her mother was fluttering and her father preoccupied. Though an only child she was not lonely. There were a lot of army children in Germany, then local children in England. She was reasonably happy at school, though not an academic success. She made friends. She knew from an early age—too early, perhaps—that she was attractive, pretty and fun, that she was admired and envied. She was not otherwise outstanding in any way, except in art class. There she was praised and encouraged. It became evident later that she had inherited this enthusiasm from her father, although at the time he had not yet taken up the brush himself.

She got into a provincial art school and then, at twenty-one, into a major school in London. That was the beginning of adult life—pubs, discos, shared and overcrowded flats, foreign films, all-night conversations, cheap wine, hamburgers, many Gauloises and a few joints, CND meetings, anti-apartheid rallies, Matisse reproductions, ethnic dinners eaten on cushions on the floor . . . it was all wild and exhausting: all, in retrospect, childish and harmless.

Harry Christie sailed into her life from distant seas, from a world that seemed more like her parents'. He was a merchant banker in a pin-striped suit, ten years older than herself. They met on middle ground, at a private view to which they had both been taken. But he was far from the stereotype her art-school friends derided. He drove an old banger, for example, with collapsed cushions and squeaking brakes; he said that in London any car got sideswiped everywhere you parked it, so you might as well start off with plenty of dents; he said that anyway the car as status symbol was middle-class mindlessness. He himself declared himself upper-class. He toiled not, neither did he spin. He was not after all exactly a merchant banker, but he came from a family once bankers. He thus permitted himself eccentricities which for middle-management-on-the-way-up would have been dangerously frivolous. He had a flat in a converted warehouse in a seedy part of Peckham, to which no business associate could have been invited. He had beautiful clothes and manners and buttonholes. On his hair there was stuff with a beautiful smell. He was funny and sophisticated. He mocked the students' gods, without revealing the faces of his own.

Only later, too late, did Josie realise that Harry's only god was himself.

He gave her dinner, he gave her clothes, he took her to the opera and to Annabel's. He made her feel that she had outgrown her friends.

He praised her work. There were some drawings he

wanted to buy. She gave them to him, proud that he wanted them. He had them framed. He stored them until he had somewhere where they could worthily be hung. Only later did she learn that he sold them.

He was regarded with suspicion by Josie's contemporaries, until one by one he charmed them off their perches and they crouched in adoration at his feet.

Josie was not completely conquered until the death of her mother. That was an accident of an appallingly frequent kind.

Josie's father had just retired. They were house-hunting. They took a rented house as a base, a place conveniently central to the area where they wanted to live, though itself isolated. Josie was in London and her father in Scotland. The mother was alone in a house strange to her. It was a winter evening, not late but already dark. There was a power failure. At least, the police and the coroner agreed that there might have been. She fell downstairs. She died quite quickly, alone in the dark at the foot of the stairs.

Of all Josie's friends, Harry Christie was the best, the greatest help, the most comfort. She was conquered.

Josie's father wanted to know more about Harry than Josie knew. He asked Harry to lunch at the In and Out. They had a long, long talk, until teatime. They had tea. Giles was retired—he could spend his afternoons as he liked: but it was odd that Harry had no office to go to. They both reported the conversation to Josie. Harry said that he had answered six million questions, and laid bare his soul and his bank balance. Giles said that he had the sense at the time of hearing everything, and the sense afterward of having heard nothing. He had been beguiled. It made him feel alarmed and annoyed. Nobody under his command could ever have got away with it. He thought Josie was beguiled, too.

She was. They were married quietly, because Josie was still mourning and her father was still alarmed. They had a honeymoon in the Andaman Islands. Harry had some kind of job there, selling property or broking yachts on commission. There in romantic circumstances Peter was conceived.

Harry got a flat in Notting Hill from a friend of a friend, and a more respectable car, from a friend of another friend. Their life was glamorous but not expensive. Harry was asked out a great deal, and now of course Josie was asked with him. They hardly ever dined in the flat; they never spent a weekend in London. Harry was a kind of mascot in tremendously comfortable houses all over Surrey. He mixed martinis and played backgammon, and Josie worked hard at not feeling left out. All the people were much older than herself, most much older than Harry.

Angelika was older, but only a little, perhaps thirty-five. She was at a few of the parties, the very grandest. Coming on from Deauville or Davos, she went to the houses with indoor Olympic pools, helicopter pads, private cinemas. She was four inches taller than Josie, with marvelous legs and figure, a thin face with startling wide eyes of the palest blue, a mane of lion-colored hair. She was kind to Josie. Harry beat her at backgammon and made her a Bloody Mary. He did not afterward mention her.

It was at this stage that Josie's father married Marjorie Holland, a widow of his own age. It seemed he had known her for a year. It came as a complete surprise to Josie. It came as a shock. It was too soon after Josie's mother's death. People remarked on that. But people said that he was a man who needed to be married, needed companionship, needed somebody to look after and somebody to look after him. The very fact that he wanted to get married was a compliment to Josie's mother: that was what people said, to comfort Josie. They did not say, but Josie thought they thought, that Giles had made an odd choice.

In the months that followed, Josie continued to be surprised when she thought about it, but she increasingly forgot to think about it. Marjorie became Step, and part of the landscape, as, to the Londoners of a century ago, the Albert Memorial must gradually have lost its power to astonish.

If Josie was surprised by Step, it seemed that Step was also surprised by Josie.

"I was told about a daughter," said Step to Josie at their very first meeting, "but nobody told me about a raving beauty with artistic genius."

This was ridiculous, but it was certainly endearing. It seemed to be sincere, and to remain so.

Harry didn't seem pleased about Giles's new marriage. Josie couldn't see that it was any of his business. Harry and his father-in-law had not become close. Josie thought they avoided one another. It was a cloud in a sky in which there were shortly to be a great many clouds.

Josie thought Harry would be pleased about the baby. But his face went stiff with anger. She had seen him angry with a waiter, and with a man who accused him, as a joke, of buying secondhand suits from Moss Bros, but never with herself.

She realized that, in the moment of conception, she had threatened Harry with prison. He would be shackled by responsibility, emotional and financial. His free-wheeling life would be impossible.

Nappies. The noise of crying in the night. Taking a carry-cot to dinner parties, and leaving before midnight. A larger flat? The wages of a nanny? School bills? A nine-to-five job? Who would give him a job?

He said, "I naturally assumed you were taking precautions."

"Why?" she said. "It's not unusual for married couples to have children. A lot of people even want them."

"I suppose you can get rid of it. I'll find out who you can go to."

"I'm not getting rid of it."

"Then you're getting rid of me. Is that what you want?"

"Do I have to choose?"

She did have to choose.

Probably Harry would have gone anyway, sooner rather than later, to join the dizzy circuit of Angelika von Stumm. Josie was a pretty girl but not an international stunner. She was respectably connected, but not related to half the royal houses of Europe. She was not a regular tenant of the gossip columns. She was not glamorous enough for Harry.

The surprise was that Harry was glamorous enough for Angelika. Presumably she fell in love with him. Presumably she continued to love him—they were still together after twelve years. They were often abroad. Angelika used kinship to shoehorn herself into houses all over the place, and Harry went along as her consort. That was how it struck Josie, from what people who saw them reported.

No doubt Harry was still making himself useful with cocktail shakers and card tables.

Angelika was kind to Peter. There was that to be said about her. Peter got on perfectly well with both of them, and they had given him some exciting holidays. Heaven knew how they had paid for them. Josie knew she ought to be thankful for that, grateful, but it was not easy to feel grateful to people who had behaved with such monstrous selfishness.

Step and Josie's father had found a house in Somerset, with a gardener's cottage but without a gardener. Josie moved into the cottage, for the weeks before and the months after Peter was born. Then she moved back to London, found a flat and a girl to look after the baby in the daytime, and got a job in the art department of a downmarket women's magazine. She could go out in the evening only occasionally, owing to the cost of babysitters. She could go away for weekends only to houses where babies were welcome. It was a very different life from her various previous lives.

She passed her twenty-fifth birthday. Harry had escaped imprisonment, but she was imprisoned.

When Peter was four she took him on a holiday to Brittany, the first time she had been abroad since her honeymoon. It was Step's idea, and they paid for it. It was not expensive. There were wonderful beaches, and a lot of families with young children. Josie bathed and sunbathed and dozed and read *Barnaby Rudge*. Peter ran shouting with other little boys, kicking footballs in the edge of the sea.

She did not at once think, when they met the Americans on the beach, that her life was about to take another large turning.

There were just the two of them—the serious, anxious father of about thirty, and the very blonde daughter of Peter's age. The children opened the door to conversation, as was normal on holiday beaches all over the world; they provided the subject for conversation, all the early conversations. It was a relief to Josie to chat in English, after efforts in French which she had not had a chance to attempt since schooldays.

It began to be a routine that they spread their towels beside one another. Each could then keep an eye on the other's child, relieving them, one at a time, from unremitting watchfulness. Robert Kemp brought lemon squash for the children, and chilled Muscadet.

The Kemps were staying at a different hotel, more expensive, the most expensive. He had hired a big car. They went on picnics.

Droplets of information accumulated, as though from a pot still. Rob Kemp was not secretive, but he was too modest to imagine his life of interest to a stranger.

He was a scientist. He taught and researched at a New England university. He was in Europe attending a conference. They had been in Amsterdam. He had brought his daughter to see the country of her ancestors, to meet some of her mother's kin. He had extended his stay by this week. If alone, he might have gone to Tuscany or Venice, but this beach was right for the child.

She had a Dutch name because her mother was Dutch.

You could maybe see that from her coloring. Her mother now lived mostly in the Virgin Islands. They had a yacht, a charter yacht. They lived on that. They took parties on cruises in the Caribbean. She preferred that to being the wife of an assistant professor in a small university town.

Josie was aware of telling Robert, in return, a certain amount about herself—her childhood, her father, Step, Harry, Harry and Angelika. He wanted more, much more, but really there was very little to tell. She was afraid of boring him. She was afraid that his questions were make-talk, good manners, not serious curiosity. She did bore Tanja, who interrupted the conversation and dragged her father along the beach to buy an ice cream.

Peter immediately trusted and respected Rob Kemp. How sure a guide was the instinct of a four-year-old? Little Tanja Kemp resented their inclusion in the party. She wanted her father to herself. She interrupted conversations between Josie and her father, and dragged him away to see things or buy things. How sure a guide were the instincts of that four-year-old? How much attention would the father pay to it?

The Kemps were due to go back, while Josie and Peter had another week at their little hotel. They appeared on the beach, after Josie had thought that they had all said good-bye. He had called America in the early evening, at a time to catch his mother midmorning when she was pretty sure to be home. The hotel was fixing new reservations on the PanAm flight from Paris. They were staying another week.

Josie was astonished at the joy she felt.

Rob Kemp was a thin man with a thin face, with mouse-colored hair and gray eyes. He was a calm man, a quiet man, but after a week Josie saw that his calm was not intrinsic but imposed: he disciplined himself to be bland, to take things as they came. Underneath the academic cool she thought she glimpsed a volcano. She liked the cool, and she liked the volcano.

She was twenty-six: young enough to be an attractive girl in a swimsuit, to wear a bikini, to go proudly topless if she had cared to; old enough to be her own mistress, custodian of herself, to give or withhold herself exactly as she chose.

She knew Rob Kemp wanted her. She knew that she excited him physically and pleased him personally, and that he was lonely.

She was ready to give herself to Rob. She was herself almost frighteningly excited at the thought of doing so. He was thin, wiry, muscled, full of electricity. She imagined her excitement was as visible to him as his to her. She knew that if they had an affair, if it was successful, if they were as compatible in bed as in conversation, then she would find herself deep in love with him. That might be a good thing or a disaster. She was prepared to take the risk, any risk. She was twenty-six and divorced. Ironically, it was impossible to arrange. They both shared hotel rooms with their children. They could get away for evenings together, hotel maids acting as sitters, but only with distasteful blatancy could they take another room in another hotel. Rob recoiled from that, and from improvisations on towels on a beach at midnight. He was fastidious, more on her account than on his own. She would have subjected herself to rolling on a towel under the sky, but he would not subject her to it. He put a high value on her, higher and higher.

Josie was sure that Tanja needed her, somebody like her, although Tanja was sure she needed nobody except her father.

They all had to go home. Rob took Josie and Peter to the ferry at St. Malo. Their farewells were scrappy and public.

Josie went back to work and Peter to his nursery school.

Rob telephoned. It was Josie's first experience of a transatlantic call. Extraordinarily, it was like any other call, except that for her it was ten in the evening and for him five in the afternoon.

He still had some days of vacation. He was leaving Tanja with his mother and flying to London. Was that a good idea?

But the expense!

He was not worried about the expense. She was not to worry about it.

Rob was either wildly in love with her, or had inherited a lot of money, or both.

The affair was shyly consummated in his room at the Hilton. He asked her to marry him that night, and bought a ring in the morning. They drove to Somerset in a hired Jaguar, taking Peter, in time to have lunch with Step and Josie's father.

Rob told Giles what Harry Christie had not told Giles, what Rob himself had not told Josie because he was afraid of seeming to sell himself. Rob's father was also an academic, a retired teacher of English, author of a few books of importance to a few people. His mother was the only child of a corporation lawyer who had made a serious fortune in the boom of the twenties, and kept it through the crash and the depression. Rob's father was the richest retired professor in New England. Rob was the richest assistant professor of biology in New England. Rob produced these facts apologetically to Giles, over thin drinks in the garden.

Giles had the lovely sense that some of his problems were being solved for him.

"But will you live in America?" said Step. "Will Peter be a horrid little American? Oh, Robert, I'm sorry. I'm only going by the television."

Rob laughed.

"I'd live in Timbuctu," said Josie.

She had known that if she went to bed with Rob her doom was sealed. She had. It was. There was nothing sad about any of it, except the Atlantic Ocean.

Peter, overhearing, misunderstood. He burst into tears, because he knew that in Timbuctu little white boys were boiled in pots and eaten.

"I've been spending the day on a different planet," said Rob to Josie on the way back to London.

Peter was asleep in the back. If they spoke quietly they could talk.

"I hope you like our planet," said Josie.

"I never actually met anybody like your father before, but of course I read about him. He's in Trollope. He's in every Trollope. He's in Kipling and P. G. Wodehouse and Somerset Maugham. He's unfamiliar to my experience, but perfectly recognizable. I don't have any difficulty believing he exists. But your stepmother? She has no known referrent. She's not like anybody I ever heard of."

"She did come as a surprise," said Josie.

"If it's not an impertinent question, what in the world brought them together?"

"Attraction of opposites."

"I never believed in that, except as a temporary extravagance. Witness my first marriage. Witness yours."

"Well, it works with Daddy and Step."

"I guess it must do."

Josie crossed the Atlantic, and joined a little closed society of campus wives. She joined many other things, too—art club, drama group, garden club. She looked after other young children; other young wives looked after Peter. With Tanja she made not so much peace as a truce. Tanja spent vacations mostly with her mother, living on board *Esmerelda* at St. Croix or Antigua or Mustique. She came home tanned and reluctant, full of the glamour of the Caribbean—millionaire charter-parties, water-skiing, candlelit diners on deck. Peter had nothing like that—no other life. Harry and Angelika were preoccupied, or bored, or broke.

In the society of that campus, Josie was eccentric both in being English and in being rich. There were advantages and disadvantages to both oddities. On balance, the advantage of being rich outweighed the disadvantage of being foreign.

Rob worked too hard, though he did not have to work at all. (Harry had to work, but did not.) He was concerned with microorganisms, and with bright students who merited extra time, and dull students who needed extra time. There were half-defined jealousies and rivalries, sometimes reaching and affecting the wives she saw in the shopping mall.

Simon was conceived in love and born in luxury.

This event, though irrelevant to him, was circuitously reported to Harry Christie. It worked a strange change in him. Perhaps Angelika worked the change. He suddenly began, after all those years, to make paternal noises. The lawyers said he had a right to make these incongruous sounds. Harry's English lawyers said that he *was* right. Peter was a natural-born Englishman. He must be brought up as such. Since his mother lived abroad, and his father was often abroad, he must go to an English boarding school. There were schools that would take him at seven years old. There was nothing bizarre or cruel about it. It was less common now than heretofore, but it had been normal for generations.

It was difficult to explain to Peter. In those two most formative years, he had become an American kid.

There was no fighting it, not without the kind of public squabble that might play hell with the child.

Duly, in September, Peter was put on board a jumbo at JFK, in the charge of a British Airways stewardess. Rob could not go with him, because the academic year was beginning. Josie could not go with him because of Simon. A forlorn little figure, trying hard not to cry, disappeared into the Departure Lounge.

He went to Harry and Angelika for Christmas. They took him skiing. He loved it.

Josie puzzled, long and long. What motivated that strange, selfish man, that predatory woman? A kind of jealousy? Angelika was childless, probably on purpose.

Was it thwarted motherhood? Could it even, possibly, be what they said it was—a genuine concern for Peter's future?

Tanja did not miss Peter, because in those four years they had scarcely made any contact.

They made scarcely any now. Josie was distressed by the thought. She drank her dry white Minervois on a rickety chair, on the flagstones of the yard, in the last of the evening sun. The old stones gave back the warmth they had absorbed when the sun was high. The old stones said: take a long view. Today and tomorrow seem important for today and tomorrow only. Unkindness comes and goes.

The ghosts of the Cathars in the farmyard said: unkindness stays.

The domestic arrangements, like the farm itself, had not been designed at one moment or by a single intelligence: they had grown or shrunk or changed as need arose or in relation to the available people. The present arrangement was of long standing and, like the farm, had an air of permanence.

An old man called Etienne thumped up the track at eight every morning in an old pickup truck. He brought Thérèse, who looked too big to fit into the front of the truck. She brought in baskets and bags and packages whatever was needed in the house. Five mornings a week Etienne dropped Thérèse and her cargoes, and went off to his job as maintenance man at a wine-making cooperative in the valley. He picked her up in the evening, dropped her in Montferaude-St-Antonin, and himself went home to Castelnaudary. Two mornings a week he stayed at the farm, fixing anything that needed to be fixed, looking after the rubbish, inspecting the water supply and the electricity, and in all ways acting as the owners' representative.

Some of the shopping was done by Thérèse in the village, most by Etienne's wife in the town. Both kept meticulous accounts in little notebooks.

There was always too much of everything. The surplus went home with Thérèse and Etienne in the evening. This was part of the arrangement, as long-established as the rest.

Etienne never spoke. Thérèse never stopped speaking, in the local accent that sounded more Spanish than French. Old Gwen Woodhouse's contribution to the welfare of the establishment was to listen to Thérèse when she cooked and cleaned.

Thérèse would have given them cassoulet every day, but Giles said that pork-and-beans twice a week was enough.

They were in daily terror that Etienne's truck would not make it up the hill. Peter thought that in the week they had been there it made more noise every morning, a more screaming complaint at the gradient. The truck was one aspect of the arrangement which was probably not permanent.

Life was easy, comfortable and quiet (too quiet for Simon) and a lot cheaper than if they had all been at a hotel.

Two days after Simon's accident, it was necessary to go shopping for things Thérèse and Etienne could not buy—Gwen needed sunglasses, Peter socks, Josie moisturizing cream, Giles tubes of watercolor (he had got through a lot of blue, rendering those flawless skies.) It was an expedition to which Josie would not submit Rob, and Tanja would not subject herself. Josie could drive the minibus—had done so part of the way down.

Simon insisted on coming, because left behind at the farm he would have had nothing to do. Step insisted on coming, because if anybody went anywhere she wanted to go too.

Father and daughter could amuse one another, or amuse themselves. They did both. They took a walk, then read in the shady part of the yard. They were companionable, ready to talk but not needing to. Rob turned the pages of his book; Tanja guessed that he was not taking anything in.

At noon, two hours after the minibus had left and an hour before it was expected back, a different vehicle hummed like a ship up the track. It was a great black Mercedes. It pulled into the yard, nearly demolishing a spindly chair which somebody had left there after breakfast. A chauffeur emerged, with blue glasses, blue cap, blue chin. He opened the door for the passenger in the back, who came out slowly and stiffly, and straightened with difficulty. She was a tall old lady, very thin, in a black silk suit, with black hat and stockings, with a thin black walking stick and black glasses. She was formidably smart, completely urban. She belonged in a certain sort of café in Paris or Milan. She looked like an insect, or like a surrealist painter's idea of the embodiment of death. She and the chauffeur and the car were incongruous in the farmyard, with the old stones, the beat-up chairs, the tubs of geraniums.

There was some mistake?

There was no mistake.

She asked for Major General Schofield, speaking in the voice of somebody not quite English, or of somebody English who has lived abroad for a long time.

"He is not here," said Rob, wondering at this visitant, this exotic.

"But he is living here? He has taken this house for the summer?"

"Oh yes, that is correct."

"So they told me, when I telephoned to his home. They gave me this address, and a number. There is a telephone here? Yes. They gave me perhaps the wrong number. At any rate I had no success with my instrument. Since it was necessary that I talk to him, I had no alternative but to come, on the off chance. It is a difficult place to find."

"Yes, we had that trouble ourselves."

"Are you then of General Schofield's party? Friends? Do you mind my enquiring?"

"I am married to General Schofield's daughter."

"You are Christie?"

"No. That ended years ago."

"Not a moment too soon, I understand."

"My name is Robert Kemp. This is my daughter Tanja."

"How do you do? I am Dorothy Schofield. I am Giles's sister. You might have heard me mentioned, but perhaps not."

"Uh . . . yes. I believe so. No more than mentioned."

"I am the skeleton in the cupboard. Partly for that reason, but also for others, I live in Buenos Aires. I do not communicate with my brother, because it would be useless, nor he with me, because it would not be permitted."

"We expect him back in an hour. Will you wait?"

"Not for an hour. I am on my way to Toulouse, to the airport. I must be in Paris for my flight home. I am committed to these arrangements. Other people are involved. How vexatious. If I could have come before I would have done so, and if I could stay longer I would do so. But really I can stay only for a very few minutes. It would have been enough, to give Giles my message."

"I can give him a message."

"Yes, I will ask you to do that. I might have written, but the words spelled out on paper. . . . In any case, I would have been nearly certain that my letter would not have reached my brother—than any letter I might write in the future would be intercepted and burned. The telephone is a useful toy, but its wires should not be subjected to some communications. You never know who may be listening. Of course I have been living in a police state, a military dictatorship, where one is apt to become paranoid."

"Will you come in? A cup of coffee? Or there is wine on ice?"

"I think it is pleasant out here, as long as one remains in the shade. If you are contemplating a glass of wine, I will join you with pleasure."

"I'll get it," said Tanja.

"What about your driver?"

"He will have brought something in a thermos flask."

Dorothy Schofield sat with caution on one of the chairs on the flagstones. She looked older than Giles, thinner, smarter, richer, foreign: but there was a clear resemblance. You could not doubt the relationship. There was, as so often in families, an echo of his voice in hers, though she was a woman and spoke in a strange, stilted way as though translating in her head from another language.

"May I ask of whom your party here consists?" she said, when she had spread her silken skirts, with an air of *salons* and of bowing ambassadors, over her stick-thin knees.

Rob mentioned Josie and her sons, Gwen Woodhouse, and Step. He referred to the last as Marjorie, although it was difficult to remember to do so.

"Josephine. My niece, of course. I remember her only as a young child. I was told that her marriage to Christie was an error speedily recognized."

"Pretty speedily rectified," said Rob.

"A son nevertheless resulted? Giles must be pleased to have a grandson."

"He has two grandsons."

"And a granddaughter? That lovely child?"

"No. She is my child from my first marriage."

"Dear me. These convolutions are strange to someone of my generation. I was brought up between the wars, and those years have nowadays a reputation for wildness which I find quite unaccountable. Did you ever see a play called *Dear Octopus?* It perfectly depicts our family. Our cousin Gwen Woodhouse, did you say? How dashing of her to be here. How very good for her. She is a person of great excellence. She remained kind to me when nobody else was. She must be a fair age. This is very unlike the scenes of her labors, though almost as hot. And then Marjorie. It is about her that I wished to speak in confidence to Giles and to his daughter. I could not do so from Argentina. Nor was I ready to do so. I tried to do so in England the other day, but they were already here. I tracked you down, and now I must trust you. On brief acquaintance I am inclined to do so, but in any case if my message is to be delivered it must be to you."

Tanja came out of the house with two glasses on a tray, already misted by the chilled wine they contained.

Dorothy Schofield took a glass from the tray. She raised it to Rob in a gesture unfamiliar to Anglo-Saxon countries. He raised his glass, in imitation.

Dorothy Schofield said to Tanja, "You may as well hear what I have to say. You will hear it anyway. You will be told it is completely untrue, and that I am crazy and bitter. But although I was in Argentina at the time, twelve years ago, I have complete and perfect proof of what I say. I was morally certain then. I wrote to Giles, but of course he did not see my letter. I have not been to the police because I have not been in Britain, and there was nothing to be gained by talking to Argentine policemen. Is this the local wine? It is refreshing. It goes well al fresco, and at this time of day. I must not ramble. The car is very fast, but I must not risk missing my airplane at Toulouse.

"To be brief, then. To be, I am afraid, brutal. My brother Giles was married at the end of the war to a gentle and amiable girl, a most suitable girl from a respectable, professional background. She was criticized only for a certain . . . passivity, an excess of meekness, a refusal or inability to assert herself, to make decisions, to live any life of her own. She was a creature out of the past, of an epoch long even before my own, of Victorian domesticity—she was a little mouse in Dickens, a voluntary slave."

Tanja and Rob glanced at one another. Rob knew what Tan was thinking: this strange old lady might have been discussing Josie.

"I dare say it was not at all good for Giles to have such a wife," said Dorothy Schofield. "He was spoiled all his life. He was even spoiled in the army. But they were by all accounts extremely happy together. I saw them only fleetingly, and that long ago, but I was pleased by what I saw. You may have heard something of this, of that marriage?"

"Yes, a little," said Rob. "Josie speaks of her mother, sure. I never met her. When I first met Josie, her mother had been dead for four or five years. From what I heard, I'd say you were overstating her humility, her lack of character. I don't think she was that wishy-washy. But I guess you're right that the marriage was exceptionally happy."

"We agree, then, on the important point. It is what makes all that follows so shocking. Now, at a date unknown to me, a woman called Marjorie Illingworth married for reasons unknown to me a man called Edward Holland. It is about this woman that I require my brother to be informed. She was, as I suppose she remains, in great contrast to the gentle person we have been discussing. She had had, to give her credit, an active and exhausting war, as I had myself. She was not a girl. She had been a driver and mechanic in some part of the army. She had served with the Free French, and was decorated by them. Not a little mouse.

"The unfortunate Holland was, I believe, an accountant. He was some years older than herself. His health was not good. He went into early retirement on that account, and they were not at all well off. She met my brother Giles when he had been married for twenty-five years and she, I suppose, a little less. The circumstances of the meeting are unimportant—the foyer of a theater, the bar of a golf club, a cocktail party in the country, introduction by friends. I imagine he gave the impression of being far richer than he was. He did that all his life. He was a man of great charm, a ladies' man. She decided she wanted him. There were obstacles to her gaining possession of him. He had a wife and she had a husband. She was meanwhile infected by a bizarre personal morality, derived from her misreading of some venerable crank, by the terms of which she was entitled to anything she desired. You understand? She thought she had a moral, God-given right to anything she wanted. She thought that her end justified any means. Accordingly she murdered first her husband and then my sister-in-law. She was thus free to marry my brother, and did so.

"I have been morally certain of these facts for a dozen years. I have recently pieced together the full and final details. The evidence is complete. It is not available for your examination at this moment, as most of it is in Buenos Aires and some in a bank in London. It includes letters, diaries, sworn depositions, and some tapes. The tapes are the missing links which have converted a certainty in my mind into a case which could be proved in a courtroom."

"What are you going to do about it?" said Rob at last,

because a response was clearly expected of him and it was all he could think of to say.

"Nothing. There is nothing I can do. I am too old and tired. I am returning to my home in Argentina, and when I get there I shall stay there. Giles must do what he thinks best. I think he should get that woman sent to prison for the rest of her life, but he may prefer simply to leave her, or to kill her."

Dorothy Schofield looked at her watch. She stood up, with the assistance of her ebony stick. She shook hands with Rob, who found to his surprise that her hand was like a hand, not a claw or tentacle. She put out a hand toward Tanja, but the child had backed away and was on the other side of the yard.

"I have done my duty," said Dorothy Schofield. "Thank you for your patience, and for the glass of wine, which I greatly enjoyed."

The chauffeur materialized—blue hat, glasses, and chin—and helped her into the Mercedes. As he backed the car to turn it, she waved in the manner of royalty.

Rob's hand twitched in a small, instinctive response.

Tanja's hands were behind her back.

The car swam away down the track and out of sight.

THREE

The yard seemed larger without the formidable bulk of the Mercedes. The dust settled. Geraniums were again visible. The little local world had returned to normal. Had it? Could it?

"Crazy," said Tanja. "Crazy and vicious."

"Yes. I want you to say nothing about this to anybody, sweetie, until I talk to Giles."

"What will you say to Giles? Will you ask him if Step murdered those people?"

"I'll say his sister was here. I'll ask about his sister."

"She said about Gwen . . ."

"Yes, I should talk to Gwen. And then, later, maybe we can talk about it to Step, Josie, Peter, everybody."

"Dad, that visit is not going to be any secret."

"Only for a while."

"Not even for a while. Thérèse was here. She saw

that car. She probably talked with the driver. You can't tell Thérèse to keep quiet about it, not without telling her why, and I don't think you know enough French to do that . . . *Don't worry about it.* We'll talk to Giles and Gwen, and then to Josie and Step."

"*We'll* talk?"

"Well, I heard it all. She wanted me to. She practically insisted. You can't handle this on your own."

Realizing what she had said, Tanja gave a short, unhappy laugh.

It was as Tanja predicted—Thérèse was by the door of the minibus almost before Josie put the handbrake on. Gwen understood her well enough, although none of the others did. Such a car, like that of the President! A lady of such elegance! The chauffeur a Toulousain, a charming man. He did not know his passenger's name—he and the car had been hired for the day, through the management of a hotel. He did not know how much the client paid, only what he himself earned. He did not even know that, he told Thérèse, as he had not yet received his tip. The lady was Argentine, but in a sense English. Was that possible?

Thérèse's description of the visitor, interpreted when feasible by Gwen, caused Giles, Step, and Gwen herself to look at one another, astonishment and consternation visible to each in the faces of the others: visible also to Josie and Rob.

"I thought we'd never see her again," said Giles. "I suppose we never shall see her again."

"I'm sorry to have missed her," said Gwen.

"Are you, indeed?" said Step.

Thérèse put on the kettle for the tea which Step had brought from England.

Robert Kemp received three different reactions to his reports of the visit of Dorothy Schofield—as different as the accounts of Simon's fall under the walls of the little castle. Tanja heard a part of these reactions, Josie a part. Peter no doubt took in some of all this, Simon only that something had happened which was strange but also boring.

Giles said, "I'm sorry you should have been subjected to that, the two of you. But it's probably a good thing that the rest of us were out. Poor old Dorothy slipped a cog at the end of the war—blew a gasket. I think 'flipped' is your word? I was in Austria and I don't know exactly what happened. Strain did it, I suppose, long hours, anxiety, the bombing, not enough sleep. She was in London all through the blitz, and then the doodlebugs and rockets. She worked at the War Office. It was all too much."

Giles tried to pick his words carefully, since he was talking to a man who had had a nervous breakdown for some of the same reasons. He found tact in this situation extremely difficult.

"It takes different people different ways," said Giles, with an unusual note of apology in his voice.

"That is true," said Rob. He smiled to show that he was not flying into a rage, or sinking among waves of lunacy.

"She went off to Argentina with, ah, a friend. I gather there was general relief, though as I say I wasn't there.

She came home a few times during the fifties. We saw her. Josie saw her, though I don't suppose she remembers. Gwen saw her, I think."

"But this story she told?"

"My dear boy, she's told wilder stories than that."

"She said she had proof. Diaries, tapes, all kinds of stuff. She said it would stand up in court."

"I wonder what kind of court she had in mind. A rackets court, perhaps. I'm afraid that joke was in bad taste."

"Giles," said Tanja, "are you telling us your sister is plain crazy?"

"It comes and goes," said Giles. "They give her pills."

"Because of bombing and stuff in the war?"

"I believe love was involved," said Giles.

"Oh," said Tanja, who could not associate the emaciated duchess with the emotion she knew about from songs.

They were climbing back to the farm from the evening stroll which Rob had suggested. They passed the dangerous electrical shed containing the transformer, the converted pigsty which housed the water pump, the big sunken tank where the water paused on its way upstairs to the cistern (if your footsteps on its wooden cover reverberated, the water was getting low). The sun was going down behind the hills in an eiderdown of clouds of custard, apricot, and blackcurrant. The sun touched like a blessing the windbreak of cypress trees and the big curly tiles of the barn; it touched Tanja's pale hair and Giles's sunburned pate, and deepened the lines of tension by Rob's eyes and his mouth. Far above and out over the valley, a kite rode the thermals rising from the sunbaked vineyards into the evening air, a spiky black crucifix against the theatrical sky.

Etienne's pickup truck had come and gone, taking Thérèse and the day's booty of cheese and cleaning fluid. Even as the pickup clanked down the track, Thérèse's voice could be heard embarking on the story of the visitor.

The shopping expedition had been successful but exhausting, Simon fretful, Peter bored, Josie getting a headache from the glare of the streets and the blare of the traffic, the ice creams hideously expensive.

"I wonder what brought the poor old thing to Europe?" said Giles.

"I understood her to say that this brought her. She came to get evidence."

"She said she made the tapes while she was here," said Tanja. "She didn't say she came here to make them."

"I suppose she's in Paris now," said Giles, "*en route* for BA. I hope she doesn't tell that story to too many Argies."

"It wouldn't matter if she did," said Tanja. "If they don't know her, they won't know who she's talking about, and if they do know her they'll know she's crazy."

"I suppose that's a kind of comfort," said Giles.

"Why would her imagination manufacture such a thing?" said Rob. "Why would she believe it?"

"God knows. Why do people think they're Julius Caesar?"

They came into the yard, in the last of the sun. The whole party was there, with a bottle of wine and a jug of squash. Everybody wanted to talk about Dorothy Schofield's visit, but nobody did talk about it.

"Of course I knew her as a child," said Gwen Woodhouse. "We were first cousins, and our families were close. Such very conventional families! Quite stifling, even for me, and I was not exactly an adventuress! Giles got away, of course, to boarding school, but Dorothy and I went to day schools. Home every evening in time for tea. She resented it more than I did, because she had a brother who was free. Could you call it freedom, being at boarding school in those days? The Schofields had money enough for one expensive education, but not for two. Of course the boy had to be given the preference."

"Why of course?" said Tanja.

"That's a good question, dear. It was Dorothy's point exactly. It explains a great deal, I think. She was already in her school days aware of the unfairness, and so she was a rebel, considered a problem. Oh, how they discussed it, her parents and mine! I used to listen, lying huddled behind the sofa. Can you picture that? I scarcely can! So when Dorothy really rebelled, I thought a little bit I understood. I think Giles might have understood, if he had known what I had known. But he was always far away, living a different life. Boys like him had a different focus. Could it have been so in America? When the moment came, I jumped at the chance to go to Africa. My family never understood that, so you can imagine that Dorothy's family never understood her."

"Where was all this?" said Rob. "Who were these people?"

"We all lived in Bedfordshire. The Schofields were

outside Luton, and my family lived in Dunstable. Only a few miles apart. Both families had cars, little Austins, identical. Dorothy and I used to bicycle back and forth at weekends. Uncle George Schofield had a job in the city. He went up by train every day. My father was an estate agent with a local firm.

"Well, we grew up. I joined a missionary society, and went to the Congo. I met my husband there. We couldn't afford to come home for the wedding, and our families couldn't afford to come out. But it was quite a merry little affair. Some Italian priests came in from their mission, and grew very overexcited. But all this time Dorothy was stuck at home."

"Why?" asked Tanja.

"Her mother was in poor health, or thought she was. Dorothy had to take charge. It was hard. There was I in the Congo and Giles with his regiment in India, and Dorothy's greatest excitement was a tennis party at the vicarage. There were young men, of course, but not the kind she wanted. There was very little money, especially as Giles was paid an allowance."

"Why?" asked Tanja again.

"As a young officer in India you had to have a private income. For polo ponies, you know, and cars, and big-game hunting. Dorothy drew a short straw. Giles never realized how short. The war came as deliverance. She could genuinely say that she had to get away, that she had a patriotic duty. All of which, as I say, goes far to explain what happened, though of course it does not excuse it."

"What did happen? She had a breakdown?"

"That was what the family said. That was what they

told the neighbors, and Giles, and me. Giles continues to believe it. It is the comforting thing to believe. I do not disillusion him. I shall not do so, and I ask you to respect my confidence. But I heard from Dorothy herself. The letter took months! She wanted me to understand. Years later I saw her in England. We were on leave, and so, in a manner of speaking, was she. Well! At the end of the war she was working for a liaison officer who dealt with neutral countries. She met in the course of her duties an Argentinian officer, a colonel, a rich, dashing playboy sort of man. He had a wife and children. But they had an affair. He set her up in a flat, and gave her all kinds of presents. It was all very scandalous, because of their official positions, to say nothing of his wife and children. She was rather blatant about it, as I heard from others later."

"She'd never had any fun," said Tanja, "and suddenly . . ."

"Yes, dear. Like a child denied chocolates. Or, which I have seen, a Primitive Methodist drinking a glass of whisky . . . I principally blame the mother, a selfish *malade imaginaire*."

"All of this rings pretty true, Gwen," said Rob, "but how does it end up with her having these vicious fantasies?"

"She must believe them to be true."

"Then she is crazy."

"That is what I cannot understand. I would describe her as intemperate, highly excitable and emotional, rebellious, difficult. Because of the drabness of her background, she put far too high a value on material things, clothes, jewels, big cars, race horses. But so mentally unbalanced as to convince herself of something so monstrous? That is not the person I knew. I wish I had seen her yesterday. I am glad she spoke kindly of me."

"Gwen has missed the point completely," said Step. "I've spoken to people who knew the families, local people, childhood friends. Everybody knew the Schofields with their dashing son and their disappointed daughter. It's not so very long ago. It's well within the memory of people who are by no means senile."

"These are people Giles stayed in touch with?"

"Oh no. He would never have bothered."

"Then how did you come to meet them, hear all this?"

"I didn't come to meet them. They came to meet Giles. They claimed ancient friendship, because he was a popular general. They told me how well they knew the family, as a *laisser-passer* into our house. I'm sorry if that sounds very grand and patronizing. But it's still the way of the world, although it shouldn't be."

"Yes," said Rob, whose own friendship had sometimes been sought because his mother was so rich.

"Gwen saw," said Step, "that Dorothy resented and envied Giles. Not only because he got away, not only because of his allowance, but also because of his charm and popularity. In a qualified sense she was right. And it's true that Dorothy was a rebel. I can understand that—I was one myself, and for much the same reason. What Gwen never understood is that Dorothy adored Giles, worshiped him. Her little brother. She was insanely possessive. It went far beyond natural family affection. Giles was totally unaware of it. Gwen, I suppose, was simply too innocent to recognize what was practically an incestuous passion."

"If that is so," said Rob, "she would have been insanely jealous of Josie's mother."

"No. For two reasons, as I understand it. She was herself at the time of Giles's marriage a pampered *poule de luxe* in Buenos Aires, her own life cocking a continual snook at her family. Very satisfactory for her. And, secondly, she managed to despise poor Alison."

"Ah. She more or less said she did do that."

"You are not obsessively jealous of someone you despise. In other words, she rationalized her inability to do anything about it."

"That does sound like the logic of the crazy."

"Yes. But even she can't despise me. So the logic doesn't work. If I'm not a doormat, what am I? Let's think of something. Oh yes, a murderess, that will do nicely."

The cold shadows were beginning to creep out of the sides of Rob's skull, as he tried to untangle the facts in this tangle of fictions.

He forced himself to say, almost calmly, "You're saying that she so violently resents you as Giles's wife that she concocts and then believes this story?"

"That's the way it looks to me."

"Then it's lucky she went back to BA."

"For my peace of mind it certainly is."

"She couldn't possibly represent any actual physical threat. She looks pretty frail. She walks with a stick. She said she was too old and tired to do anything about this."

"Rob, she's rich. Her boyfriend was a millionaire, and think of the stranglehold she had on him, a married man, a senior officer, a practicing Catholic. She's only got to send to Nice for a couple of Corsicans. This is an isolated place in empty country. I should hate to think there was somebody about with bottomless money and a poisonous hatred of me. I'd be happy to get confirmation that she's back in Buenos Aires, but I don't know how to go about that."

"I guess Giles could."

"He'd never see the need. He'd never bother. He's too busy painting and tasting the wines. I daresay he's right. They're rational occupations. There are much worse hobbies he could have, and probably did have. Dear old boy, he does need a keeper."

"So do I," said Rob.

"Yes. You've got one, and very nice too."

The weather continued brilliant. The kites wheeled and the grapes ripened. In the valley, the big bricks of the villages changed color throughout the day, and in the hills the stones of small ruined castles went from black to silver to black.

They were busy in various ways. Step claimed to be busiest, on mysterious archaeological researches. She poked about, in her ancient cotton hat, among the rocks on the flat piece north of the farm. Unless they were going somewhere, doing something special, she spent hours a day there. She lowered herself to the ground, put a pillow behind her back, leaned against a rock, and pondered. Pondering was what she said she was doing. She was very busy at it.

A passing balloonist would have seen a place of marvelous peace.

But Dorothy Schofield's visit had done something to

the atmosphere. Josie was not, as far as she knew, the least bit psychic, but she detected a trace of strange, new, unvoiced hostility in the very flagstones of the yard, in the monoliths behind the farm, in the plumping melons and the blackening olives.

It seemed to her that the spirit of the place had tasted them and found them unpleasant. She had never in her life felt such a thing before. If she was imagining it, why was she suddenly imagining it?

She did not discuss it with Rob; it was unfortunate, even calamitous, that he should have been subjected to the mad-woman's ravings; to worry him with these new fancies could be really bad for him. She did not discuss it with Giles, who had never in his life been aware of an atmosphere. She did not discuss it with Gwen, who was supposed to be having a happy and restful holiday, a last treat. It was not a thing to discuss with children, planting fears and uncertainties in half-formed minds.

She mentioned it to Step.

"Good gracious, yes," said Step. "Something really malign sets up the most dreadful jangles. The whole crowd is aware of it."

"The whole crowd? Well, yes. Obviously that visit wouldn't have been on the therapist's program for Rob. Tanja was upset more than she lets herself show."

"Giles, too."

"And me, though I wasn't there. And Gwen."

"And me, I assure you," said Step. "You can imagine how I feel about it. But I wasn't talking about the family."

"Who then?"

"You don't suppose we're alone here, do you? There

are scores of people here. I just hope they don't blame us for Dorothy."

"Private," said Gwen Woodhouse gently. "Of no interest."

She would not tell them about it. She was sweetly inflexible.

She had received a letter. It was not the first letter any of them had had, but it was one of very few.

Peter had had a letter from his father, from Norway. Angelika had added a message of love, with a dashing signature. Of course they knew where he was. Of course he knew where they were. Harry was working pretty hard at his new role of caring father. They were staying with friends in Norway. How else would they stay there? There was nothing private about the letter. Peter showed it to his mother; he did not mind the others reading it. It was not about anything very much—the weather, birdlife, fishing, hopes that Peter was having a great time, good wishes to everybody. After Norway they were going on to Iceland. They would send a card. They would be back in England in time for Peter's return, in time to have him for a few days in London before taking him to school.

Reading between the lines of Harry's letter, Josie glimpsed something she had known all along, which she had been glimpsing for years—something strange and sad and terribly predictable. Harry was consumed by jealousy of Rob. His jealousy increased as he moved into a useless, directionless, impoverished middle age. Jealous of Rob not for acquiring Josie, for having another son, for being younger and cleverer and American, but just for being rich. Harry would have loved to be rich. He had a grudge against Providence that he had not been born a rich duke. He was a man of great crudity, of simple and raw ambitions, without having any will or ability to achieve anything. He wanted to be rich, and he was a professional mixer of martinis in other people's houses. Oh dear. Harry's spiritual pilgrimage was long outside Josie's charge, and it was of no interest whatever to any of the rest of them, even Peter his son.

Tanja had a letter from her mother. The news was news indeed, though after a moment hardly surprising. The owners of *Esmerelda* had decided to offer her for charter in the Mediterranean all summer. It was normal. Many of the bigger charter yachts wintered in the Caribbean and summered on the Côte d'Azur or in the Greek islands. The letter was postmarked St. Croix, and dated the 21st of June. It had taken a long time to arrive. It could be assumed that Tanja's mother and stepfather had crossed the Atlantic, part of an elegant and predatory fleet, and were now in Europe, serving candlelit dinners on the afterdeck and laughing at the terrible stories of their clients.

They did not own the boat. They never would own any boat. They never would own anything.

It was another letter which gave news, asked questions, and said nothing important or private. Tanja showed it to her father; she did not mind the others seeing it.

Josie, reading it, wondered if something nasty was growing in her character. She saw regret and resentment between the lines. Anna had been bored married to Rob, living that life enclosed by those narrow academic horizons, so she had left her husband and infant daughter and gone off with Dickie Hamlyn in his yacht (not his yacht). So she got sun and rum punches and silver sand and waving palms and steel bands and all that, and so there was no money at all. Now Josie had got Rob and Rob's mother's fortune, and Anna would have liked a bit of that.

Rob knew all this perfectly well. Tanja knew it. Tanja had heard her mother, late at night on the foredeck after a few drinks. It was no business of any of the rest of them.

A week after the letter from the Virgins, Tanja had a card from Turkey. It had only taken a few days. They were cruising that coast. Many charter yachts did. A number of the greatest classical sites were visitable only from the sea. *Esmerelda* was more than a thousand miles from Languedoc. As far as Tanja was concerned, her mother might as well have been in the Virgins. It was to be hoped that Tanja did not wish too intensely that she was in *Esmerelda* off the coast of Turkey.

Peter received the promised card from Iceland, a lurid photograph of a volcano, a frivolous message about being bitten by the midges.

Josie herself had received one letter, from her father-in-law the Professor Emeritus. It was coherent, even witty, shakily written, a chronicle of books read and small New England doings.

Rob had received no letters, because everybody knew that he was to be left in peace.

Giles and Step had received no letters. Letters would be piling up on the hall table of the house in Somerset—dividends, invitations, charity appeals, bulletins and newsletters of countless organizations, as dull a collection as anybody could imagine. They had decided before they left to have nothing forwarded. The housekeeper knew where they were, in case of crisis. No crisis at home was predictable, except the burning down of their house, which they could have done nothing about.

Gwen had received no letters, because her friends were either too old or too busy to write. But now she had one. It came up from the village with Etienne and Thérèse. It was given by Thérèse into Gwen's hands, Thérèse being well able to distinguish "Gwendoline Woodhouse" on an envelope from the names of the others, strange as they were. Nobody else saw it. Thérèse knew nothing about it except that the envelope was typewritten and addressed to Gwen. Gwen said nothing about it.

"Private," she said. "Of no interest."

The others did not know if the stamp was English, French, Zairien or what. Gwen did not tell them.

It was, perhaps, because life at Montferaude was so quiet that Gwen's letter became a subject of discussion and speculation among the others. It was a mystery.

It was not a mystery to Step.

"I'm not sure, but I'm sure," she said to Josie and Giles after dinner, while Josie shifted plates and Giles drank Armagnac at the kitchen table. "Gwen had some tests before she came. She didn't tell me, but I know the woman who took her to the hospital. They were going to send the results to her doctor, and the doctor was sending them here. These are the results."

"If it was good news," said Josie, "she'd tell us."

"I know."

"Damn and blast," said Giles. "Why does it have to happen to the very best and nicest people?"

Gwen was low. She would not discuss the contents of her letter, but she was depressed by them. She was apathetic and preoccupied.

It was surprising to Josie. In a way it was disappointing. She had come to appreciate Gwen as a very rare spirit, a saint with a sense of humor. By all accounts her whole life was full of faith and courage. She had often faced death by plague, drowning, or black drunkards. She had stared him in the eye. Now she seemed to quail. She was old and weak and penniless. Josie had thought her indomitably brave. But now she was afraid.

Even Simon lowered his voice when Gwen was by. He slowed his run to a walk, muted his clumping to a tiptoe. They were all instinctively, half consciously, treating Gwen as an invalid. She knew it. She was distressed. She told them to bang about and laugh; she told Simon to run, and to make a merry noise.

The sun blazed and the grapes ripened as though everything was quite all right.

Gwen continued interpreter. She interpreted, in one of Thérèse's monologues, a chance remark that there was in Montferaude-St-Antonin a lady who had been a hairdresser in the biggest *salon* in Toulouse, a female most expert in cutting, washing, setting, drying, dyeing, waving the hair of other females.

Gwen herself had never had her hair done in her life. Josie's hair was cropped short for the summer; all it needed was a shampoo once a week. Tanja's was even shorter. She gave it a shampoo twice a week. But Step was delighted. Her hair was thin. It had always been a problem. She hated walking about in rollers. She had resigned herself to going without a hairdresser all summer: but a little woman in the village, an expert semi-retired, was too good to miss.

Etienne took Step to the village in the pickup. Rob would collect her later with the minibus. Rob meanwhile took Gwen, Josie, and the children to a place where it was said that they could swim. Giles was left alone with his easel in the yard, while Thérèse clashed cymbals in the kitchen.

The telephone rang, which it had scarcely done since they arrived.

Giles sat tight, willing the nuisance to go away.

The bangs in the kitchen stopped, and then the ringing of the telephone. Good.

Bad. Thérèse appeared in the door, waving her arms above her head as though directing the landing of a fighter on the flight deck of an aircraft carrier.

Giles sighed, rose, crossed the egg-frying flagstones of the yard; he was unsighted by the darkness indoors; he groped for the telephone, and picked it up with distaste.

The caller was a woman, high-voiced, perhaps old, speaking English with a strong foreign accent which Giles could not identify. She asked for Mademoiselle Dorozy Schofield.

"She's not here," said Giles. "She came here for a short while a few days ago, but only for a few minutes. She's in Buenos Aires."

"She is not in Buenos Aires. I 'ave spoke to zem in Buenos Aires."

"Then she's in Paris."

"She is not in Paris. She 'as not come to Paris. She is in Languedoc, I zink. She is not wiz you?"

"No. No, she's not here. Absolutely not. No."

"She is in Languedoc. Ah. Zank you. Good-bye."

"Good-bye," said Giles, after having hung up the telephone.

"Did she say who she was?"

"No."

"Why didn't you ask?"

"I don't know why I didn't. The conversation didn't go that way. Does it matter who she was?"

"How on earth did she get this number?"

"Dorothy must have given it to her."

"Why? Dorothy wasn't expecting to stay here."

"Oh, why does Dorothy do anything?"

"Was she calling from Paris?"

"I took it that she was. Yes, I think she must have been. The system's automatic. You don't go through an operator. You can't tell where a call's coming from. But she knew that Dorothy hadn't got to Paris. The suggestion was that Dorothy was supposed to be meeting her in Paris. Yes, I'm sure the call came from Paris."

"But Dorothy might have gone anywhere," said Step. "How did this mysterious woman know she's still down here?"

"She didn't. She said she thought Dorothy must be still down here."

"That's bad enough."

"Why bad? What's bad about it? What does it matter where she is?"

"It matters to me," said Step. "I'm the one she hates."

"She's a harmless old bag with a bee in her bonnet."

"She's an old bag with a bee in her bonnet," said Step. "But she's not harmless."

It was strange to see Step frightened, as it was strange to see Gwen frightened.

Gwen was not frightened but aghast. She was perplexed. She was undecided, as seldom before in a life in which the right thing to do had nearly always been obvious. She was confused. What faced her was too horrible to contemplate. She recoiled from what was apparently happening, from the future, from what was being asked of her.

She prayed for guidance and strength, but God was silent.

The problem was what she did with what was left of her life. Pain given, pain received, seemed inevitable. These monsters, when faced, should have grown less, but they grew larger.

The moment would come for her—certainly it would—to make the agony endurable by sharing it. Other hands must take part of the burden. It would become too much for her alone. She would confide in her blood relations, in Giles her cousin and Josie his daughter. It would be difficult to make them understand. Gwen felt exhausted at the thought.

She had tried to convince herself for an hour, for a day, that the letter was wrong. There might be a mistake. There might be hope. But the habit of honesty was too strong. There was no hope. There was time, but not much.

Confusion and unhappiness drove Gwen in on herself, making her bad company. She excused herself, therefore, from an expedition which involved a long time in the overcrowded intimacy of the minibus. They all exclaimed: of course she must come. There was a tinge of relief in their regrets.

Thérèse's conversation filled a good deal of the day. Thérèse was restful company, requiring an audience but not a response, knowing nothing about the contents of Gwen's letter, not bothering to make any guess about about them.

Gwen lunched alone in the shady part of the yard—an omelette, salad, mineral water.

There was no sound of traffic, no airplane, no radio. There was hardly a buzz of insect or pipe or bird. Even Thérèse was quiet. It should have been the nearest to absolute peace that Western Europe could provide—quieter by far than the incessant chatter and shriek of tropical Africa. There was no peace in Gwen's troubled old heart.

Step said there were ghosts in the yard, bodies under the flagstones. Gwen was not haunted by them. The demons were in her head.

The illusion of stillness was broken by the stammer of the telephone. This was a coincidence—calls on successive days after so many days of silence.

Thérèse took it. She handed it to Gwen as though it might explode.

It was another woman, long-winded and gassy. She

announced herself as Lydia Ross. She was American. She asked for Tanja Kemp.

"Tan is not here," said Gwen. "They are all out for the day."

"Oh, shoot. Maybe you can tell me. Does Tanja have any news of her mother?"

"Oh yes. They are on their yacht, off the coast of Turkey. At that end of the Mediterranean, at least."

"You're a little out of date. They brought *Esmerelda* right along by Sicily, Naples, Sardinia, Nice, Marseille, and to Sète."

"I'm sure Tan had not the slightest idea they were doing that."

"Well, it wasn't in their plans. We were on board, there in Turkey, my husband and I and the kids. Kids! In a lot of ways they're older than we are. Dickie and Anna had another charter that fell through. Two weeks, straight after us. They were pretty downcast. Mackintosh has just retired—"

"Who?"

"My husband, Mac Ross. So we kept the boat another two weeks. We came all the way west. Why not? New places. A lot of fascinating contrasts. Anna looked after us just beautifully. They were picking up a party, so we went ashore. With regret, let me tell you! So crowded and noisy, when you gotten used to having the ocean to yourself."

On and on this went. Gwen could see no point in any of it; she did not understand why she was being asked to listen to it.

The point emerged at last, like a small gift in a large wrapping. *Esmerelda* was now at Sète, halfway between

Marseille and the Spanish frontier. The professional crew was on board. Dickie and Anna Hamlyn were not. The two crewmen had no idea where the Hamlyn had gone. Presumably another charter had fallen through. Sète was only seventy miles away from that farmhouse in the hills, a pretty direct road, two hours in a car. They took a swing across southwest France to see the kid. Mrs. Ross needed to establish urgent contact with the Hamlyns. She had to track them down.

"They surely called," she said.

"No," said Gwen, "I am sure they have not."

"They called or wrote."

"Tanja had letters from Turkey, but no hint of this."

"Uh, Mrs. . . . Woodhouse? Uh, I think Anna must have called her daughter and you were out of the house."

"It is objectively possible. I think it most unlikely. Telephone calls are a rare event in this household. If Tanja's mother had called, if she were expected here, there would have been talk about it."

Mrs. Ross gave Gwen a number. It was the hotel where they were staying. If Anna arrived—*when* Anna and Dickie arrived—they were please, please to call Lydia and Mac on that number.

"*Esmerelda* tied up only seventy miles away?" said Tanja. "Let's go."

"What for?" said Rob. "To talk to the crew?"

"The crew will know where they've gone."

"Seems not."

"Mom and Dickie *must* have said where they were going."

"If so, they told the crew not to pass it on."

"But that's impossible."

"I agree it's strange. They live on the end of the radio-telephone. The business depends on it. This is the height of the season here. They wouldn't drop out of sight, leaving the boat, your mother not saying a word to you ... How long have they been there, Gwen? When did they get there?"

"I'm afraid I have no idea. I think it cannot be long."

"Long enough to get here if they were coming," said Tanja. "Two hours away."

"Do you want them to come, Tan?" asked Step.

"My own mother? Sure I do. Of course I do."

Sure she did. Of course she did. Rob's own feeling were mixed. He felt for Anna little of the abiding anger which Josie had for Harry Christie. It was a different ballgame. The two marriages had different beginnings and different ends.

With Rob and Anna, nobody had swept anybody off their feet. They had met as equals, in New York, of the same age and with some of the same friends. Anna was pure Dutch, but educated in America and working in New York. Her family had gone home to Hilversum; she had stayed with her PhD and her whizz kid job in publishing (mass-market paperbacks, every jacket resplendent with metallic inks and deep embossing).

The first time they had dinner, he said, "I wonder if I can say what I want to say without sounding patronizing and insufferable."

"From my experience of academics, I doubt it."

"I'll take a swing at it, and hope not to be slugged by

the Chablis. I never expected to meet anybody in your trade as intelligent and responsive as you are."

She pretended to fly into a rage, half stood up, reached for her bag.

Everybody in the restaurant was looking at them. Everybody had been doing that anyway, because to look at Anna was pretty special. She was five-nine, slim, long-legged, blond, with a face more Slav than Dutch in the breadth of brow and cheekbones; she was dressed conventionally for New York in 1974 (red silk shirt, navy skirt, dark tights, black court shoes) but she somehow made these career-girl clothes look exotic and extreme. A touch of the foreign came and went in her voice, according as she was excited or amused. Her favorite composers were Monteverdi and Mozart, her painter Georgia O'Keeffe, her poet one Rob had never heard of.

She was often excited, often amused, often beautifully relaxed.

She shared an apartment off Washington Square with a girl who worked for a dentist, and made more money than she did.

She startled Rob, the Puritan New Englander, by the amount she drank. She showed no sign of it. She said everybody in Holland drank like a fish and nobody ever got drunk. It was a triumph of selective breeding, inherited hardness of head. This explained the genius of Rembrandt and Vermeer, the victories of Van Tromp, and the fact of a tiny country having a huge empire. She only drank wine in those days. She knew a lot about wine.

He took her home to New Hampshire, for a weekend,

then another. She was a bird of paradise on campus and at parties. Everybody wanted to meet anybody in publishing. She spent a morning with the president of the University Press.

They skated. She had skated as a child on the Dutch canals, like the people in seventeenth-century paintings. When they came afterwards, her color was high from the cold. When he kissed her, her face was cold. The thought of not having her had become intolerable, not suddenly but gradually. He asked her to stay forever, and she said it was funny he should ask, because it was just what she wanted.

Rob was sure, then and later, that Anna was not influenced by his family's wealth. She had welcomed it without greed, and she abandoned it without regret. The regret came later.

What was wrong, in the end, was his life, which was the life he had. It was not so much himself, although his preoccupations must sometimes have made him boring. It was not Tanja, whom Anna had had nearly the whole of every vacation. It was the size of the horizon, the faces in the shopping mall, the dinner parties. It was the campus wives taking note of the number of drinks she had. Three years were all she could take.

The court gave her custody of Tanja—inevitably: the child was tiny. It was Anna's decision that Tan be educated in America, in her father's care.

She sailed away into the sunset on Dickie Hamlyn's yacht. She thought at the time that it was his yacht.

Dickie had things going for him. He was forty, but lean and tough and bronzed. He was a competent and experienced skipper, unflappable, charming in a laconic, man-of-action way. He stepped straight out of an advertisement for cruising in the Virgins.

The Caribbean sun did great things for Dickie, but a dozen years of it had not been kind to Anna's complexion. There was no wine in that life. There was plenty of gin, whiskey, run at duty-free prices. There was no money in that life, and never would be.

Rob knew what Anna allowed herself to feel about him and his money, and about Josie. He knew that Dickie Hamlyn faced despair. He did not like the idea of them lurking somewhere out of sight in southwest France.

Tanja was another one to be puzzled and distressed. Knowledge that her mother loved her was emotional bedrock. Anna might be rackety and directionless, but she had been throughout Tanja's life a good and reliable mother. Now her mobile home, her only home, was tied to a jetty seventy miles away. And not a word from her, not a sight of her.

Mom was bored with being bothered about Tanja? She was so resentful of Josie that she wouldn't come near them? Dickie was up to something? Mom not only knew where Tanja was, she gave the address and telephone number to strangers. There were two possible reasons she didn't make contact, over that little distance: she couldn't, or she didn't want to.

This came on top of the visit of the horrible old witch. Tanja was appalled at the effect of this kind of thing on her father. She was not crazy about the effect on herself.

These two things were pretty well ruining the summer.

Of course Peter didn't notice how upset she was, and

wouldn't have cared if he had.

Giles didn't notice, but maybe he would have cared.

Josie was too busy worrying about Rob, and he was too busy with the monsters in his head.

Gwen noticed and cared, but Gwen was being eaten up by private misery. Probably anybody felt like that if they knew they were dying, but Tanja had expected from Gwen a kind of gaiety in the face of death.

This left Step, who lived in another world.

They had a small expedition planned next day, another little castle, twenty minutes' driving. Gwen would come. It was only the morning, the second half of the morning.

Tanja was inclined to want to stay within reach of the telephone.

"Thérèse can answer the phone," said Rob. "Your mother speaks French. We'll be back by one. Thérèse knows that."

"Suppose she just comes?" said Tanja.

"She wouldn't do that, without calling."

"Dorothy did," said Step.

"Do come," said Peter to Tanja.

Tanja was surprised. Peter had never seemed to want her company. She was pleased. She was as surprised at herself at being pleased as she was at Peter.

She saw an exchange of glances between Peter and Josie. Aha. Josie had put Peter up to being nice to Tanja. It didn't mean a thing. It was a phony. He didn't care if she came or didn't, and would probably prefer it if she didn't. On that basis she said she would come.

Gwen made sure that Thérèse understood that Tanja's mother might call on the telephone or come in person.

*   *   *

The castle perched on a crag, itself on a hill. It was ruined but not flattened. From a distance it was just like many others.

In close-up it had a difference. On the hill, under the castle, were a stone building like a garage and a corrugated-iron shed. Rob parked behind the building, beside a beat-up truck.

An old man passed, deeply weatherbeaten, in rubber boots and sagging overalls. Rob asked him in gestures if it was all right to park where they were. The old man gestured widely, indicating that the whole hill was theirs, for parking the minibus or any other purpose. He was very welcoming.

Simon, already out and exploring, called round the corner, "Hey, it's some kind of laboratory."

This was not to be believed.

The rest of them climbed out into the tremendous sun. They walked round the corner of the building to the crazy, improvised shed. It was almost open to the sky, with walls on two sides only and an incomplete roof. There were vats and troughs and tanks, all linked up with bright plastic tubing that was centuries younger than the rest. They were cleaning it all out, the old man and a young one who needed a shave.

It was a winery. They were preparing for the new season. They explained it, showed it off, used to doing so, proud to do so. Gwen interpreted.

A monstrous roaring approached up the hill, out of sight behind the building. Motorcycles. The engines cut. Rob could not remember if he had locked the bus. He went round the corner. Three motorcycles were there, by the wall. The riders were not to be seen. They were already climbing to the ruin.

Rob got back in time to hear Gwen say that the men of the winery were father and son, heirs of antiquity. They had inherited the hill and the crag and the castle, and a large area of vineyard at the foot of the hill. Some of the grapes went off to the cooperative, but the best they used for the wine they made here, with these improvised plastic pipes, under this sky-punctuated roof. It was a sparkling wine, the method centuries older than that of Champagne. They would try some?

The old man's French was stranger, more Spanish even than Thérèse's. He spoke with great clarity and emphasis, as though to dull children. He was easier for the Anglo-Saxons to understand than a Parisian, because he separated words from one another, and sounded consonants which to a Parisian would have been silent. His words dropped like friendly stones, jagged and distinct, into the edge of his sunshine. He did not seem like a Frenchman at all. He was not a Frenchman. He was *Languedocien*. His people had been conquered by the Albigensian Crusade nearly eight hundred years before, but they had not been absorbed.

They tasted his wine, half made, last year's, no bubbles yet, no merit either, a rancid and acid taste.

There were bottles, thousands of bottles, in the building like a medieval garage, which was their *cave*. Giles bought three bottles, for which Rob paid thirty francs. The bottles had no labels, although there were labels. The labels had not been stuck on because there was no glue. The labels were well-printed, restrained, professional. They suggested a different kind of wine-making.

Buying the bottles was a gesture of friendship. Giles had no idea what they would do with them.

Of course they should examine the castle. Other visitors were presumably even now doing so, those who had arrived on the noisy machines. There was no charge. The castle had been pulled down and was now useless. Some of its stones had been used to build the *cave*. But it was important to the old man and his amazingly young son.

"C'est un château des Cathars! Des Cathars! Tous morts."

The old man sounded the "s" in *tous* and the "t" in *morts*, with the effect that they all understood him.

"Vous êtes Cathar, Monsieur?" said Step, in her best and almost only French.

But the old man did not understand, or pretended that he did not understand.

They fanned out from the winery, breaking one by one bonds which the old man wanted to make permanent. Giles took the key from Rob; he deposited the wine, and got easel, box and camp chair from the minibus. Gwen saw wild flowers; Step made her borrow the ancient cotton hat. Step herself, in Giles's panama, was archaeologist, explorer, historian, rock climber. Josie kept an eye on Simon. Rob and Tanja and Peter began separate, dilatory scrambles.

They were all out of sight of one another, except that Simon was in Josie's sight. None of them saw the other visitors, the ones with the noisy motorcycles.

Some later said they had seen, some that they had not seen, the all too explicable tragedy.

A small, light body, a pillowcase stuffed with rose-petals, floated rather than fell down the steepest flank of the crag on which the castle stood, of the hill on which the crag stood. It came to rest four hundred feet below the foot of the castle walls, a crumpled bundle of washing, as quiet as the ghosts in the castle.

All of them heard three motorcycles explode into life and snarl away down the hillside.

FOUR

Josie had done first aid; Step also, but long ago. It did not take an expert to know that Gwen was dead, though it might take an expert to know why.

Having climbed down one by one from various points, they stood in a shocked circle. Giles was the last to learn that something had happened, the last to arrive. Josie supposed that she ought to have shielded Simon from the sight of death: but, until they got there, they did not know it was death. There was nothing macabre or disgusting about the little undignified body.

By Gwen's open, upturned hand there was a bunch of flowering grasses—brome, quaking grass, cat's-tail, feather grass. She had held the bunch while she fell, held it until she stopped falling.

Step picked up the bunch and tidied it, and put it on

Gwen's breast. Near the body she found a clump of St. Bruno's lilies, white trumpets on reedlike stems, more impressive than Gwen's sad grasses. She put the lilies on Gwen's breast. There was nothing else helpful that any of them could do.

They were there for the rest of the day, and some well into the evening.

Things might have been quicker and easier if anybody could have been found who spoke English: or if anybody but Gwen had died.

The first problem was the telephone. There was none in the crazy little winery, in the *cave*, on the hill, in the vineyards—none nearer than the wine maker's house in the village three miles away. None of them in the meantime knew what to do with the body. What was the French law? Should it be left until examined by doctors and policemen? Giles said it should, remembering the body of his first wife at the foot of the stairs, people all day stepping over it. The old wine maker thought he knew, but he could not communicate his knowledge.

The doctor was like a terrier, the first policeman like a basset hound, his superior (arriving much later) like a bullmastiff. The police made a great show of executive efficiency, barking commands at one another.

It was hard on the children. It was hard on them all.

The exact positions of all persons on the hill at the moment of death? They climbed about, indicating where they had been. Scrambling on the crag was hot work for the uniformed policemen. Giles knew exactly where he had been; his camp chair was still where he had been sitting. The wine maker and his son knew where they had been, cleaning their equipment in the shed.

No one had seen the motorcyclists. No one had examined the machines, or taken the numbers. They had come from nowhere and returned, leaving no mark on the memory except the noise of their engines.

The body was taken away in an ambulance which was a mockery.

It was with difficulty established that Giles was the closest living relative of the deceased, and that neither he nor anybody else in the world benefited from Gwen's death.

Rob was at last allowed to take Josie and the children home. He would return for Giles and Step. The children seemed to have been sandbagged. They all felt sandbagged.

The circumstances had to be regarded as suspicious. The police, humanized by the spectacular evening, did not seem to think so, but the law required them to act as though they thought so. Any violent or sudden death had to be thoroughly investigated. It was the same in all civilized countries. The medical report was awaited. The motorcyclists would be traced. Meanwhile, the English and Americans had plans to leave the area, the country? No? Good. They must not do so until investigations were complete.

How long would that be? Ah. Languedocien shrugs were easier to understand than, without Gwen, Languedocien French.

Late, late Step and Josie went through Gwen's things. It could have been left until morning, but neither of them felt like sleep. Gwen had a couple of drawers of neat, threadbare clothes, a Bible, a toothbrush. She had not brought anything else. Practically, she did not own anything else.

There was no sign of the letter. Gwen must have burned her letter.

They were on their way at last to bed.

Rob said, from the depths of fatigue that clogged like treacle, "Simon said he was pushed."

"It wasn't true," said Josie. "It wasn't possible. None of us believed him."

"I believed him," said Step.

"What?"

"Of course he was pushed."

"Who by?"

"I don't suppose we shall ever know."

They were too tired to pursue it. They were almost too tired to sleep.

After breakfast, in the yard; a feeling of lassitude, as though they had all taken too many sleeping pills and not properly woken up.

Gwen would not have wanted them to leave simply because she had left. They could not leave, without the consent of the Chief of Police.

Peter snapped at Simon and Josie at Peter. They apologized to one another, muted, abashed. They were all a little unnatural. They did not know how to behave in the face of tragedy.

Was it tragedy? Gwen had been doomed, terminally ill. Brave as she was, she would not have been happy in that ward of that hospital.

"Maybe she had a heart attack," said Rob. "The effort

of climbing. That heat. Maybe she was dead before she fell."

"No," said Josie. "She was holding on to those flowers. I'm afraid she was alive when she fell."

Rob nodded. Josie was right. Peter was listening. Was this proper? Rob thought it was okay that Peter should listen. Better he should hear reasoned, adult speculation than spin terrible childish fantasies of his own, monsters that would invade his dreams.

Giles speculated rationally, too rationally. He said, "I think Step was right about that letter. It came from her doctor, and it quoted or enclosed the result of those tests. If you were Gwen's doctor, you'd tell her the truth, wouldn't you? I think that's what he did. The prognosis was as bad as could be. That's what I think."

"Nothing but misery ahead," said Josie.

"Pain. Uselessness."

"No!" said Step. "If you mean what I think you mean, you're utterly wrong. Whatever that letter foretold, Gwen would have faced it with courage. You know that, Giles! Gwen didn't jump off that hill. No. Not Gwen."

Peter was listening intently. He nodded. He agreed with Step.

Josie agreed with Giles. Giles had not given an explanation, but he had pointed at a possibility. If it were so, it was sad but not bad. Nobody could call that a sin. No God Josie could believe in would bar His gates to Gwen.

Rob said, "I agree about the heart attack. I agree with Step. But those guys on motorcycles. They went up the castle terribly quick, the moment they arrived. Usually a rider will take off his helmet, stamp around for a little, take a stroll, light a cigarette. Most people would take a look at the shack, like we did. But they went zoom up the hill. And away they went zoom the moment after Gwen fell. And how is it we never saw them?"

"It's all folds and creases and outcrops," said Josie. "Except for Simon, I never saw anybody."

"Yeah, but it's still extraordinary that *none* of us saw *any* of them."

"Not if they meant us not to see them," said Peter unexpectedly.

"That was what was in my mind," said Rob.

"I think that's fanciful," said Giles. "Three yobs from Toulouse, garage mechanics or builders' laborers—what possible connection could there be between them and Gwen?"

"You know, what we've all been forgetting," said Step after a pause, "is that Gwen was wearing my hat."

Later Rob said, "Gwen was disguised as you, Step, to the extent of wearing a distinctive hat that belongs to you."

"Yes."

"But only disguised for the benefit of somebody who knew you well, saw you regularly and recently. How would a stranger know that hat, or think that it was you that was wearing it?"

"They only had to watch the farm," said Tanja. "One man, with binoculars."

"Why would they do that?" said Giles. "What would be the point?"

"To put the finger on Step."

"Oh, come!"

"I was here when your sister came, Giles. I heard what she said."

Josie said to Rob, "Did anybody follow us yesterday? Did you see anybody behind us?"

"No. But you wouldn't have to tail very close in country like this. There's only one road for ten miles either way, any direction you're going. They *could* have picked us up here and followed us. It's not a thing I ever tried, but I think around here I could do it myself."

"I bet the police never find those men," said Peter. "I bet nobody saw their faces, anywhere. Just helmets and goggles, like spacemen, and false numbers on their bikes."

"I agree," said Rob, "which means they could come again. I agree with Tan about Dorothy Schofield, the way she talked. You should be careful, Step."

"Pooh. Gwen wouldn't want my holiday spoiled, and I won't let them spoil it. I'm as safe as a house."

"Which house?"

"Any house. This house. I've got friends."

"Why, sure, but unless you stay with us, or we with you, we're not all around you twenty-four hours a day."

"My other friends are. Scores of them. I'm one of their own. They won't let anything happen to me."

"'Gwen wouldn't want our holiday spoiled,'" quoted Rob to Josie. "It's already ruined. How can we stay here?"

"I don't think we can," said Josie. "Gwen's death is getting to me more and more. She's everywhere I look in the house, in the yard. We can't stay here."

* * *

Peter said to Josie, "We can't stay here. None of us can bear it."

Tanja said to Rob, "We can leave a message for Mom, with Thérèse."

"Leave a message?"

"When we go. We are going, aren't we? We must go. I can't stand it here any longer."

Giles said, over a lunch which none of them wanted, "I suppose the police will let us leave in a day or two. Step's right that Gwen wouldn't have wanted us to go on her account, but she wouldn't have wanted us to stay if it made us wretched."

"A day or two," repeated Rob blankly. He wanted to leave at once. Josie and the kids wanted to leave at once.

"From what I've heard about the French police," said Step, "it might be a bit more than that."

Shocked though he was by the tragedy, Giles felt a shaft of thankfulness. His old cousin had been spared the indignities and agonies of that slow promised death. Anybody would prefer to die suddenly, in the sun, with a handful of flowering grasses.

He did not take seriously their notions about his poor crazy sister.

He had no idea whether to take seriously Rob's uneasiness about his ex-wife and her sea captain. He had never seen those people. Accounts of Anna were barely credible—a film star, something between a Valkyrie and a character played by Mae West. Giles could not picture Dickie Hamlyn. He had never, as far as he knew, met a professional yacht skipper. Into his mind drifted images of earrings, red bandanas, hooks instead of hands, wooden legs. That was a pirate. Rob said he was a failed pirate. Rob would not be a reliable source on that subject. Rob himself had recently been a little crazy. He was not yet quite himself. Shocks like Gwen's death were most exactly what the doctor did not order.

A quiet life. They all wanted that, even the children. They wanted to be left alone. They wanted no more telephone calls. One of those had thoroughly upset Step; one, for different reasons, Rob and Tanja. They wanted no more letters. One had distressed Gwen and possibly killed her.

Grumbling, Giles set up his easel by the track below the farm.

Step resumed her communion with the rocks behind the farm. She had emerged from her dismay that Dorothy was somewhere near. She had acquired a new strength. She had found new confidence, though her account of its source was ridiculous.

She had lost her favorite cotton hat, once florally patterned, later paint-daubed. Gwen was wearing it when she fell but not when she landed. It was somewhere on that hillside, or blown to another hillside; it was stuck on a cypress or an olive tree, perhaps, or a church tower or a ruin or the horn of an animal. Step would not in any case have worn it again.

There were other hats, but Step did not like them. She liked Giles's panama, but he wanted that.

She found, instead of a hat, a big umbrella in the barn, a parasol. It advertised Martini in red and white. It had come from a bar, no doubt, discarded because it was stained and slightly damaged. Simon wanted it; Giles also; but Step said "Finders keepers," and took it with her to the hilltop.

Giles coveted the Martini umbrella, which was just the thing for a painter; but Step seldom let him use it.

Two uniformed policemen came, in a car with signs and searchlights and sirens. They brought an interpreter. They had some things for Giles to sign, and a copy of the postmortem report. The interpreter read it to Giles. Gwen had not died of a heart attack and then fallen. The cause of death was a fractured skull and other multiple fracturing.

No trace had yet been found of the motorcyclists. It was unfortunate that there was no description of them.

The investigation remained active, the file open, as the law required. But there was now no objection to the interment or cremation of the remains. Had the deceased left instructions in the matter? What was the feeling of the relatives?

They wanted to ask Gwen.

For much of her life, Gwen had expected to die in West Africa and to be buried there. She would not mind lying in Languedoc. That little broken body in the morgue was not Gwen; she was quite elsewhere. Rob offered to pay to have the body taken back to England for burial, but it was a hassle of a kind that would have seemed to Gwen preposterous. There was a Protestant cemetery in Toulouse, fifty miles away.

* * *

Making the arrangements was difficult. They badly needed Gwen, to sort out with the undertaker the details of her own funeral.

A bleak little service was conducted in the cemetery chapel. The minister had adenoids, and spoke no English. They tried to dress suitably, but they had brought nothing suitable. No one had anticipated a funeral. Thérèse came, shaming them in a magnificence of black. She was puzzled and shocked by the Protestant ceremony.

Etienne would have come, but could not. He was gloomy at having tenants with whom he could hardly communicate. He seldom spoke, but when he did the matter was important—electricity, water, drains, mice, paint, the roof.

They went afterwards to a café, Thérèse with them. They sat where they could see a corner of the great red Romanesque cathedral. The eight of them sat at adjoining tables out of doors, under umbrellas smarter than Step's. The streets were full of a bustle and animation which made a great change from Montferaude, though there was less activity than there would have been with all the university students there. Josie was glad it was the summer vacation, the students dispersed: they would have unsettled Rob, especially on top of that service, that burial.

"That cathedral," said Step, "was the church of Raymond de Toulouse, our greatest general."

"Whose?" asked Peter, out of politeness, knowing the answer.

"He led the defense of his friends and subjects, against

conquerors who called themselves crusaders."

"Well, the Cathars were heretics."

"Oh, that was simply their excuse! That's why it all makes me so angry. It was an international conspiracy, the purest power politics."

The others were now listening, because of the passion in Step's voice. Even Thérèse had an air of listening.

"The King of France," said Step, "wanted to gobble up the independent princedoms of the South. No wonder. They were rich, and full of gallantry and gaiety, music, poetry. They were the one civilized, tolerable part of Europe. All the rest was barbarous misery. Of course the King of France wanted them. The Pope gave him an excuse—the Cathars lived here. He could call his bare-faced aggression a crusade. Raymond de Toulouse was fighting for the whole civilization of the South, which happened to include the Cathars. That was why he was backed by King John of England. England didn't want to see the French crown suddenly twice as rich and powerful. That's where Simon comes in."

"Mm?" said Simon, startled.

"Simon de Montfort was a French subject but also an English Earl. He quarreled with King John and he lost his English inheritance. He was burning to get back at the English. That was why they picked him to lead a war against an ally of the English. He was delighted to be given the job. He was just the man for it, the only possible man. It was an extraordinary, calamitous coincidence that that man, feeling as he did, vindictive as he was, greedy as he was, with his military experience, should have been in that place at that time. Without that coincidence, the whole gigantic tragedy would never have happened."

"I guess you could say the same of Hitler," said Rob.

"Of course you could. And Peter the Great and Stalin and Pol Pot. If Hitler had never reached manhood, think of the saving of human misery. I'm going to have a closer look."

Step got up to look at the cathedral from another angle. She strolled off alone. None of the others was inclined to go out into the glare, to leave cool drinks for blazing pavement.

She was gone five minutes, the ice in her vermouth melting.

She came back thoughtful, perhaps unhappy, as though the cathedral had disappointed her or something had shocked her. She was unusually silent all the way back in the minibus, the gap filled by Thérèse. It could be gathered that Thérèse was telling them about the funeral as though they had not been there.

Josie was putting Simon to bed. Peter and Tanja were playing badminton in the barn; they seldom did things together, but the funeral seemed somehow to have brought them closer. They knew they felt exactly the same about Gwen, although they disagreed about everything else. The shuttlecock hit the immense beams, or lodged in the cobwebs between them.

Step said to Giles and Rob, "I haven't said anything till now because I didn't want to upset Josie and Peter. But I suppose I shall have to tell them."

"I can't advise you," said Giles, "until I know what you're talking about."

"I had a very great surprise this afternoon."

"By the cathedral? Yes, you did seem a little bilious when you got back."

"Nothing like as bilious as Josie's going to be. I saw Harry Christie. There was a woman with him. A tall, striking blond, not in her first youth. I suppose Angelika, but I've never met her."

"Did you know Harry?" asked Rob.

"Yes, of course. Josie was married to him when I married Giles. He hasn't changed at all. Put on some weight. Rather puffy. Very brown. Smart clothes. She's *very* smart. Deadly chic, I think you'd call it."

"They're in Iceland," said Giles. "We know that. Peter got a card."

"They've left Iceland."

"Are you absolutely sure?"

"Do you think I'd forget the face of a man who treated Josie like that?"

"No," said Rob. "That's a face you wouldn't forget."

"Did he see you?" asked Giles.

"I don't think so. I didn't go up and say hello. It doesn't matter if he saw me. Everybody knows we're here. He knows Peter's here. What is Peter going to make of this?"

"What Tan made of the same deal," said Rob. "He'll be puzzled and hurt."

"Yes. What on earth does Harry think he's about?"

"This is all too much of a coincidence for me," said Giles. "I don't believe in coincidences."

"It must be coincidence," said Step. "There's no reason Harry should ever even have heard of your first wife, Rob, let alone her husband. Or the other way round. Would Anna know anything about Harry and Angelika?"

"I don't think so," said Rob. "I can't see how. If I see her it's to talk about Tan, not gossip about Josie's first husband. There can't be any connection at all."

"Yes, there can," said Giles. "One of them could have made a connection. Harry could know about Rob, all he wants to know, all there is to know, from Peter. He'd know there was a first wife. He could easily find out the name. He could get a brochure from a yacht-charter company, so he'd have an address, the name of the yacht, everything. He could have done that any time in the last ten years. Or it could be the other way about. It might all have started with that pirate—what's he called? Hamlyn."

"What might all have started?" said Step.

"Whatever they're doing together."

"I don't think they're doing anything together," said Rob. "But it would be interesting to know if Anna's in Toulouse."

"I don't suppose Harry's staying in Toulouse," said Giles. "Who would? They're sponging off somebody with a house in the country. But if they came to see Peter, why aren't they seeing Peter? If they came for other reasons, they'd surely see Peter as well. They'd surely tell him they were coming."

"Anna didn't tell Tan," said Rob.

"I wonder where Dorothy is," said Step. "Whether Harry knows about Anna or not, he certainly knows about Dorothy. He was married to her niece. He couldn't have met her, could he?"

"He could have met her now," said Giles. "I still don't like coincidences. All these people from all over the world, popping up out of our past, all together in a remote place like this? I *don't* like coincidences. Also I don't like or trust Harry Christie. Hum. I can see why you didn't tell Josie straight away, darling, but you'll have to tell her."

Peter at first flatly refused to believe it. He did like and trust his father.

Convinced at last, he said, "Well, they've only just arrived. They've only just got here from Iceland. I expect they called up when we were out, when we were all at the funeral. They'll try again this evening, I expect. Or tomorrow."

The telephone was silent all evening, and all the following day.

"I know how you feel," said Tanja.

When a group stays in a strange place, it develops habits, rituals. This happens even when there is no director, no natural leader, no commanding intelligence who decrees who shall do what and when. At certain moments a bottle of chilled white wine will materialize in the shady part of the yard; at others coffee, a chessboard, a sketch pad. There come to be times when postcards are written, hair shampooed, ghosts consulted.

For Rob, the pleasantest of all these rituals was the nightcap under the stars with Giles. The children were long in bed, Step and Josie going to bed. The men drank Cognac-Perrier with ice, having settled on this well-proved *digestif* after learning the local price of Scotch whisky. They sat on the rickety chairs by the rickety table in the yard. The flagstones of the yard, night-storage heaters, rendered and remembered the heat of the sun, and insects chirruped in the accent of Languedoc. Often Giles had two drinks.

The two men were as different as they could be, in age, background, country, career, tastes, interests, financial circumstances; they had never had a chance to know one another well, but they were so congenial that no conversation was necessary and any conversation was possible.

Rob said, out of a long silence, "I know what happened to Josie's mother. It happens every day all over the world."

"Yes. Accidents in the home. A major killer."

"But what happened to Step's husband? How did Dorothy fantasize murder out of that? Did he just die?"

"No, it was an accident."

"Another one of those."

"Also, alas, common enough. He was fishing. It was poor old Edward's one passion, his only hobby, practically his only topic of conversation."

"What kind of fishing? Out in the sea?"

"Oh no, very purist, salmon and trout, only used a fly. People were kind to him, I think. He could never afford good fishing of his own. He was asked to various rivers. That time he was on one of those fast, treacherous East Highland salmon rivers. Findhorn, Spey, Deveron, I'm not sure. Slippery rocks, very tricky wading, the hell of a current. He was a bit doddery for that sort of thing. He should never have been alone. They found him ten miles downstream, caught in somebody's illegal net."

"I thought when it was dangerous you went out on the end of a rope."

"Yes, with a gillie at the other end. He had a rope.

He tied it to a tree. He didn't know how to tie a knot."

"That's one thing fishermen do know."

"Knots in rope are different from knots in gut. It came undone. He took the rope with him. It might have snagged on something. That might have saved him. All very silly and avoidable. Step blamed herself, for letting him go out on his own. Nobody else blamed her."

"Was this before or after Josie's mother died?"

"Just before. So we comforted one another. Why are you asking?"

"We were talking about your sister. That story of hers. The question occurred to me. I'm sorry if I seem ghoulish."

"Not ghoulish. But you've given me a thirst."

Still the telephone was silent, and no letters came.

From the open side of the yard, from the top of the track, the hillside sloped unevenly, steeply, yellow and gray by day, until it flattened into vineyards and melon fields.

Josie stood looking at the evening. The sky was by Tiepolo, theatricality in pastel colors. There were two wheeling kites, miles away, miles apart.

Peace. Peace?

If Josie had an enemy in the world, she supposed it was Anna Hamlyn. If she had another, it was Angelika Christie. If Rob had an enemy in the world it was Harry Christie. If another, it was Dickie Hamlyn. If Step had an enemy it was Dorothy Schofield.

The Kemps were rich. The Hamlyns worked hard for a thin living, though they did it in a nice climate. The Christies probably worked even harder, being courtiers and toadies all over Europe.

The Hamlyns were supposed to be in Turkey, the Christies in Iceland, Dorothy in Argentina. What drew them all here? *Could* it be coincidence? Why no sign, no signal to the children? Josie was distressed for the children: those pigs of parents. Were they hiding, waiting, watching? Why were they?

Somebody was watching. There were eyes on the farm. Josie was aware of scrutiny. There was no watcher, only dry grass and rock and olive trees and the flat ocean of vineyard.

Josie's spine crawled ever so slightly, in the stare of malevolent eyes.

They had another month at the farm, the whole of August. That was what Rob had paid for. They were obliged to stay, while the obscure procedures of the law nibbled at the death of Gwen.

The children were becoming dark brown. Tanja's hair and eyebrows were white. There was enough for them to do if the minibus was continually used. It drank a lot of gas.

Simon, an intelligent child, constructed a world of his own in the barn and among the rocks, so that he did not depend on the intermittent patronage of the older ones. He had cities and castles and armies, among which he squirmed, to which he made speeches.

He seemed to have invented a language for his private games. He would not talk about it. He was frightened, perhaps, of derision, dismissal. He had the prickly dignity of young children with active imaginations; he was protecting a flimsy world against the killing breath of adult comment.

So absorbed was he in this world of his making that sometimes you would have sworn that he was talking to somebody, that he was carrying on a conversation, that he was not alone.

Step said that he was not alone, that none of them was alone.

Simon addressed persons of his fancy, giving them names of his fancy. One of his imaginary friends was Antonin. That was the local saint, who had given his name to the village: an easy choice, almost automatic. Then there were Valerien, Marius, Domitien. The French forms of Latin names. Such names had survived in Roman Provence, until the Albigensian Crusade smashed the ancient Provençal civilization.

Step explained it all. Step talked an awful lot of nonsense. Simon had got the names from Thérèse, perhaps.

In a strange way, Gwen was more vivid to them for not being there. One had grown used to turning to her, pointing something out, asking her to laugh at something. She always reacted quietly, kindly, responsively.

Now all of them turned to share an ephemeral comedy with Gwen, a fleeting beauty, a cloud like a camel; and there was an empty space where she had been larger than the space she had occupied in life.

"What's your father doing?" said Tanja to Peter. "Why does he want to hurt my dad?"

"He doesn't. He wouldn't hurt anybody."

"He hurt Josie."

"He didn't mean to. He's told me all about that. It was a long time ago."

"It was horrible."

"It's none of your business. What's your mother doing?"

"She must have a very good reason for going wherever she went."

"I believe you know what she's doing."

Tanja could not resist. She was putting herself one up. She was only twelve years old. She was competitive and suspicious. She said, "Maybe I do."

Peter said that, after all, he didn't believe a word of it. It was almost true. But a little bit of him believed her.

Josie was the only person Peter could discuss it with. Grandpapa would be painting, and thinking of nothing but painting. Step would be talking to ghosts. Rob wouldn't listen to any suggestion that Tan was hiding something from him. But Peter did not want to bother his mother about it. She was worried enough already. She said she wasn't, but she showed it in little ways.

Giles was not sensitive to atmosphere, as Step was, as Josie perhaps was. But he had a trained and logical mind, a masculine mind. The women were intuitive. That was not without value—it was different and complementary, and it could find a short cut to an answer. But you used what you had, and Giles had a methodical brain.

Mathematically, what were the odds against the purely coincidental presence of all those people in Languedoc? The figure was astronomical. It was impossible.

Links could be hypothesized. On the face of it they

were improbable enough, but a lot more probable than coincidence.

It was rum. It was not worrying, but the effect on the others was worrying—on Step, Josie, Rob, on Tanja and Peter, who seemed both to have had slaps in the face. Simon would not worry, at his age, but the worry of the others would get through to him. It would be very nice to hear that all those people had gone away.

Assume they had come for a purpose, a common purpose. You had to assume that. They would not go away until they had accomplished it. What was their purpose?

Giles did a bad drawing that morning. Even he knew it.

Piqued, he tried the same subject the following morning. He said he had been distracted by the glare; he needed the Martini umbrella. Step surrendered it with only nominal protest. She said that she was entitled, under the circumstances, to borrow Giles's panama. Giles wanted both hat and umbrella, but eventually surrendered the hat.

Rob took Josie and the children off to the place where they could swim.

The parasol had been designed to fit into the middle of a café table. It had no struts to make it free-standing. This was never a problem to Step, who shared it with a spike of rock or leaned it against a bank. It was a trial to Giles, who was obliged in the end to build a small cairn of rocks in which to bed the pole. Even then, an incautious movement of the camp chair had the whole thing over. He persevered, with military grit, keeping his temper with the stupid stones.

His position was well and ill chosen. From halfway

down the hill below the farm, on the steep part to the west, the angles of the roofs were a lovely study for a skilled architectural draughtsman. A sophisticated grasp of perspective was required, as was an allowance for the irregularities of the old buildings. Giles in his previous effort had made too much allowance for these oddities, disciplined by too little regard for the rules of drawing, with the result that he had made the roofs look rubbery, flexible, concave. The desired effect was massive solidity. He was determined to rise from the ashes of this failure, to protect himself from the glare and to put all those damned *revenants* out of his mind.

Usually he was at once too proud and too impatient to start with a careful pencil. His teacher in Somerset, a bouncy female, approved of banging in with a pen. But on this occasion, chastened, Giles drew the major lines with a pencil and even a ruler, stood back a few paces to contemplate the effect, erased a line and replaced it, all with a twinge of guilt. At last he reckoned he had fused various disparate vanishing points. He put aside the pencil and picked up a pen. He liked a good big pen with a good broad nib; he used Winsor & Newton "peat brown" ink, which had the authority of black without its severity. He inked in his pencil lines, and then many more lines, details round the windows, some of the stones of the walls, part of the tile-hung eaves. It was interesting but difficult to draw a group of buildings from below; it gave the artist a crick in his neck.

Giles let his ink dry, which, even in the shade of the umbrella, it did very quickly in that heat. He made himself wait until he was sure all the ink was really dry. So often he had been impetuous, his cuff spreading ink over the drawing, no good for the drawing, no good for the cuff.

He erased all traces of pencil. He owed it to himself to do that. He would not, if brought to the point, precisely deny having used a pencil, but he would not volunteer the information. He brushed away the rubbery crumbs. He contemplated his drawing, and found it excellent.

Sky. The tone should strengthen between horizon and zenith, and be broken by clouds. Today there was no horizon and there were no clouds, and the sky he could see was merciless unaltering blue. Nature must be improved upon. He mixed a squeeze of Winsor Blue with water in his palette. With clean water he wetted the area of the sky, steering the point of his brush carefully round the knobs and juts of the buildings. Much care was needed; speed was needed, to paint the sky before the paper dried. He sloshed blue paint on to the wetted paper, spread it about with the brush, dabbed at it with a Kleenex. The result was more an English than a Languedocien sky, but it had more interest and variety than the monotonous original.

Another pause. This was not a moment when he wanted colors to run into one another. He washed his brush. He stood up to stretch his legs, and stepped back to look at his sky.

At the very moment he did so, there was a crash, an explosion, a tremendous impact. Easel and umbrella were smashed. It was a rock the size of a football. It had missed Giles by a yard. The things it had hit were flimsy—the easel now matchwood, the drawing rent, the umbrella ruined. Giles was pretty flimsy, too. In the

Italian campaign he had seen brains spread over rocks in the Apennines. He did not have to imagine how his own would have looked, but only to remember. He was trembling so that h[illegible] to sit down on the ground, though he knew he would have trouble standing up again.

A trickle of little stones followed the big stone, dislodged by its passing. Then the silence was absolute.

FIVE

Giles was for a long moment unable to think or stand or stop trembling. He was disgusted with himself. He had been shot at and bombed without going to pieces like this. Was it age? He would have expected to be braver, not more cowardly, having less to lose, having known so many deaths. He would have expected to outface death, as Gwen had done until her last and lost and dreadful letter: and here he was whimpering on the ground with his damned hands flapping like palm fronds.

His drawing ruined. His old friend the easel.

At last able to think—not yet able to stand—Giles looked up. His eye followed the steep slope of the ground. It was pretty obvious that the rock had come from the crag on which rested the western end of the farm buildings, an outcrop dotted with boulders which sloped gently and then sharply. Nobody had thrown a thing of that size. It had come loose and rolled. Come loose? How? No other rocks had come loose.

There was nobody at the farm, except Thérèse.

Step appeared, hurrying, below Giles on the hillside. She was fanning herself with the panama as she crossed the uneven ground and began climbing to his level.

As soon as she was near enough, she called out, "What's been happening?"

Giles, still sitting on the ground, flapped his hands at the ruin of the easel and parasol.

Step crossed the remaining yards and looked at the havoc.

"Good God," she said. Then, "That's my best umbrella. What did you do, fall over it?"

Giles pointed at the rock which had done the damage. Step immediately looked up to see where it could have come from.

She said, "Thérèse wouldn't have dropped a stone on your head."

"No."

"I knew something was wrong," said Step. "I got a sort of telephone message. I ran like a goat. Was it loosened by rain?"

"What rain?" said Giles, the first words he had managed.

"The rain that came down when it last rained. I wonder if Thérèse saw anybody. We'd better go and ask her."

"Give me a minute," said Giles.

"Poor old boy. You'd better have your hat back."

Thérèse had seen nobody. As far as could be understood, this became grounds for complaint. She was lonely with nobody to talk to all day.

It was not to be expected that Thérèse would have seen anybody. She worked pretty hard in the house, and she never looked out of a window. For her it was all too familiar to be worth looking at. Anybody coming to push rocks down the hill would have watched for a while, seen the minibus away, made sure the house was empty except for Thérèse, and then moved stealthily, out of sight of the windows. It would be easy to approach the farm unseen, from almost any direction.

"I didn't hear a car," said Step.

"Nor I. No kind of engine. Nothing."

"If somebody came they walked."

"From where? The village? A town?"

"From wherever they left their car."

"You can't hide a car in this landscape."

"You can hide a bicycle or a scooter. Shove it in a vineyard."

"They bust up my easel."

"And my umbrella. They nearly bust you up. The others will want to know what's happened. What are we going to tell them?"

"Why should the others know anything happened?"

"Easel. Umbrella. Rob and Josie ought to be warned."

"What against?"

"That's what we don't know. Do you still think there's a conspiracy? All those people here, all keeping quiet?"

"I still don't think it's coincidence."

"Anybody who'd been watching this farm," said Rob that evening, "would know who's usually under that umbrella. And if they were above, they wouldn't have seen who was under it today."

"That thought," said Step, "had occurred to me."

There was still no sign from Tanja's mother, or Peter's father, or Giles's sister.

Josie said, "Simon said he was pushed. I thought he was fibbing. Now I think he thinks he was pushed."

"What changed your mind?" asked Rob.

"I don't know. Step. Simon himself. Something in the atmosphere."

"The atmosphere is not what it was," said Rob. "I give you that much."

The atmosphere in that bedroom in the farmhouse seemed all right. They lay in a big hard bed looking up at a delta of cracks in the plaster of the ceiling, an impossible river, a plan of the veins of a strange animal. The walls were painted a cool pale green, but they had the air of walls more used to a heavy floral wallpaper. Some of the furniture was so solid that an axe would have bounced off it, some so flimsy that a dropped match would have broken it. The large window opened on screaming hinges; to a smaller one in another wall somebody had given an incongruous Gothic arch.

These things were lit by a bedside lamp with a frilly, amber-colored shade. It was a kind light; it was a kind room. Here more than in the yard or on the hillside one could have the illusion of peace.

Josie's mother had told her about days in Kent during the war, in 1940 and 1941 when things were blackest, bombs falling, invasion imminent. You could look at whitethorn and apple blossom, hear birdsong, and not believe that any war was going on. That the enemy was barely thirty miles away, across the Straits of Dover. How far away was the enemy now? One mile? Ten yards? Who? Why?

They were tired, but too shaken by the story of the falling rock to be sleepy.

They had all looked at the place where they thought the fallen rock must have come from. There was nothing to be seen, only rocks and a feathering of dry yellow grass, any bit of hill in any hot, dry place. No window from the farm gave in that direction. An army could come and go. No footprint showed in the parched ground, no mark or memorial or clue or pointing finger.

They searched about in the last of the sun, not knowing what they were looking for. A trace of engine oil, a book of matches, a letter with an address, a perfumed glove?

"What I mean is," said Josie lying in bed, "nobody could have mistaken Simon for Step."

"No."

"Gwen they could. Daddy they could. Not Simon."

"No."

"Then why was he pushed down the hill?"

"Honey, Simon wasn't pushed down any hill."

"Oh. Nor he was," said Josie, confused. "But still he thinks he was."

"It's another coincidence which is too much for me," said Giles after breakfast in the kitchen. He was hunched over his third cup of coffee.

Josie stacked plates. Thérèse and Etienne had not yet arrived. Step had taken her second cup of tea upstairs, to go back to bed with it and with one of her books about medieval France or the system of the Manichaeans. The children were out, Simon intent on his warring cities, visible to Josie through the kitchen window. Rob took one of his pills in a glass of mineral water.

"Gwen in Step's hat, you under Step's umbrella," said Rob, after swallowing his pill with difficulty.

He did not dislike those pills particularly. He disliked the fact of pills, the need for pills. Josie was strict with him about the pills, and he tried to be strict with himself. Tanja also supervised Rob's taking of his pills, in a way which showed her concern for him, to a point that threatened to be boring.

"Probably Gwen felt giddy and lost her balance and fell," said Giles. "My rock had been prising itself off the hillside for six centuries, and it happened to fall when it did. Can you believe that conjunction?"

"Yes," said Rob.

"Gwen happened to be wearing Step's hat. The circumstance of my sitting under Step's umbrella was the result of my choice, my insistence, unpredictable to anybody, unpredicted even by myself. These fluky, accidental events triggered the same result. Very nearly the same result. Gwen's dead and I missed death by a yard. Don't you see cause and effect?"

"You're introducing logic where the writ of logic doesn't run," said Rob.

"Why doesn't it?" said Giles. "We're talking about events, observed phenomena, three-dimensional things in exact places at exact times, hats on people's heads, stones falling down hillsides. What excludes logic? We're talking about mathematics."

"Are we?" said Josie from the draining board. "Which of us do you mean by 'we'?"

"The odds against these coincidences," said Giles.

"In biology, in the whole of genetics," said Rob, "chance plays an enormous rôle. The existence of this planet, as a possible environment for human life. Human life itself."

"Chance?" said Josie.

"Sure."

"Where does God come into it?"

"I don't know," said Rob.

"Nor do I," said Giles. "Step does, but the God she has in mind is a bit different from the one I was brought up on. Do you know the *Ring?* "

"Are we suddenly talking about Wagner?" said Josie.

"Yes, of course. It has several themes. Retribution. The liberation of man from the old order, his discovery of his power over his own destiny. And the rule of law. The law controls even the gods. The gods broke an immutable moral law, so they destroyed the basis of their own authority. They cheated when they paid the giants for building Valhalla."

"That," said Josie, "has as much to do with what's going on here as strawberry jam or *Alice in Wonderland.*"

"You miss my point," said Giles. "I'm miles ahead of you. I'm going too fast for you. Mathematics, as I understand the matter, is an abiding reality in the context of which the entire universe functions. Mathematics includes the laws of chance. The laws of chance exclude the possibility of coincidence as an explanation of what's been happening."

"Then, as we've all been saying," said Rob. "Step should take care."

"Yes, but how are you going to make her take care?"

"At the same time," said Rob, "you don't believe Step about your sister. You don't believe Tan and me about your sister."

"It's wonderful how one's views are modified," said Giles, "by rocks falling out of the sky."

Step refused to take care. She had emerged with a vengeance from the shadow of fear, as though she had consulted a spiritual counselor, and been given assurances about her safety. She was ridiculous, admirable, and a serious liability. An eye had to be kept on her quite as much as on Simon, but she evaded eyes and hid behind rocks and went away scrambling on her own.

"I am too old to have a nanny," she said. "Let alone so many nannies. None of you understands. I am perfectly safe."

Sometimes she wore pink cotton trousers, sometimes a denim skirt. She had sensible sandals and a tapestry bag full of books. She wore Giles's panama hat, and various pairs of spectacles.

Of Thérèse that evening Step said, "In another life she will be silent, a creature incapable of speech. A mute swan. Like the swan, she will sing only on her deathbed."

"Poor Thérèse," said Josie. "It's probably lucky for all of us there's no such thing as reincarnation."

"No such thing?" said Step. "What nonsense you do talk, dear."

"Do you truly believe in reincarnation, Step?"

"Certainly we do. For some individuals, not all. You may need another life, or many other lives, to come out into the light. The Buddhists overcomplicate the matter, but they have a glimpse of the truth. Redemption is an entirely personal matter, you see. It's simply a comfortable illusion that a Redeemer in heaven has done all the work for us. We've got to do it ourselves. We must struggle for light against darkness in the world round us and in our own souls. There's a touch of Mani in Calvinism. We're not exactly on our own, because there are angels of light sent to help us. Jesus Christ is quite one of the most important, though the Christians make excessive claims for him. There are instruments of darkness, too, children of Satan. The whole of human history is the war between the two. They fought quite a battle here. The forces of darkness seemed to win. They conquered the ground, but not the souls of the people, not the ones they left alive or the ones they killed. They didn't leave many alive. 'The grass in the fields was dyed red as roses.' "

"Step, are you drunk?" said Giles.

"Probably. We despise material things, but we always made good wine."

The light in the kitchen was harsher than that in Josie and Rob's bedroom directly above, but it was still a benignant place. Thérèse left dinner in the oven, or ready to put in the oven or in a pan or on the grill. It was a formula devised long before. It worked perfectly well. Thérèse would have resisted any change, in the direction of her doing more work or less or something different. The big table was so deeply scarred that no further damage to it mattered. It must have been assembled in the room—it was too big for doors or windows. The chairs teetered on the stone-flagged floor, from the medieval irregularity of the surface. Though the walls were plastered, they somehow gave evidence through the skin of their stony massiveness. The pots and pans were cast-iron or copper; they hung from hooks in the wall like sloths or giant bats, décor of a genre painting, more often dusted than scrubbed. There were modern pans in a cupboard for the electric cooker.

They all stared at these familiar things, which they had come to love, which they had come to hate.

It was extraordinary that a prison could wear such a comfortable face.

Their communication with the outside world was by minibus and Etienne's pickup. There was a bus stop in the village, but the bus went nowhere near the farm. There was a bicycle in the barn that had collapsed onto itself like an umbrella after a hurricane.

It was possible to walk to the village, but in that heat it was a weary way.

The telephone was usable but scarcely used. The post came with Thérèse, but there was scarcely any post.

Isolation, absolute quiet, was the whole point of the place, but . . .

"I must have my hair done again," said Step. "I'll call Madame Thingummy. Etienne can take me and someone can collect me."

"You despise material things," said Giles.

"Certainly. I'm thinking of the rest of you."

She came out of the house two minutes later. She said, "It doesn't work. It's dead. There's nothing."

Giles sighed theatrically, and went indoors.

He came out saying, "It's dead. There's nothing."

"Thérèse can report it."

"She hasn't got a telephone."

"There's one in the bar."

"She never goes to the bar."

"Etienne can report it."

"I have a feeling," said Giles, "that in this area, at this time of year, the telephone may take a long time to fix."

"Never mind," said Step. "When did we last use it?"

Tanja minded. The hope had not died that her mother might call.

Peter minded. His father might call.

Josie minded. She wanted to be able to shout for help, although she did not know to whom to shout, or against what she might need help.

Etienne said that he had reported the failure. It was not a fault at the exchange, but either at the farm or somewhere along the line between the farm and the automatic exchange in the village. It would be investigated, and action taken. But the service was short-handed—many persons were on vacation. It was not an emergency. They were not doctors or government officials. It took a long time to extract this information from Etienne, who divulged it reluctantly, drop by drop, giving them pauses for alternative translations.

Etienne's own responsibilities did not extend to the telephone, and he had never touched it; he was, he believed, forbidden to meddle with it, that function being exclusive to properly qualified engineers.

Rob tried to trace the telephone wire among the snaking wires which entered or left the house. It lost itself among them. If he had identified it, he would not have known what to do with it.

He was used to having contact with the world when he wanted it. He was uneasy at isolation. He did not believe in watchers or conspiracies, but he understood the merit of Giles's logic and the reaction of Josie to the atmosphere. He took his pills and napped in the afternoon and beat down the chilly shadows at the edge of his mind.

Thérèse fell silent. Her silence was relative, not absolute; she was certainly a good deal quieter than she had been.

Josie thought she was the only person who noticed the change. Her father had not been given to listening to Thérèse; Step was not given to listening to anybody (to anybody clothed in flesh); with Rob and the children the question hardly arose—they were simply not around for Thérèse's monologues. Josie had not been around much, either. She kept out of Thérèse's way. She knew very well that servants constantly supervised became resentful, mistrustful because mistrusted, suspected of scamping the dusting or sweeping cigar ash under the hearthrug. Nobody could suspect darling old Gwen of being suspicious, so that she had harmlessly and usefully been Thérèse's sounding board.

Was Thérèse mourning Gwen, wearing silence like her monumental black?

Was Thérèse deterred from speech because she knew

nobody could understand her? Unlikely. It had never stopped her before. She had been more voluble when Gwen was there, but hardly taciturn when Gwen was out.

The full burden of Thérèse fell on Josie. She could not ask any of the others to share it. Josie was a dependant wife. She had had a career of a kind, simply because she had to support herself and Peter; she had relinquished it with thankful joy. She was much better and happier at doing what she was doing, being a wife and mother. Part of that role, in this particular context, was being the audience for Thérèse. It was not brave or glamorous—feminists of both sexes would have derided Josie's view of her function—it was what had to be done, and by her.

Of the little Thérèse now said, there was little Josie understood. That little she was slow to understand, because it was bizarre. When she had understood it, she was not sure that she had done so. Thérèse thought, it seemed to Josie, that they blamed her for the rock that nearly killed Giles.

Thérèse was at the time alone in the farm. No doubt about that. She herself said so. The rock came from the jut of ground just west of the farm; not much doubt about that, either. To this extent, circumstantially, there might be grounds for suspecting Thérèse. But none of them had done so, not for a second. They might have, but they just plain didn't.

Josie said all this to Thérèse, painstakingly, in awkward schoolgirl French. Thérèse turned with a face of stone back to scrubbing potatoes.

* * *

Rob said, "I didn't notice this silence, but I take your word for it."

"Of course you haven't noticed it. You're here to not listen. Not to listen. You know what I mean."

"Maybe she thinks we're mad because she takes a little loot home in the evening."

"Oh. I don't think it's that. That's almost worse. How can I explain that we don't mind her stealing a bit?"

"Don't try. She doesn't think it's stealing."

"Well, exactly. How do I say, to someone like Thérèse, 'We understand, we don't mind, we know it's a perk.'"

"We didn't know how much we needed Gwen."

The kitchen was a painting by Bonnard—brilliant southern sun, shadows of green and purple, strong colors of ceramics, reflected glare of metal. Thérèse at the sink was Flemish, head enwrapped, huge arms up to the elbows in dishwater.

Josie knew she had to do it.

Haltingly, she said that they could easily spare a proportion of the carpet shampoo, the courgettes, the butter.

Thérèse did not raise her head from the sink. It was impossible that she had not heard Josie, almost impossible that she had not understood her. She was quiet with a vengeance. That which had been mentioned was unmentionable. Thérèse pretended that she had not heard.

That evening, both Thérèse and Etienne left the farm ostentatiously empty-handed.

* * *

"I made things worse," said Josie.

"You showed moral courage," said Rob. "It was probably a mistake. It usually is."

Step sent a message by Thérèse to the lady in the village who did hair. At least, she thought she had done so. It was not clear if Thérèse had delivered the message, if an appointment had been made. Thérèse's words were still fewer, and her accent more opaque.

Step said she would take a chance. Rob took her to the village in the minibus, arriving at eleven. She would be an hour. He would wait, look around, look at the church, have a drink.

He had looked around before, inspected the church, had a kir at the village's single gloomy bar. He was prepared to do these things again, to save six miles driving in the midday heat.

There was not much of Montferaude-St-Antonin—a few acres of squat, secret houses, side by side and back to back, built of big pink bricks. There was a Romanesque church, heavily restored, with a fat square tower of unguessable date. The church flanked the one *place*, where there had been a market, where the bar had no parasols outside, where heavy rock music pounded from within, where the *patron* dropped ash from his cigarette as though laying a trail for draghounds.

Step disappeared inside the house of the lady who did hair. It was exactly like all the other houses in the village. Its windows were shuttered. It was blind to the immediate world but not to the larger world: it had a television aerial on the roof. They all did. The door closed behind

Step, and silence fell. It appeared the gamble had paid off.

Rob strolled about the village, by little streets named for Napoleon and de Gaulle. He tried to keep in the shade. There were ancient women in black, and a few parked cars. They were not motorist cars. There were no tourists. Children could be heard from somewhere, shouting with the special intensity of the French at play.

Were the people away on holiday? Where did you go on holiday to from a place like this? What could you afford? What would you look for? Noise, life, crowds? These people had a different perspective. Rob tried to think into their minds—this as home, those fields and vineyards as frontiers—and found it as difficult as imagining the emotions of a Martian.

There was a poster of Chirac and a bigger one of Mitterrand, both weathered and defaced. A Dubonnet advertisement had been painted on the side of a barn a very long time before.

The terracotta tiles of the roofs were like the waves of the sea in Baroque stage machinery. Within the confines of the village there was no living green thing; but immediately at its edge was the paradox of a parched red desert bursting with grapes and melons.

The door of the church was open. Rob went in, pulling off his khaki safari hat. It was dark. It was not cool, but it was cooler than the glaring *place*. The interior of the church was bleak, almost unadorned, the altar simple, the windows small and uncolored; no pews or benches, but a few rows of rickety chairs with cane seats: no pictures, few candles. To Rob it had an almost Calvinistic feel, familiar to him from Puritan New England.

Had Step's Cathars used this place for their heretical worship, those ascetic people who did without pomp and vestments and golden ornaments? That was the feeling the place gave, as though it had been untouched by the Albigensian Crusade and the Counter-Reformation, as though it had gone on in secret simplicity while the world rolled fatly forward in incense and embroidery . . .

An old woman materialized from the shadows of a side chapel. She was, no doubt, the reason for the church being open. (Another reason might be that there was nothing in it worth stealing.) She gave a start when she saw Rob, standing with his hat in his hands in the middle of the church. She dropped her broom. He stepped forward to pick it up for her. She gave a gasp—a little shout: if it was a word Rob did not understand it. She turned her back on him; she put herself between him and the broom, as though to protect the broom, to save the church's property from the marauder.

Rob did not like being cast as a robber, a Vandal. He was a little nettled. He had meant only to help. She was a very old lady.

He said carefully, "*Bonjour, madame.*"

She turned. She stared at him through the gloom. Her head was draped like a nun's. Her hands were deformed with arthritis.

"*Vous êtes l'anglais?*" she said suddenly, loudly, her voice surprisingly deep.

"*Je suis américain.*"

"*Ah! Hé! Dieu! Allez! L'église est fermée! Personne permis!*"

Her voice was nasal. Her "R"s rolled against her teeth,

and she sounded the "S" of *permis* with the sound of a "Z."

She picked up the broom, straightening painfully. She waved the broom at him, minatory, driving him out.

"*Mais, madame—*" Rob began, as soothingly as he knew how.

"*L'église est fermée!*"

It was simply untrue. The door was open. She was there, in the house of God.

"*L'église est fermée!*"

She crossed herself as he backed deprecatingly through the door.

On the corner across from the church were two little shops, apparently identical, village shops selling everything. For most things that were wanted it was necessary to go to a town, to send a list to Etienne's wife.

Rob passed the first shop. He did not want to buy anything, anything that was in this shop. He looked in through the window. A thin girl with dyed hair was putting something in the window, something for sale. She saw him, and looked away. She moved away from the window, taking with her whatever she had meant to display. There was no doubting that he had driven her away from the window. In God's name, why?

Rob went into the shop, curious, piqued. The girl was already barricaded behind the till. She looked wary. She did not look like a girl employed to sell things. Rob had been in the shop a few times before, and he had no memory of anything odd—of anything like this nervous hostility. He thought he remembered this particular girl behaving as girls do who work in French shops—almost too polite, showering them with thanks for their patronage.

She waited for him to say something. That was reasonable. He had come into the shop. He looked round for inspiration—wine, various aperitifs, stacks of cans, oil, fresh vegetables, pâté and sausage, cheese, bread. There was no bakery in the village. The bread came daily from the town. Possibly this bread was fresher than the bread Thérèse had brought in the morning.

"Du pain, s'il vous plait."

"N'y a pas."

No bread? But there was a stack of yard-long, cigar-shaped loaves.

"Déjà vendus," said the girl.

She repeated it, in a flat voice, as though she had been hypnotized. All the bread was already sold.

Rob walked out of the shop into the *place*, where the sun hit like a ball bat.

Two of them.

Did he suddenly look ridiculous, obscene? Some smear of grease, pants unbuttoned, new horns? He checked his reflection in the window of the next-door shop. He could see nothing unusual; he looked more or less the way he had always looked. His clothes were decent and his haircut conventional.

He altered focus, seeing through his reflection and into the shop. A little dark man stood among his shelves, looking out at Rob as though warned, as though ready.

The thought came into Rob's head that he should defy this nervous little dragon—that he should go into the shop and tackle the man.

With what? Looking out of his window? With an old

madwoman dropping a broom? With all the bread in the next-door shop being already sold? An infinity of embarrassment gaped, and a probable failure of communication.

Rob crossed the *place* toward the bar, called the Hôtel de Commerce although it served no food and had no bedrooms. It was a quarter to noon, the sun directly overhead, the sky mercilessly blue. The door of the bar was open, pink brick framing an oblong of impenetrable darkness. Two motorcycles leaned by the door. Business was being done. Two women and a young man were in the *place*. The man and one of the women stood staring at him, watching him cross the cobbles. The other woman, older, turned and scuttled away as though hearing a telephone, remembering an appointment, seeing a monster.

Rob met the eyes of the starers. He had a right to do that. They did not move or speak. It was their town; if they wanted to stand and stare at visiting Americans they were allowed to. It was odd, perhaps discourteous, but it was breaking no laws.

Aware of scrutiny, Rob continued toward the bar with a certain self-consciousness. He felt that his shoulders were hunched and his toes turned in. He tried to walk with absolute naturalness, and felt, as people do, more unnatural with each step.

A figure appeared in the oblong of the doorway: the *patron*, M. Leroux, in a white apron, cigarette ash falling like blossom from a fruit tree. He disappeared, and so did the black oblong, replaced by a green-painted door.

The bar was closed.

The one bar in a village, in an area famous for merriment, open at a quarter to twelve on a weekday morning, shut at ten to twelve?

Rob stopped, turned, and looked slowly round. Where there had been two people standing and staring at him, there were now five—seven—a dozen. They did not arrive but materialized. None of them moved or made a sound.

Rob felt dizzy. The sun. He was still holding his hat. He put it on his head. It was not a dignified hat. Rob tried to walk with Yankee dignity toward the house where Step was having her hair done.

"Yes," said Step as they drove home. "Yes. I know what you mean. Of course I only saw Madame Thingummy and the girl who helps her, but . . . yes. They weren't rude or hostile. I should think not, the amount I pay them. But *wariness*. Did you say wariness? Yes, they treated me as though they thought I might explode."

"I was going to do that," said Rob. "But I had a damp fuse."

"I had a long one, fortunately. Usually it's all too short. If people are going to treat me warily, my fuse is going to get shorter by the minute."

"Has Thérèse been talking to them," said Josie, "or has someone been talking to Thérèse?"

"It started here or there or somewhere," said Step. "Which came first?"

"Chicken and egg," said Giles sleepily. He was not closely following the conversation round the kitchen table after dinner. He was exhausted. He had spent most of the day trying to repair his easel, failing, and flying into a rage with wood and tools and himself. He knew it was an old man's impotent rage, which annoyed him even more. He sought and found comfort in the red wine of Corbières.

"I wonder how much I imagined," said Rob suddenly.

None of the others answered, because he was a man who had just had a nervous breakdown.

Step was up early, looking at the dawn in her nightdress. She woke Giles, who grumbled from his pillow. She was not usually an early riser. He, since he retired from the army, was never one. Much of his active life had been spent getting ready for action an hour before first light; enough was enough. *Aubades* were not his music, nor Aurora the subject of his brush. At home in Somerset, he attempted nothing before ten. Even here he was seldom downstairs before nine. If the others were bent on making an early start, they could leave without him.

The room faced east, toward the sunrise, toward the birthplace of Mani and his teaching. Step was not looking eastward as a Muslim faces Mecca when he prays. The Cathars would have ridiculed the notion that it mattered in what direction you faced.

Step made a little exclamation, a sound like that of a small child clearing its throat. She had seen something other than the sunrise flooding up into the sky, the growing definition in the faces of the rocks, the apricot blush spreading over the vineyards below.

"Giles, come and look."

"I'll be damned if I do."

"We may all be damned if you don't."

There was enough urgency in Step's voice to drag

Giles's spindly old legs out of the sheets onto the floor, send his toes groping into his slippers, thread his arms through the sleeves of his cotton dressing gown.

He joined Step in the window. He saw a rosy blur. He muttered, and looked for his spectacles.

"Can you see him?" said Step.

"No."

"Beside the track. There's a kind of bush, and a rock. He moved! He's in the shade, in the deep shadow. Surely you can see him."

Giles was not sure. Step's certainty made him almost sure. Something did seem to move. Did something glint in those first sunbeams, glass or metal? It was difficult, staring into the first small segment of the sun hoisting itself over the hills. Giles had the wrong glasses on, the reading glasses he had brought to bed.

"Binoculars," said Step.

"We haven't got any. It's one of the things we forgot."

"No, but he has."

"What a bloody impertinence."

"Yes. It's been going on for weeks."

"You've seen him?"

"I don't think so. Not until now, not properly. But it's a thing you're aware of. I think Josie's been aware of it."

"I wish him joy of looking at my dressing gown."

"I wish I could feel joky about it," said Step, "but I can't."

Their voices had woken little Simon; he came in rubbing his eyes to see what the fuss was about.

Simon was sure he could see a man crouching in the

shadow of the bushes, by the rock, with a pair of binoculars.

Giles might have kept quiet about it. Step might have tried to do so, though it was not in her nature to keep quiet about things. Simon was certain to tell all the others, immediately, importantly.

Binoculars? He was an innocent bird-watcher? There were practically no birds, except the kites that rode the thermals over the valley.

What sort of man? How dressed? Giles was not sure, not sure at all. Step said dark clothes. Simon said with certainty a camouflaged flak jacket.

"I don't like being spied on," said Tanja.

"We don't know anybody's been spying on anybody," said her father.

"Yes we do," said Simon.

A watcher with binoculars in the dawn fitted much speculation, the soberest, the most outlandish. None of them liked being spied on. Too many things were happening.

People were suddenly silent, bars were suddenly closed, a telephone went dead. They could do without the monologues, the drinks, the telephone. Binoculars? What did it matter? Their lives were blameless. There was no basis in the farmhouse for blackmail. Rob had paid for another month. Go or stay? The question was academic, since they were not allowed to leave until the file was closed on Gwen's accidental death.

Peter wondered, sometimes half audibly, where Tanja's mother was and what she was doing.

Tanja wondered about that, and about Peter's father.

Rob and Tanja wondered about Dorothy Schofield, and it was evident that Step did, too.

Rob tried to make like a scientist, to construct a hypothesis which fitted all the known facts and was itself credible at a commonsense level. His theories foundered in puzzlement, and in the wary hostility of the village.

Simon played by himself, in the barns and the yard, with imaginary armies with names that were almost Latin.

Giles was still shaken by the rock falling out of the sky. He burned the useless fragments of his easel, and then regretted having done so.

Josie? Josie felt responsible for them all, to a degree which was unreasonable and reasonable, to a degree which was a burden. Her father was an old man, Step a dreamer touching reality seldom and at few points, Rob sick, the children children. After silent days, Thérèse left empty-handed in the evening with a silent Etienne.

SIX

It was one of the mornings when Etienne was there, doing odd jobs and maintenance. He inspected the outbuildings morosely to see what damage the children had done. He looked at the water pumps and the ground-level tank and the attic cistern, and prodded into the dangerous electrical headquarters. He said nothing, but this was no indication of a change of feeling.

Using a pocket dictionary, Josie wrote out a shopping list for Etienne to give his wife. There were particular dry biscuits that Giles liked with his cheese, electric lightbulbs, soap flakes, fresh vegetables from the market.

Etienne crossed the yard towards his pickup, parked just outside the yard at the top of the track; he was satisfied that the farm was still standing and its systems functioning. He could do no more about the telephone:

nothing about the telephone. Josie intercepted him as he reached the pickup. She held out the list to him. He made no move to take it. There was no expression on his face. He wore overalls and a cloth cap and incongruous elastic-sided boots. His face was brown and deeply lined, his hair sparse; he had eyes like olive stones, and long stringy arms. His arms hung at his sides, although Josie was most obviously holding out the shopping list.

"*Pas possible*," he said. His expression was neither hostile nor apologetic.

"*Pourquoi pas?*" said Josie, after a moment's search for the words.

"*Pas de temps.*"

Etienne pronounced it "*tamp*," but the meaning was clear. Etienne's wife was unable or unwilling to do the shopping.

Josie tried to ask why, suddenly, Etienne's wife had no time to do the shopping. She must have time for her own shopping. It was only a few extra minutes. Had she suddenly got a job? Was she unwell? Josie stumbled over these questions, knowing that she was speaking badly and inaccurately, knowing that a Frenchman like Etienne would make no allowances for a foreigner who was not fluent in his language; she was sure that she could be understood, that she was understood.

Etienne did not answer any of the questions. He felt no need to give any explanation. Probably there was no explanation.

"*Pas de temps*," he said, and climbed into the pickup.

* * *

"It's monstrous, it's intolerable, it's pure bloody-mindedness," shouted Giles. "I'll talk to him."

"How?" said Step.

"He must have given *some* reason."

"No," said Josie. "'No time.' That's all he'd say."

"Somebody's been talking to him," said Giles.

"There's a lot of it about," said Step.

"It's a bore," said Step, "but it's not the end of the world. Giles can have bread with his cheese. If there are things we absolutely need, we can go into the town and get them."

"Oh yes. But it's just so odd. Here's a system that seems to have been working for years and years . . ."

"Things are changing all the time," said Step, "and they're going to change more."

"What do you mean? What's going to happen now?"

"We shall just have to wait and see. I don't know what's going to happen. I just know that something is."

Josie had the same feeling. But she did not know whether she had hatched it in herself, or Step had hatched it in her.

"Probably she's mad because she lost her share of the loot," said Tanja.

"She's only lost it because Etienne didn't take it," said Peter. "It's not our fault."

"She doesn't see it that way. Etienne told her we were mad. So she climbed on her high horse."

"That's absolutely childish."

"People are."

Peter nodded. Tan was not often right, but she sometimes was. The childishness of adults was startling—some of the masters at his school, Thérèse on *her* high horse, Grandpapa and his rage at a harmless hammer and some broken bits of wood, Step and her crazy religion and all her ghosts, Rob clenching his fists so the knuckles went white, looking ready to scream for no reason.

Rob, Tanja, and Peter wanted to see the early-morning spy. Josie for some reason did not want to see him. She wanted to be told about him but not to look at him.

The three thought they might rush out and collar the man. If he was innocently there—bird-watching or whatever—he would tell them. If not, they would at least get a look at his face. Josie was alarmed at this plan, but they reassured her. Physically Rob was tough and active, probably in better shape than he had ever been. The children were both as agile as spiders, and if they had to they could run back to the safety of the farmhouse. Josie was still against the whole thing, but she was talked down by her husband, son, and stepdaughter.

Tanja was very nearly rude to Josie, telling her not to fuss over them like an old hen.

Step was rather in favor of the project. No earthly harm could come to the children if Rob was with them. She was curious to know who was looking in through their windows with binoculars.

If they caught the man, Peter would do the talking. His French was that of a twelve-year-old English schoolboy, but it was a little better than that of the others.

Simon wanted to come too. That was a bad idea. He could watch with them, but not rush out with them.

Giles said he would not even watch with them.

They woke each other up at first light. It was no hardship to see that dawn. They watched from the attic windows. They drew a blank. Simon said he thought he saw something, but the others were sure there was nothing.

They watched three successive sunrises, and then grew tired of it.

The man with the binoculars, perhaps, had seen all he wanted to see. What had he wanted to see? What was there to see?

Rob took Josie and Step into town, to buy light bulbs and other things not to be found in the village. Step disappeared into a church, and was later found looking at the florid memorials in the cemetery.

Nobody in that bustling, overheated place was wary of the strangers. No girls hid behind cash registers, no doors were shut in their faces. It was a relief to meet indifference, absence of curiosity; to move among people who were busy moving in orbits of their own, who did not stare or spy or run away or keep resentfully silent.

It was a comfort to know that they could all escape, in three-quarters of an hour, into normality and anonymity.

"You told me you had a perfect command of French," said Giles to Step, suddenly, at dinner. "I remember being greatly impressed, as the gift of tongues was withheld from me by the fairies."

"I've never had the least command of any known language, including English," said Step. "I never said such a thing. When did I say it?"

"Before we were married."

"Ah, well, I expect I was boasting in order to increase my charm. You did a bit of that, too."

"Never. I am a man of unimpeachable honor and integrity. I would never lie to a lady, except under special circumstances."

"They were special circumstances. We were courting, if you can use the word of people of our age. You led me to believe that you had a large private income and an aristocratic background."

"You leapt to the conclusion that I had those things," said Giles, "because of a certain effortless and indefinable charm which led you to assume that I was the son of a millionaire duke. If I said I was, I must have been carried away."

"You will be carried away," said Step, "if you drink any more of that wine."

This sort of flippancy was a kind of banner they carried, in order to pretend that everything was all right.

Some policemen came again when they were all out, Thérèse reported laconically. She was shocked. She had never had dealings with the police. Only criminals did so.

They came again the following morning, two in plainclothes suits made of gray paper, two resplendent in kepis and piping and pistols. Step and Josie were darning socks in the yard, Giles painting with an easel improvised from a card table. Thérèse was in the house. It was not one of Etienne's days. Rob had taken the kids off to swim.

The police had no interpreter. The interpreter was on vacation.

A new atmosphere came into the yard with the police. They were not friendly. The commander was a small, brown middle-aged man with graying hair *en brosse* and severe steel-rimmed spectacles. He had not been to the farm before. There was a suggestion that he had been brought in because of the seriousness of the investigation. The others called him *Patron*, pronouncing it *Pat-rang*. He was aloof from the questioning, but he looked long and hard at them all and murmured into a tape recorder.

Josie presently understood that they were cross at having come all this way the previous day, to find the house empty except for a cook. They had tried to telephone before coming. It was annoying that the telephone did not function. It was necessary to police enquiries that the family of the deceased be available for interview. The telephone was therefore essential. They had an obligation to cause the telephone to be repaired.

This took a long time to get through. When she thought she understood, Josie was speechless. They were being blamed for the failure of the telephone, almost accused of criminal negligence. This could not really have been the serious sense of what the police were saying, but that was the way it got through to Josie.

The two uniformed officers, young men, glanced often toward the house. Did they think there were people hiding there? It came to Josie that they were expecting Thérèse to emerge into the yard with a tray of coffee and wine glasses and little cakes. Josie was sure Thérèse would stay where she was. It did not improve the atmosphere: the police had driven a long way.

But the new grimness of the police was not to be

explained entirely by the failure of the telephone and the absence of refreshment. Something had made them more suspicious. They had new information, perhaps, new grounds for doubt about the circumstances of Gwen's accident.

Josie asked, hesitantly, if they had learned more about the accident. She did not understand the reply, but, interpreting the tone, she took it that she was being told to mind her own business.

She asked if the three motorcyclists had been traced. It seemed to her that she was told it was discourteous to question police efficiency; from this it appeared that the motorcyclists had not been traced.

Even in the midst of the miserable tragedy, on the sun-baked hillside under the castle, the police had seemed slightly ludicrous—pompous, officious, histrionic, harmless. They did not seem harmless now.

They went away with an air of dissatisfaction; they looked as though they would be back.

"Why exactly did they come?" said Step. "I couldn't in the least make out what they were after."

"Nor could I," said Josie. "But they said a lot I didn't understand."

"I thought they were our friends."

"I thought so too. Something's changed their minds."

"Somebody's been talking to them," said Step. "Somebody's been doing a lot of talking."

Angelika Christie spoke fluent French, being the hanger-on of international jet-setters. Anna Hamlyn spoke fluent French, like many people from Holland. Rob and Tanja had heard Dorothy Schofield speak to her chauffeur in what sounded like fluent French. Any of those could have spoken to the police, singly or in various combinations. It was hard to think why they would do so; it was harder to think why anybody else would.

It was just before lunch, the hour of the aperitif, when the two men arrived in a red Peugeot. One was middle-aged, one young. The older wore a black suit, the other a white suit, so that they looked as though they were about to embark on a song-and-dance act in the farmyard. But what they wanted was to inspect the property, in order to value it on behalf of the owner, who was considering an immediate sale.

The young man had worked in London, and spoke good English. It was he who had taken the instructions by telephone from England.

"But the owner's in Australia," said Giles.

"I spoke to a lady, a Mrs. Falconer."

"Oh. That's the owner's wife. They must be back. How odd of them not to tell us this was happening."

"They perhaps tried," said the house agent, "as we ourselves also tried to telephone, as a courtesy, before coming."

"They could have written."

"They have perhaps done so."

"They never said anything to us about wanting to sell. It's damned odd. Step, you said they loved this place."

"Well, they told me they did," said Step.

"I understand that they do," said the agent politely. "We do not know at all the circumstances that have led to this decision."

The implication was that Giles did not know them

either, and that the house agents wanted to get on with the job.

They had, of course, nothing in writing from the owners. Written instructions would no doubt follow, as would the name of a lawyer acting for the owner.

They made a thorough inspection of the house and outbuildings, the younger man making notes to the dictation of the older. They made a sketch map of each floor of the house, and of the yard and barns. They inspected the attics, the dovecote, the water tank and cistern and pumps, the electrical installation; they inspected the condition of the track down the hillside, and the rocky plateau to the north. The younger man took many photographs with a Polaroid camera.

Giles was incensed, but the others took it pretty calmly. It was a normal sort of thing to happen. Neither the owners nor the agents intended to upset them. There might be all kinds of reasons why the Falconers had made this decision, and why the letter they must have written had not arrived. Only Step had actually met the Falconers, and that only once. The rest of them said all this to Giles, but on top of everything else the business unsettled him.

"How do we know they were estate agents?" he said.

"The guy showed me a card," said Rob.

"Anybody can show a card."

"They knew the owner's name."

"Hundreds of local people do."

"If they weren't house agents," said Josie, "what were they?"

"Somebody," said Giles, "now has an exact, detailed description of the house and the barns, an exact picture of how everything works, and a set of large-scale maps."

"That's consistent with valuing a property," said Rob.

"They *looked* like what they said they were," said Josie. "They acted like it."

"They'd take the trouble to do that," said Giles. "Whoever they were."

"Well, who do you think they were?"

"Before a military offense against a position," said Giles, "a commander finds out everything he can about the place. Supply lines, lines of communication, reserves, strengths, weaknesses. The process is known as intelligence."

"Oh pooh," said Step.

But the idea, once planted, stuck in the skin like the tiny thorn of a bramble.

Peter was angry at Tanja's rudeness to his mother. She was a spoiled, rich American brat with stupid ideas about everything.

She was more than that. She might be worse than that.

It seemed to Peter that she had been trying to make friends with him, to ingratiate herself. Why would she do that? To put him off his guard? It was obvious to Peter that he understood Tan better than any of the others, even though he had scarcely known her until a month before. He was the same age. They had to do a lot of things together, whether they liked it or not. Peter's mother was preoccupied with Simon and with Rob and with running the house. Rob himself was very decent, but he was half barmy, and naturally prejudiced in favor of Tan. Simon was too young to understand anybody, and Step and Grandpapa too old. Of course Peter understood her best, and if she was up to something he would be the one to notice.

He thought he had noticed. He thought she was up to something.

Of course it was the influence of that mother, that stepfather, drunken layabouts, half criminal, hiding somewhere. They were gunning for Peter's mother, probably for Rob's money. Tan was their fifth column. She said she hadn't had any contact with them since they came to France, but it was perfectly possible that she had. They could have got a message to her in a dozen ways. She could be in touch with them secretly almost every day. None of this was proved, but it was a screamingly obvious possibility. It explained an awful lot of things. It could explain the "accident" to Simon, the "accident" to Gwen, the sabotage of the telephone, which stopped them checking up. It might explain why Thérèse never talked any more. It might be tied up with the man in the dawn with binoculars, and with the "house agents" who came and poked their noses everywhere. Peter's theory didn't *necessarily* explain everything, but it *could* explain all that had happened.

The hopeless part was that the only person with whom Peter could have discussed any of this was Tan herself. He still would not add to his mother's burden. But he could help his mother and the rest. He could keep an eye on Tan. He could pretend to respond to her tacky efforts at friendship, and in that way keep her under observation. It was not a very nice thing to have to do, in a family, when you were supposed to be on holiday and enjoying yourself.

* * *

Josie was pleased to see that Peter was much happier with Tan. They should be good for one another—he a bit less of a school prefect, she a bit less of a little madam.

It was nice there was something to be pleased about.

Step saw again the man with binoculars in the dawn.

"I think he saw I'd spotted him," said Step. "I was leaning out of the window to get a better look. It was stupid of me. He scuttled away like a crab."

"Why didn't you wake us up?" said Peter. "We could have rushed out and grabbed him."

"That, dear, is exactly why I didn't wake you up. The more I thought about that plan, the more I agreed with your mother. There is one reassuring thing, though. If they're sending men with binoculars, they're not sending false house agents."

"It depends who you mean by 'they,'" said Peter. "It may be two different people sending people to spy on us."

"Just coincidentally, just here, just now?" said Giles.

"Oh no." Tanja felt isolated and vulnerable, even though her father was there. He had to be protected from worry. That was still Josie's job, but the least Tanja could do was not to add to the stress which had made him sick.

Peter had suddenly gotten friendly, too friendly. There was something phony about it. He wasn't a terribly good actor.

Peter spent a lot of time with his father and stepmother. They were obviously creeps, spongers, greedy and treacherous, dangerous. You only had to read between the lines of what everybody said about them. Peter had been with them in Britain before he came out of France.

What was the point of it all? Hatred? Jealousy? Money? Some kind of blackmail? There was nobody she could ask. Kidnapping? That went on all over, in Italy and Spain, the kids of rich families, the rich men themselves. They could kidnap her father or Simon, or herself. The place was miles from anywhere and the telephone was dead. They could hide the prisoner in a hut in the mountains, or an isolated barn almost anywhere.

Tanja had not forgotten, would not forget, the crazy venom of old Dorothy Schofield.

That old witch and Harry and Angelika and Peter could all have made a plan together in Britain, and now they were putting it into action.

Tanja wanted to warn her father, but she knew that if she did he would clench his hands until his knuckles went white.

Josie did not know what to make of the house agents, real or false. She knew nothing about those Falconers, the owners: she had no idea whether they were likely to make a sudden decision to sell. Her father said not, but he didn't know them either.

There were too many other things to ignore. If you turned your back on them, they did not go away.

She had sensed a hostility which was impersonal, which could be the result of too much sun or too many melons or too much worry about Rob, the result of the strain she herself had been through with his crack-up: lots of things could have caused a kind of hallucination of malevolence in the ground. But now the thing was personal, fleshed out, three-dimensional. A man with binoculars was not the result of anybody's disordered liver.

The reality of something unfriendly out there dispersed the hostility to which no name or face could be given, as a bad dream is forgotten in the reality of a fire alarm or a robbery. But bad dreams can return; Josie's did. Whenever she was alone, in or near the farm, she was aware of suspicion and scrutiny.

She did not know if there was a real and personal threat. It seemed impossible—it seemed more and more likely. She did know there was a real impersonal one, the voice of which she could sometimes almost hear as a strange language inside her head, the eye of which she could feel in the small of her back.

Thérèse, wordless, produced a letter for Step. She drew it from the capacious bag of imitation leather which she still brought every day, although she took it home empty.

The letter was from Monica Falconer, written from Sydney only thirteen days before. Mrs. Falconer gave some news of their adventures in Australia. She hoped the farm suited them all, that all was well with Thérèse and Etienne, the water and so forth. She said that they might come to the farm for Christmas. There was no hint in the letter that they were returning to England immediately, or that they were thinking of selling the farm. Quite the reverse, in both regards.

"Now do you believe me?" said Giles.

The weather continued glorious, almost merciless. There had never been such a summer, even in Languedoc. Giles put clouds in his skies with a Kleenex, but he lied.

They were all overwhelmed by the heat, though Rob and Tanja and Simon were used to the blazing summers of America, Josie had become used to them, Giles had served in the tropics. They were all, by the heat, reduced to slow motion, to looking for shade, to rejecting the hearty option. All except Step. In Giles's panama hat she scrambled among the rocks, picked wild flowers, communicated with ancient victims, and suggested visits to ridiculous places. Her forehead and forearms were vividly freckled. She was tireless, indestructible, and impossible to protect.

Thérèse continued to do the basic shopping, bringing the groceries with Etienne in the morning. They missed the special extra shopping which Etienne's wife had done. That episode was still unexplained and vexing. It was all the odder because Etienne still evidently considered himself the owner's representative, committed to the place, keeping an eye on the tenants.

Giles expostulated with Etienne about the shopping. Etienne either did not understand, or pretended that he did not understand. Giles's voice grew loud and his gestures wide, but Etienne stood leather-faced, expressionless, silent.

There were definitely gaps in the larder. There was the minibus and there was the town: but the idea of the drive in the heat appealed to nobody. There was a certain lifting of the spirits in being there—in being ordinary and accepted and ignored—but heatwaves do not suit cities.

Josie thought they could get by with the shops in the village. She was not sure what had happened to Rob that morning in the village. She did not think anything had happened to him. She thought the notion of hostility had blossomed in his mind, as people under stress imagine insults and treacheries.

It was difficult to know which to prefer to think. If what he described had really happened, then it was puzzling and frightening. If it was all inside a mind with its bogie wheels still uncertain of the rails, that was frightening too in a different way. Setting off for the village with Giles and Tanja (he to supervise, she to help) Josie did not know what to hope.

Rob had wondered too. Giles and Tanja were wondering. Josie and Tanja made bright conversation in the car. Giles was unusually silent.

Rob had half wanted to come, to face evidence of reality or neurosis. He thought he should have the guts to do that. Josie thought it was a bad idea. Rob agreed with a kind of relief that he had better stay to hold the fort: a phrase which, after he had used it, he regretted.

Obviously, in a literal sense, the fort needed no holding. Thérèse might have turned sour, but she would stand no nonsense from strangers. Peter could look after Simon and Step could look after herself. All the same, it was quite a good idea to have a man about the place.

Josie parked in a street off the *place*. There was nobody about. The village was always quiet; now it seemed dead. The men were all out, of course, in the fields or working where they worked. The women had done their shopping early, before the full impact of midday: they were now cocooned in their little brick houses, among shawls and family photographs and religious pictures.

Tanja jumped out from the back of the minibus. She

was curious. She was not going to be outfaced by any of the things her father reported. She looked more confident than Josie felt, because Josie seemed to herself to be facing a choice of evils.

Giles was slow getting in and out of cars. He did not like to be hurried. He did not like to be helped, either; he just wanted to take his time.

Tanja was visibly impatient. Josie understood. She wanted to get on and face whatever it was, while she was still in a mood to be brave.

"Josie," said Tanja suddenly.

Josie, following her eyes, saw it too—the face in the window, looking through a gap in a curtain. The face was not looking at the sky or the ground, but at them.

"Look," said Tanja.

There was another, and another: faces peeping round the edges of window blinds, through shutters partly opened. All the little street was watching them.

"Old women with nothing else to do," said Josie to Tanja, speaking, as she immediately realized, a little too loudly. She went on in a more normal tone, "They spend all day peeping out, hoping to see something they can gossip about. French peasants are always suspicious of strangers."

"Yeah," said Tanja, not believing a word.

Josie did not believe herself either.

Straightening slowly on the curb beside the minibus, Giles had no eyes for eyes. He was concerned to find biscuits that he liked, better olives, Armagnac. He was in any case a man well used to being looked at by women.

The silent, half-hidden faces watched them along the street and into the *place*.

There were houses in the *place*, two sets of squat, secret façades at right angles to the church. There were faces to be glimpsed in the windows.

There were faces in the windows above the shops, and above the bar.

Tanja stopped. She stared defiantly back at one of the peeping faces. The face disappeared. Tanja turned. Josie saw from the corner of her eye that the face reappeared, a gray face with a shrouded head.

All the faces disappeared if you stared at them, and reappeared if you looked away, like mountains far off or sails on the horizon.

Both shops were shut. One had a sign hanging in the window, *Fermé*, cut-out letters pasted on cardboard. The other had no sign but it was just as shut.

"Damn and blast," said Giles. He banged on the door of the shop with the sign, and on that of the other.

Josie thought the message had somehow been conveyed from the watchful women in the windows to all the other women and to the people in the shops. She dismissed this idea as ridiculous.

They went to the bar. The bar was shut. Josie could have sworn it had been open a moment before, when her father was childishly banging on the doors of the shops. Now the black oblong of the doorway was replaced by a slab of wood, exactly as Rob had described.

Rob had not imagined anything.

They went to the church, for something to do, to give a point to their pointless journey. The church was locked.

"Did God lock us out too?" said Tanja. "I'm sorry. I didn't mean to be shocking."

But Josie thought it was a good question.

Peter meanwhile was looking after Simon, who did not care to be looked after. Simon was as perfectly American as Tanja, although his mother was perfectly English. He expected to be allowed to do anything he wanted, and to be applauded when he had done it.

Peter was used to dealing with bumptious little boys. As a prefect at school he had been left in charge of dozens at a time. But that was in a Hampshire valley, where he felt at home and confident, where climate and countryside were familiar and people predictable. This was all strange. Time passing made it not less strange but more so. The earthmen on Mars in Ray Bradbury's stories found that their roses turned green, and then they themselves became black-skinned and slender and golden-eyed: they spoke a strange forgotten language and lived different lives. They were chemically different. They were not people any more, but something different. That was happening to all of them here.

It made Peter feel less able to cope with Simon, and Simon less willing to be coped with.

Simon wanted to climb among the beams in the barn. Peter had to stop him by physically grabbing him. Simon struggled. It was too hot for that kind of thing.

Peter tried to keep his temper, to be reasonable. "You'll fall and hurt yourself," he said, "like you did on the hillside."

"I did not fall," shouted Simon. "I was pushed."

"And you lied about it then and you're lying about it still."

"I did not, I did not, I did not!"

It was at that moment, just at noon, that with a terrible noise the motorcyclists arrived.

There were four of them, men, young men, in black leather and studs and macho boots, in spherical black crash helmets with tinted visors so that their faces were invisible. Their bikes were not very big but they were very noisy. They came up the track in single file, close together, in low gear. They came into the farmyard, slowly, the noise of the four engines suddenly shattering at close quarters and within the old walls. They went slowly round the farmyard, clockwise, changing position, arrogantly expert, slipping into neutral and gunning their engines to make the noise almost unbearable.

Peter pulled Simon back out of the way, back into the barn. Two of the motorbikes came by at a walking pace, almost into the barn, almost hitting the boys. Peter pushed Simon behind himself. He tried not to show that he was frightened. He did not know where the others were, Rob and Step and Thérèse. He was on his own, responsible for Simon, with these invaders, these bullies on their great machines. They went half a dozen times round the farmyard, weaving in and out, exhibitionist, terrorists on juggernauts, utterly anonymous behind the tinted visors.

Then like dive-bombers they peeled off one by one, and dropped out of the yard down the track toward the road. They accelerated away on the road, changing up through the gears, the great noise fading. They left behind a pall of exhaust fumes and sickening fright.

Simon was crying.

Rob, Step, and Thérèse arrived in the yard, from different directions, almost at the same moment.

"*Des gars,*" said Thérèse, without emotion.

Thérèse sniffed the exhaust fumes, looked as though she was about to make a comment, made none, and went thudding back into the house.

It was as though Thérèse knew them, even as though she had expected them.

Did she? Had she? Did that make it worse or better?

Step tried to comfort Simon, but he wriggled away from her, clinging to Peter, which he had never done before.

Rob's hands were shaking. He was trying to keep still the muscles of his face, but they twitched as though driven by clockwork.

The ritual glass of wine before lunch was a muted, uneasy occasion.

Rob did not know whether to be relieved, angry, or frightened by Josie's account of their reception in the village. There were grounds for all three. Josie knew very well to be angry and frightened about the motorbikes.

Could Thérèse have known the men, expected them?

Characteristically, Josie asked Thérèse.

"*Des gars,*" said Thérèse, and would say no more.

Giles and Rob did not have their usual nightcap under the stars. Giles went to bed early with a sleeping pill. He sometimes took one and sometimes not. His doctor prescribed them, but he disliked dependence on little gray pills. He took one when something told him he would have a bad night without. That night was going to be bad. He was thoroughly ruffled by the events of the morning, those he had seen and the others. He was cross and uneasy, which was as bad a start to a night's sleep as lobster Thermidor.

Step deplored the pills. She deplored any drug. Sleeping with a pill, Giles snored.

Rob was trying to wean himself off tranquilizers, but this was not a night to go bravely to bed without help. Worrying in the dark in the small hours was visibly bad for him—everybody could see that he was a wreck in the morning—and it was purposeless.

Josie lay beside him, listening with relief to slow, even breathing. There was no other sound. If there were hunting owls or prowling animals, they were silent.

Josie was happy about Rob getting a good night, but she was unhappy about a lot of other things. Purposeless as it was, she lay worrying. Endless discussion of the morning's events had only confused them all. Too many things had happened; too many things were still happening.

Something was happening now.

The bedroom's big window opened over the yard. It was wide now, the open curtains unstirred by any breath in the air, the square of the window not quite black on the black of the wall. From the yard, from below, there was a sound, a chink, a click, a movement. There was somebody there, a prowler, a man or an animal, at two o'clock in the morning.

Josie got out of bed, moving gently so as not to disturb Rob. She crossed the floor to the window, trying to avoid the squeakiest of the floorboards.

There was no moon, but a scattering of amazing stars. Some of the starlight was diffused by a milky mist.

The outside doors were locked, but the house would not be difficult to burgle. The "house agents" had exact maps, plans of every room. What was there worth the risk, the trouble? A couple of cameras, a couple of clocks, a drawerful of cheap holiday cutlery?

Peeping round the side of the window, like the women in the village in the morning, Josie tried to penetrate the darkness in the yard below. She saw nothing, but she heard movement, stealthy, loud in the absolute silence.

She was intensely reluctant to wake Rob. He would be groggy from the tranquilizer, and probably take a long time to come fully awake. Her father was knocked out for the night with one of his pills. Step would say breezily that it was the ghost of a Cathar, one of her friends, although she had not said that about the motorbikes.

It might simply be a passing hobo looking for somewhere to sleep.

But nobody passed the farm. You had to leave the road and climb the track.

Movement. He was still in the yard. No animal made clinking and chinking noises. He did not seem to be attacking the house. There was nothing of value in the barn, since Etienne brought his own tools. The key to the minibus was here on the dressing table. The bus was unlocked, but there was nothing in it except a couple of maps.

Josie waited and watched for a long time, wondering whether to wake the others, wondering what was happening, wondering how much she had imagined, until she was almost too tired to stand.

In the dawn she crept downstairs. Tired as she was, it seemed a necessary thing to do. Her nerves were at full stretch. She searched the shadows of the ground floor. The front and back doors were both locked. All the windows were shut and latched. Nobody had come in.

She unlocked the front door as quietly as she could. The mechanism gave a loud thunk when the lock pulled back into its socket. She opened the door a crack, then wide. The barn was still in deep darkness, although the sky was rapidly paling. The yard was empty.

There was a big flashlight on the table in the hall. It was a weapon as well as a light. Josie slipped out of the front door, barefooted, frightened, intensely curious, holding the flashlight like a club.

There was nobody in the barn or any outbuilding. There was nobody sleeping in the minibus.

In the strengthening light Josie could now clearly see the wobbly tables and chairs they used in the yard. On an iron table were a half a loaf of bread and a bottle. The bottle was uncorked, and a third full of red wine. The bread was not cut, but had been broken. There were crumbs and little pieces of bread littering the table top. The bread had been broken here. Half of it was gone.

SEVEN

Giles said at breakfast, "Is it our wine? Is it our bread?"

"I don't know," said Josie. "It's Corbières. It's the sort we get, but it's the sort a lot of other people get too. The bread? One French loaf's like another. I don't know if it's ours. It can't be. Everything downstairs was locked up."

"I simply don't get it, I don't begin to understand."

"Dear me, you are slow," said Step. "What does bread and wine convey to you?"

After a long and astonished silence, Giles said, "Are you seriously suggesting that somebody held a communion service in our yard at two in the morning?"

"It's not our yard," said Step. "It's their yard. I agree it's an odd time. But if you're worshiping in secret, that's what you're doing. What's your explanation? A solitary tramp having a solitary dinner, and leaving half of it? That's *quite* incredible."

"But the Roman Catholic mass only lets the priest drink the wine," said Giles. "The laity aren't allowed to. One of the causes of the Reformation. Your priest must have drunk two-thirds of a bottle."

"Who's talking about the Roman Catholics?" said Step.

"Oh."

"But," said Josie, "there were no people, no prayers, no psalms or anything, just one man prowling about."

"The Cathars don't have a ritual," said Step. "Set prayers and all the mumbo-jumbo. Nothing like that. It all comes between you and God. Incense and vestments and statues of the Virgin, gobbledygook in old-fashioned language, they can't be bothered with any of that. They just come together in comradeship and love. They break bread and drink wine as a symbol of that love. You must have felt it."

"No," said Josie. "Actually, I didn't."

"Were these people alive or dead?" said Giles.

"Perhaps a bit of both," said Step.

Peter said, "There should be fingerprints on the bottle."

"Mine," said Josie apologetically. "I didn't think about that. I picked it up and pawed it and had a good look at it."

"Anyway, what do you say to the police?" said Tanja. "Somebody left this wine at our place, send the prints to Interpol?"

Peter was silenced. He saw the force of what Tan said, and therefore wished somebody else had said it.

* * *

Step had sounded serious. Could she have been serious? Could anybody believe what she said she believed?

"We've never really talked about Step," said Josie to her father, "ever since you were first married."

Giles cleared his throat. He gave the impression that he did not want to talk about Step, which might have been because he knew she was crazy or because he knew she was not.

"These Cathars," said Josie.

She felt she was walking on eggshells, even talking to her own father.

"Hobby," said Giles. "Gives her an interest."

"Not now," said Josie.

They had maintained throughout Josie's life a kid-glove relationship, no gushing confidences, no embarrassing questions. There was no coldness between them, but there was a wall of good manners. Giles had never, to Josie, expressed all he thought about Harry Christie; Josie had never, to Giles, expressed any of her doubts about Step. Josie could not now say, "Has Step gone really crazy?", and if she had said it Giles would have pretended, politely, that she had not.

If there had been pigeons in the dovecote, they could have had the rest of the bread. It was hopelessly stale, after two days and a night, turned into wood and sawdust; it went into the plastic bag which Etienne would take away in the pick-up. Thérèse put the rest of the wine into the casserole they were having for dinner, not knowing where it came from, why it was there. Josie, eating it, felt obscurely blasphemous.

* * *

"There must have been a human intruder," said Rob, already drowsy from his tranquilizer.

"Yes," said Josie. "The bread was real bread, only about a day old. The wine was wine. I didn't taste it, but it couldn't have been open long. It was a modern bottle with a new label, the ordinary label. Just a brand-new bottle of supermarket plonk."

"I don't like the idea of a stranger prowling around under our window."

"Nor do I, but this one was pretty harmless. He even did us a favor."

"I'd rather not have his visit and not have his wine."

"Nothing like it has happened before. I don't suppose it'll happen again."

It seemed stupid—they all agreed it would be stupid—for any of them to sit up all night watching a farmyard which was in any case in pitch darkness. It might have seemed desirable to leave a light on in the barn, but there was no socket in the barn or anywhere outside the house. They were unwilling to risk flattening the battery of the minibus by leaving its headlights on. They could not do that night after night, even if they did it once.

They checked the locks and the downstairs window catches. They settled themselves uneasily to sleep.

Josie, short of rest after the previous night, fell asleep before midnight, knowing that Rob was already asleep.

"Valérien!"

It was a thin scream, the cry of a bird, a young voice, frightened.

"Valérien!"

A voice from the yard but from very far away, moving, echoing, almost too high to hear.

Josie was wide awake, her heart thudding. Simon. She ran to his room, switching on lights. He was there, awake, sleepy, puzzled. Peter and Tanja were in bed.

Step was up, too, padding along the passage in her slippers.

"Did you hear it?"

"Just outside our window," said Step.

"It was outside our window, in the yard."

"I wouldn't have heard anybody your side. I don't think you could have heard anybody our side. They were both sides. I heard a child's voice."

"Yes."

"Two children."

"The one I heard screamed 'Valérien.' "

"A name. A Roman name, one of their old names."

"What did you hear?" asked Josie.

"I don't know what mine said. A name, yes, I suppose so. It was something like 'Parapet.' "

"A frightened voice. Terrified."

"Yes. Two terrified children, at the moment of their slaughter."

"Children from the village," said Josie. "Coming for a dare, then getting lost and frightened."

"Children from the village," agreed Step. "Lost and frightened indeed. Lost and frightened for a long, long time. What a terrible thing to hear."

Everything downstairs was locked up tight. There was nothing unusual in yard or barn.

* * *

Giles and Rob, with their different pills, had heard nothing. Peter and Tanja, deeply asleep, had heard nothing. Simon said he had heard a sort of a scream, but it was possible the idea had been put into his head.

"Simple imagination," said Giles. "Something coming out of a dream."

"How could both of us imagine the same thing at the same moment on different sides of the house?" said Step. "And you're the one who doesn't like coincidences."

"Then it's somebody's idea of a joke."

"I don't know what it was," said Josie, "but I don't think it was a joke."

"I know exactly what it was," said Step, "and it was not a joke."

The spirits of massacred children trapped for eight centuries in these stones? The benevolent after-breakfast sunshine did not make the idea ridiculous, not after the note of despairing terror Josie had heard in the night. Josie looked at the phrase book, as she often did, to prepare for the ordeal of a conversation with Thérèse. Her eye lit on *"par pitié"*—"for pity's sake," "have mercy."

Screamed by a child with a Languedocien accent, by a child cut off in mid-scream, that could come out as the "parapet" Step had heard.

Men came to mend the telephone.

Three men came, in an official vehicle of formidable power. Thérèse spoke to them as she had not spoken to the family since the day of her sudden silence. One of the men was forty, mauve-chinned, balding, garlic-scented, with a sporting emblem embroidered (perhaps glued) on the breast of his shirt. His colleague was younger, more cheerful, of Arab appearance. The third remained unseen because he never left the truck. His purpose was unexplained, or, if explained, not understood.

To the obbligato of Thérèse's voice, unleashed like a torrent which has burst its dam, the two active members of the party tried the telephone, reported to one another on its nonfunction, and then lost themselves among the snaking wires which entered and left the house.

There was no doubt that they were genuine telephone engineers. They brought with them the smell and sense of earthy reality. As they squeaked about in rubber-soled boots, grumbling and smoking cigarettes, they banished the screams of ancient children into the mists of the absurd, drowning out that midnight fantasy with everyday orchestras of drills and wrenches. They were comforting.

After a long and perspiring search, punctuated by drinks brought unbidden by Thérèse, they found the fault. They debated, exclaimed, explained, exhibited. The wire was severed. The injury was in an obscure place behind a panel; it was no wonder Rob had not found it.

Giles and Rob looked at the two ends, held out to them with a gesture of triumph and tragedy. It did not look like a clean cut, done on purpose with a wire cutter, or by accident with some other tool, or by act of God. It had a chewed, nibbled, informal look, the plastic sheathing of the wire irregularly gouged as though by small teeth.

"*Animal,*" said the older engineer.

Yes, but what animal would chew a telephone wire in the back of a cupboard in the hall? There was no granary, no feed-store, no clamp of potatoes or turnips: so there had been no problem with rats. There might be mice; certainly there were bats in the dovecote. Had anyone ever heard of a mouse eating plastic and wire?

Its wire replaced, the telephone functioned. There were calls from the engineers to the exchange, from the exchange to the engineers. There were drinks and smiles and affable failures of communication. These two fellows came from the town. They had not been influenced by the local virus. Normality reinvaded. Giles drew up a list of telephone calls to make.

"I feel a lot better about everything," said Rob.

They all felt a lot better about everything.

The sun went down behind the hills of Gascony, the light reddening as it faded, through a spectrum of all the colors of tropical fruit. A new moon rose from the Pyrenees into the sky like a bruised grape. There was a lovely, sleepy silence in the farmyard, broken only by the chink of ice in glass. Simon played a solitary game in the deep green shadows in the barn. It was a silent game. Tanja and Peter were silent. Step for once was silent, pierced by the beauty of the evening.

Giles came out of the house with his list of telephone calls.

"Those bloody fools," he said. "Those incompetent slaves."

"Don't say it's gone again?"

"Dead as mutton. Silent as the grave."

"What's silent about a grave?" said Step, but so quietly that only Josie heard her.

The rest of them sat in continued silence, no longer tranquil but dismayed—Rob, Tanja, Peter. Giles sat down, sighing and then silent. Simon was by them, silent.

Giles had wanted to call the Falconers in England, if they were in England, to find out if the house was really going on the market, if the estate agents were real. He wanted to find out about those agents. He wanted to know from the police the state of their investigations into Gwen's death, and whether the rest of them were allowed to leave. He wanted to get hold of a plumber, whose number was one of several on a card by the telephone, because pipes thrummed if a plug was pulled at night.

Step said she wanted to call here and there—to Buenos Aires if necessary—to find out what had happened to Dorothy Schofield.

Rob and Tanja wanted to call the customs or the *capitaine du port* to find out the movements of the yacht *Esmerelda*, of Anna and Dickie Hamlyn.

Josie and Peter wanted to know where Harry and Angelika were, though it was not easy to guess what number to ring.

It might become necessary to telephone shops, garages, travel agents, airlines, doctors, lawyers. It was intensely desirable that it should be possible to make contact with such people, to know that it was possible before need arose.

With the flashlight, Rob inspected the new section of wire. It was intact, gleaming whitely in the recesses of the cupboard and along the angle of the ceiling. If another animal had bitten through it, it had done so somewhere else. They could search better in the morning. They now knew where to look, and the sort of thing to look for. Etienne could report it again.

It seemed to Josie that the telephone had a psychological importance to them all, outweighing its practical usefulness. For a few hours they had been part of the world. They could reach out to it; it could reach in to them. Now they were once again on a boat in an ocean, the water full of unknown things.

The new moon, narrow as a nail-paring, should have been reassuring. But she had an air of neutrality, indifference. She was a cold presence in the warm sky. If she had relationships with people, they were not warm, living people.

Josie made a conscious effort to thrust away these fancies. But she could not thrust away the chilly sliver of moon, nor recent memory, nor the mountain of the unexplained.

Rob had no better luck in the morning. You needed a special instrument to locate a fault in a line. Everything he could see looked all right, but the telephone responded to no amount of banging on the hook.

Etienne said something about the children. But the children wanted the telephone, too.

Millions of people went without telephones. But none of the people at the farmhouse ever had. Giles had had some sort of radio wherever he went in the army. Tanja's stepfather's yacht had a radio. There were telephones in all the places where Peter went with his father and stepmother.

People went on holidays to escape from the telephone. Josie had often felt like doing so, when she worked as a designer and during both her marriages. The reality of isolation was surprising. It was something to be chosen, not forced on you. It was something you had to be able to terminate at will, like a television program or the noise of a blender. Josie shared her father's anger with the bungling of the engineers, but it was useless anger, like most anger, leading only to headaches and bad digestion.

Nothing had happened in the night. Nothing happened in the morning.

Josie and Rob took the children down to the Canal du Midi, broad and tree-lined like the approach to a palace, lively with small blue barges full of cross self-catering families. They parked by a lock, and watched the barges traveling westward rise up out of the depths, and the barges traveling eastward sink down to them. When there were no barges, the water was so still that the reflected leaves of the plane trees were carved out of green copper. A hoopoe flapped across the water with feathers like fingers.

Josie was not sure that they ought to have come. She had an instinct that they ought to hurry back. She found herself afraid for Step and her father, although she did not know what to be afraid of.

Before, going to the town, she had found that she could run right away from fear, leaving it behind like a piece of litter or luggage. Now it came with her, perched like a parrot on her shoulder with its claws digging into her flesh. She could see it reflected among the leaves of the plane trees in the canal, and feel its breath on the back of her neck.

Josie laughed and relaxed with the others, pretending a liberation she did not feel. She was frightened of the past and of the present and of the future.

There was something new and peculiar in the atmosphere when they were driving home. It was something between Peter and Tanja. Rob would not have noticed it because he was driving, Simon because he had his own concerns.

Was it new? Josie thought so. Peculiar? Josie tried to observe the children without seeming to do so. It was something between them that had happened, was happening, was going to happen. Nothing physical, precociously romantic. Almost the exact reverse. It was at a mental level, and it was more like suspicious neutrality.

The children made Josie think of moments in Westerns when two characters in a barroom keep their hands poised near the butts of their pistols: the long moment of suspense before one draws and one or other is killed.

They were watching one another.

It was depressing and distressing. Josie had thought that they were becoming friends, brother and sister. They had been going through the motions, perhaps, for the benefit of the grown-ups. It was the difference in background, of language and interests and upbringing, which ought to have been bridged by now. It had been bridged, Josie thought, and the bridge then demolished as though it dangerously linked two jealous sultanates.

Josie had no idea what was going on in either child's mind; she knew that she could never find out by asking.

Josie's instinct was right. Nothing had happened before they left, but something happened while they were out, at three or four or five in the afternoon: the most innocent hours of the day, the time when heaven and hell and ghosts take a siesta.

Giles had a nap, by mistake, in a camp chair in front of his improvised easel.

He was drawing—as they all knew, because he had told them—a complex and testing subject, the grouped monoliths behind the farm which might once have been the basis for defensive works, bastions provided by nature between which curtain walls had been stretched. That at least was Step's idea, and there was obvious merit in it—the rocks showed signs of the mason's chisel. The result was disturbing and surreal: not a ruin but a place defended by aliens. A literal drawing, Giles said, would be almost incredible, so that he would expose himself to ridicule, but a stylization would be a waste of the subject. It was not clear from his preliminary work how literal he intended to be.

In the late morning and early afternoon of his second day's work on the picture, he had advanced considerably. There was much detailed penmanship in the faces of the rocks, some gnarled by nature, some smoothed by man. You could begin to see the artist's intentions. That is, you could have done so, but someone while Giles slept had taken a knife to the pad.

There was perhaps some design, pattern, symbol in the slashes.

It was apparently Giles' own Stanley knife that the vandal had used.

Thérèse had seen and heard nothing. She never did see or hear anything. Step was herself asleep at the time, in the shade on the other side of the farm, though a nap after lunch was not usual for her.

A child? Would a child take such a risk to commit so pointless an outrage? A child who had played a practical joke on them with a loaf and a bottle of wine, who had amused himself by screaming in the night? A disturbed teenager, a passing lunatic? These were not welcome theories; in any case hardly credible.

Had Giles slashed his own picture in his sleep?

"When you take an image of something, you catch its soul," said Step after dinner. "You magically snare it. That's why primitive people won't have their photographs taken."

"But you're talking about savages," said Giles. "The evil eye and the Great Spirit and places which are taboo."

"Some funny things came here from the Balkans," said Step. "Remember it was in the middle of the dark ages."

"But the Cathars weren't superstitious in that sort of way, were they?" said Josie. "You make them out so full of common sense. They didn't believe in magic."

"How could you live in a place like this," said Step, "and not believe in magic?"

"Why don't we just go away?" said Josie in bed.

"The police wouldn't like it."

"Don't you want to leave?"

"Part of me does. Yes. The scared part. But I don't want to be chased away by somebody slashing Giles's drawing. It was a terrible drawing anyway."

"That really isn't the point."

"I know it. What I do think is that we should stay together more. Keep an eye on one another."

"I don't know what you're admitting. What threat you're seeing."

"Neither do I."

Rob drifted into sedated sleep.

Josie knew that her father would be doing so also. He had had more of a shock than he admitted, too many shocks for a man of his age. He was an old soldier but a tired one, turned sedentary and nervous. Step would oppose the pill but he would take it.

Josie lay waiting for sleep. She had no reason to be physically exhausted, but there was too much on her mind and at the edges of her mind—too much that, like the faces in the windows in the village, disappeared when defied and reappeared at the fringes of the mind's eye.

She decided to believe, and announce, that they were the victims of a series of tiresome practical jokes. The theory had come and gone; it could come again and stay. If it left too many coincidences for her father, then he must make the best of it or think of something else.

So. It was late. It was really time to sleep. There was the distant nibbling of an insect or a small animal somewhere in the structure of the house. There was the low prairie noise of Rob's drugged breathing.

There was another sound.

Josie listened, rigid with attention on the big hard bed.

There was not one voice but many, from one side and another of the yard, a child, an old woman, young women, softly wailing, names and unknown words. No voices of men. The men were away fighting. Footsteps perhaps, not the crash of clogs but the whisper of soft leather on stone, the bat-squeak of bare feet.

Josie crept once again to the big window. The young moon had set. She knew she would see nothing. She saw nothing. She knew that if she went down into the yard she would see nothing, even in the midst of the voices: that what was there would not be lit by a battery of the most brilliant arc lights.

A voice from the darkness below called softly, "Josie?"

"Step!"

"I can see your face in the starlight. But I couldn't see them!"

"Nor I."

"They've gone. I tried to tell them that we were friends, that we meant no harm, that we were sorry about their troubles. But I think they are in a strange wild mood."

"Good God, they have moods?"

"How would they not have moods? Terror, and defiance. Even among the women and young girls, a most marvelous courage. But not always."

"Not tonight."

"No. Why are we talking like this, a scene from a play?"

"Because you are down and I am up."

"I have had an exhausting and frustrating time," said Step. "I shall make myself a cup of tea."

This was more extraordinary to Josie than all the miserable mysteries.

The story could not be kept from the others, certainly not from the children. Josie had to tell Rob; Step had to tell Giles. The children were bound to overhear scraps—to be aware, almost by extrasensory perception, that something weird had happened. It was better that they should hear the exact story.

It was all new to Tanja and Peter, as it was to Giles and Rob. They could not exactly disbelieve it, if only out of politeness. Simon said he thought he had heard a lot of women and children calling in the yard in the night. Simon hated being left out of anything.

"No sign of the visitants," said Rob, inspecting the yard and barn.

"What do you mean, 'visitants'?" said Step. "We're the visitants. They're residents."

It was true, Josie thought, that they were transients, tenants. Were they intruders, trespassers? Did anybody think so? Did the live in the village think so, as well as the dead in the stones? She wondered if anyone was actually buried under the flagstones of the yard. From what she understood of the crusade, it seemed highly likely. Were they having drinks and parking the minibus on the graves of women and children? How much would those people mind? What would they do about it?

Josie continued to think of herself as practical and unimaginative—her father's daughter. This made it all the odder that she should hear so clearly and feel so sharply the people in the sun-baked stones.

* * *

Giles was practical and unimaginative, and intermittently logical in his process of thought. He tried to be logical always, but he thought that was impossible except for a robot. It could be impossible even for a robot. His grandson Peter had lent him science-fiction books about robots, which, to his own surprise, he had enjoyed. Interesting stuff, based on intellect rather than fancy. Robots sometimes got above themselves—not failure of logic, but excess of it. Giles, sitting somnolently in the shade after lunch with the heel of a bottle of Minervois, pulled his mind with an effort back from the year 4000 A.D., back to 1989, back to 1210.

Let us be logical.

Rob had tried to examine the thing (was it a thing? Could you call it a thing? What name did you give what they were involved in?)—had tried to examine their situation and experience by means of the scientific method. He had told Giles so, having a nightcap under the stars. That meant devising a hypothesis to explain observed phenomena, and then subjecting the hypothesis to criticism derived from those phenomena and from known rules. A pompous way to go about things, if essentially sound. Rob had tried that, he said, in order to arrive at a tenable theory to explain . . . Yes, all those things. He got bogged down. It didn't work at all. Simply no good. Came up with nothing. Hardly surprising. All of it outside the legitimate area of the physical sciences. In any case the poor fellow was still half barmy, jumping at sudden noises and needing pills for his nerves.

Giles relied not on scientific training but on military and administrative experience. Take the interpretation of military intelligence. There it all was, a wodge of stuff pushed at you by a junior officer with spectacles and a receding hairline. On it action had to be based. Therefore it had to be evaluated. A view must be taken as to relative credibility, importance, relevance. A subtle and demanding task, requiring cold objectivity, intellectual honesty, and at the same time receptivity to hint, suggestion, intuition. These also to be scrutinized, evaluated, treated with suspicion: but an intuitive element was part of all military genius. Not a job for a boy, a nut, or a woman. Too much intuition there. Giles recognized himself as the only one of them who could make sense of the situation.

A battle was a game of chess, following rules but infinitely unpredictable. In this game you reached for a piece and your finger and thumb met, unimpeded by substance. House agents. Bread and wine. The village. Dorothy. On and on. Some events observed, some reported. Some possibly irrelevant. Gwen's death irrelevant?

Giles tried working from the events to an explanation. This was so hopeless that he had a nap, hands limp on his knees, mouth wide.

He tried working outward from the personalities involved.

Anything could be believed of Harry Christie and his Kraut wife. By all accounts, anything could be believed of Dickie and Anna Hamlyn. Item: they were greedy and malicious. Item: they were all hiding somewhere in Languedoc. Why this mischief? What in God's name is the point?

And how?

There was only one answer to that. An ally in the

garrison, a fifth column. Who?

Giles recognized the obvious with great reluctance. He rejected it furiously, until honesty obliged him to accept the logic of the thing.

What after all did he really know about Rob, his son-in-law? Bare outline of his background, his professional career. Scraps of hearsay about his domestic and social life with Josie. Of Josie herself and of Step there could be no doubt. Giles knew them through and through. Who did that leave?

Motive?

The man was a nut or he wasn't. If he was, he didn't need a motive in the ordinary sense. If he wasn't, he was pretending that he was, and that itself was a rum carry-on.

He had plenty of money. He could buy any help that he and his allies needed, "house agents", yobs on motorbikes, the hurling of boulders, even children screaming in the night.

Once born, this idea wouldn't lie down.

Tanja? A stunning child. Secretive. Bad blood. Evidence and intuition suggested her involvement. Sad, really. Heredity. Environment too—that father, that mother, that stepfather. The poor child had never had a chance.

None of this amounted to a theory. It was a hypothesis achieved by the process of elimination, based on the observed psychology of the people involved. It was common sense. It was saddening and worrying. It was frightening for Josie, Peter, maybe Step and himself.

Did it suggest a form of action? Finger and thumb met, unimpeded. More needed to be known. The thing was observation and alertness. Meanwhile they all had to be looked after without a word said to anybody.

"Your Dad suspects me of something," said Rob to Josie.

"Of course he doesn't. How could he? What of?"

"You know the sensation of being under scrutiny? No, probably not. Probably you never were. As far as I know I never was, until now. You can't mistake it. Your father's not a terribly subtle man."

"He's subtle in some ways," said Josie loyally.

"Not in hiding suspicion. I feel like one of those Hollywood writers in the days of Joe McCarthy."

"You're being paranoid. It's bad for you. Stop it."

"The trouble is that I'm an outsider. I don't have a London club or a regimental tie."

"For God's sake take a pill."

"No. Tonight I won't."

So it was that Rob heard the voice, and Josie, short of sleep, breathed quietly through it all.

It was two-thirty. The sound was high and thin as a wire. It came from the yard. Rob lay rigid with a fear that made him feel ill with shame. The voice was not human. It was not animal but it was not human.

Yes it was. It was a child. It was a joke. It was a pest. It had gone on long enough.

"*Paara-peetiay.*" Then a wordless scream, very light and high, a thread of sound which was almost beautiful and almost unbearable.

Rob forced himself out of bed. He blundered a little, as anyone does suddenly roused from sleep. He did not think he had woken Josie. He shut the bedroom door softly behind him, and only then turned on the lights. He forced himself out into the yard, with the big flashlight from the table in the hall.

What were the rules in France? If you grabbed a mischievous child, what did you do? Keep it prisoner and take it to the police in the morning? A great way to be popular locally. Belt it with a strap? Probably against the law. Rob convinced himself that the question was not academic. There had to be a child out here. There had to have been one.

The beam of the flash jumped all over the old buildings and flagstones, and ran like an animal into the recesses of the barn. Partly Rob was intentionally waving the flashlight, to catch the child lurking or creeping or running; partly his hand was shaking because he was not convinced there was a child in the yard.

There was no child. There was no sound except Rob's own troubled breathing. He tried to silence the harsh rasping in his throat, because it showed to himself that he was scared. He tried to hold the beam of the flash steady on one corner of the barn.

He felt cold and defenseless in his cotton pyjamas in spite of the warmth of the night. He was cold because he was scared and scared because he was cold. He thought he was cutting an abject figure. He was doing no good. He went back into the house, locking the front door behind him.

At the top of the stairs was Step, in a floor-length dressing gown, with a shawl over her head. She was looking at him oddly. She had not heard any voice from the yard.

* * *

On the table in the hall, by the useless telephone, stood a large faience vase, pleasing enough, slightly garish, the only bright object in the dark hallway.

Josie had never particularly noticed it. It was part of the landscape, like the distant mountains. Coming down early to squeeze oranges for breakfast, she noticed its absence. Sleepily she saw that something was missing; after a moment she realized what. She was nearly sure that the vase had been there at bedtime. It was under the light in the hall. She could not specifically remember seeing it when she went upstairs to bed, but she could not remember not seeing it. It was not terribly important, but it was puzzling.

Occasionally Thérèse washed the vase, leaving it to drain and dry beside the sink in the kitchen. Josie did not think it had been there at dinnertime. It had not been there. It was not there.

Josie unlocked and opened the front door, as usual. It stood open all day unless the house was empty. Sweet morning sunshine filled a third of the yard. It fell on the little rickety table where the bread and wine had appeared. There on the table was the faience vase, lurid, friendly, harmless.

"I just didn't," said Rob. "Circumstantially I admit that it's possible that I did. Circumstantially you'll say that it's evident that I did, because there's no other way it could have moved twenty yards through a locked door. But I didn't. There has to be another explanation. I picked up the flash. I was holding the flash when I went out. I wasn't holding anything else. I could have been, but I just wasn't."

"Was the vase there when you took the torch?" asked Josie.

"I don't know."

"You must know. It's almost a yard tall. The flashlight was beside it. It was there or it wasn't."

"I don't know if it was there. I don't remember. I didn't notice."

Rob looked round the table at the others—Josie, Giles, Step, Peter. Tanja, flushed, was looking down at her plate. Simon had already left the table and run out into the sunshine.

The others were all quite sure that he had picked up the vase and carried it into the yard.

It was not a terrible thing to have done. The vase had come to no harm. It was supremely pointless.

"I wasn't sleepwalking," said Rob. "I wasn't doped. I was wide awake. I can remember exactly what I did, what I saw and heard, everything that happened."

There was pity and concern in the eyes of the others.

It was one of Etienne's days. He parked his pickup outside the yard, pulled off the top of the steep track which snaked down to the road. He was wearing new blue overalls, so that he looked as though he was on his first day at his first job. He tried the telephone. He shook it as though like a watch it might come to life. In the wrinkles of his hands the traces of diesel oil were probably ineradicable. The open neck of his shirt revealed a throat like that of a plucked game bird, with a sudden line of beige where the deep suntan ended. Usually his neck was buttoned. He must have lost the button that morning, after leaving home; he had never before been seen in an open-necked shirt. Possibly this circumstance had soured his temper. He was certainly in a rage with the telephone.

He had the cover off the main pump, which filled the tank behind the barn. He tightened things. It was probably unnecessary, but he was conscientious. He spent all morning with the pump.

It was not possible to say exactly where they all were when the fire started, because it was not possible to say when it started. The pickup was out of sight of the house, of any of the windows, of anywhere that Thérèse might go, indoors or out; out of sight of Etienne by the pump; only just visible from only one part of the yard.

Giles was sitting painting behind the farm, or was on his way back for a drink having been painting. Step was sitting in the shade writing a letter to an English acquaintance, a journalist involved in psychical research. Rob was sitting with a book unseen on his lap, wondering whether he had carried the faience vase out into the yard at two-thirty in the morning. Josie was, or had been, trying to talk to Thérèse about vegetables; she also went upstairs a couple of times to collect things that needed washing. Peter was trying to do a woodcarving; his subject started as a dog but turned into a cow. Tanja was sunbathing, something of which she decided she had not done nearly enough. Neither of the two did nothing else all morning, but those were the things they were mostly doing. Simon was busy in the yard under Step's eye. Thérèse was in the kitchen, or perhaps upstairs, and Etienne by or near the pump.

Josie came out into the yard. She did not at once see Simon. She went to the gateway where there was no gate. Simon appeared from somewhere and joined her, seeing that she was looking for him.

Simon said, "Etienne's truck must be red hot."

"What, darling?"

"See the heat above the hood. It makes everything sort of wobble."

"So it does."

The distant gray hilltops visible over the bonnet of the pickup were dancing, shimmering, as the metal gave back the glare of the sun. All the air over the front of the truck was rippling with heat, bending and liquefying the images of things beyond.

Reflected glare? So very hot? The pickup had only been in the full sun for half an hour, and Etienne had parked it two hours before.

"It's on fire," said Simon.

EIGHT

After a moment of disbelief, Josie saw that Simon might be right. No visible flames were licking up from the engine, but no flames would be visible in that brilliant sun.

The tank. Explosion. You read about it.

"Get back," said Josie loudly. "Right away. Into the house."

Josie herself hung on her heel for a moment. Everything flickered in heat that was too intense to be the sun.

Josie ran through the yard and behind the barn to the pump.

"Etienne! La machine! Il y a du feu!"

Etienne looked up from the humble machinery in its box. He looked like a tortoise and he moved no faster. He did not believe his truck was on fire. He thought it was a stupid woman in a panic.

"Nous avons vu les flammes!"

It was almost true.

Etienne said something about *la chaleur*, about *le soleil*.

Some urgency, some distraction in Josie's manner convinced him at last that he should look at his truck.

"Merde," he said as soon as he saw the pickup.

There was a fire extinguisher in the barn. It had been serviced a month before, according to a ticket tied round its neck. Etienne ran to get it.

Josie's voice, shouting at Etienne, had perhaps alerted the others. They drifted toward the action from various directions, Giles holding a drink, Peter his carving, Step her pen, Thérèse a wooden spoon. Tanja was minimally dressed for sunbathing. Etienne waved them all back. He waved Josie back. With the heroism of the uninsured he squirted the fire extinguisher at the front of his pickup. It should have been foam, but, intended for the fabric of the barn, it was water. He used up all the water. There was a great hissing as the water seeped through cracks and gaps and rust holes onto the fire, onto pipes and pumps and engine where the fire was.

Etienne filled a bucket from the tank. He poured half a dozen buckets of water over his truck. He would not let Rob or Peter help, waving them back into the yard.

The hissing subsided. The heat waves steadied over the bonnet, so that the hills were no longer dancing. There was a smell of burned rubber.

Etienne unlatched and opened the hood of his pickup. He looked at the damage with passionate dismay. Rob looked at it. There was comprehensive destruction of rubber and plastic, radiator hose, distributor, plug leads, wiring. Rob thought it could be repaired but that it was not worth repairing. The truck was a write-off.

Etienne walked round and round in a small circle. He stopped and pointed an oily finger at Peter, at Simon, at Rob. They stared blankly back at him. They did not know what they were supposed to do.

"He thinks we started it," said Peter suddenly.

Yes, he thought one of them had started it, and he was very angry.

The pickup would have to be towed away to a garage in the town. The minibus could do the towing. Etienne had a towrope. Getting down the track would be ticklish unless the pickup's steering and brakes were still in perfect order. Rob guessed it was a long time since either had been very good. Without a telephone it was the least they could do—all that they could do.

Now Thérèse would have to be fetched and returned daily in the minibus, and Etienne fetched and returned twice weekly. It was tiresome and time-consuming and expensive, but it was possible and necessary. Rob felt a great weariness at the thought of all that driving in the heat. He disliked being accused, albeit wordlessly, of having set fire to the pickup, but allowances had to be made for a man whose transport had just been burned out.

They stared at the reeking corpse of the engine, singly and in groups. There was no guessing why it had caught fire. Perhaps it had overheated on its way to the farm, smouldered for two hours, reached the temperature for combustion after half an hour in the full sun. Perhaps there was a bit of glass or flint or mica which had sent a reflected, concentrated beam onto some little smudge of escaped gasoline.

Perhaps it was a prank, most recent of a series. Persecution by pranksters. This was still the theory they wanted to believe—could almost believe, during the hours of daylight.

Rob glanced at Giles when Giles was staring with morose ignorance at the wreckage. Giles raised his eyes and caught Rob's, he looked away at once.

Rob thought: Giles thinks I carried that damned big vase into the yard without knowing I was doing so, without remembering I had done so. He thinks I lit a fire in this engine, probably without knowing I was doing so, without any sane reason for doing it. Disturbed people set fire to things, commit arson on a gigantic scale as an unconscious shout for help. Giles thinks I'm that sort of nut, in which case I could be responsible for any sort of motiveless destruction.

Rob was almost certain that he had not started a fire in the pickup.

Peter thought: *Why?* Etienne never did her any harm. He was not a friendly person but he looked after the place. Why did her mother and stepfather want Etienne's van sabotaged? All it meant was more driving for Rob. Was that the idea, simply to get Rob bored and exhausted with driving? Could anybody be so mean and childish?

Or was it to get Rob right out of the way, so that they could do something at the farm?

The footbrake, handbrake and steering of the pickup still seemed to work. Etienne said they worked. Rob took the minibus down the track to the road. Then all of them together pushed the pickup onto the track. Rob pushed hardest, Thérèse least hard. Etienne was at the wheel. The slope carried the pickup down the corkscrew bends of the track and almost on to the road. Rob backed the minibus toward it, and they tied the rope from bumper to bumper.

Tanja went with Rob in the minibus, having put on some clothes. They set off on the tow. Rob hoped Etienne had driven a towed vehicle before, so that he would neither keep a foot on the brake nor run into the back of the minibus.

It was a very slow business, towing Etienne to the town. Rob had to keep an eye all the time on the rear-view mirror, because Etienne could neither sound his horn nor flash his lights—if anything went wrong he could only wave. A lot of things might go wrong. The bottom could drop out of the pickup. It had looked on the point of doing so. The brakes or steering could fail. Etienne could have a fit. These were only the most obvious dangers.

When they reached the town, Etienne had to guide Rob with signals to the garage where the truck was serviced. This method was inexact, and resulted in long detours. Etienne's signals in the rearview mirror were baffling. Etienne lost his temper and Rob came near to doing so. Rob had a titanic struggle with his temper and with his nerves. Tanja saw the whiteness of his knuckles as he held the wheel. This was exactly the sort of strain he was not supposed to be under.

The garage was on the far side of the town, a kilometer beyond the center, on a glaring major bypass road. There were few cars, but those few were going very fast. It was hazardous crossing the oncoming traffic to the forecourt of the garage. A mechanic at last came out of the darkness of the garage to look down the throat of the pick-up. Colleagues joined him. They talked quietly. There was a mood of pessimism.

"*Je paye,*" said to Rob to the mechanics.

"That's ridiculous," said Tanja.

"Etienne doesn't think so."

After a long time, spent mostly in total inaction, enough agreement had been reached for Etienne to be taken home. He lived in a little postwar house, one of a row in a street near the station. He did not thank them or ask them in.

Etienne said and repeated something. Rob understood at last that Etienne expected to be taken to his wine co-operative each morning and returned each evening: anyway he was trying it on.

Rob said, "*Mercredi, neuf heures.*"

Etienne unlocked his door and went in.

As soon as they got back to the farm it was time to take Thérèse home to the village. She wanted to be dropped at the edge of the village, not taken to her door. She indicated that she was to be collected at that spot.

"It's not the end of the world," said Step. "I did it for years—went for the daily in the car three times a week."

"I usually went for the daily," said Giles.

"Not in this heat," said Josie.

"It's okay," said Rob. "But I must get gas tomorrow."

Rob went up to change his clothes. His wallet as expected was in the top drawer of the chest he used as a dressing table. Almost idly, almost automatically, he checked that the credit cards were there. Three: AmEx, Visa, Diners Club. None were there. The little purpose-made pockets in the billfold were empty.

He sat down on the side of the bed and tried to remember. He had used a card for gas four days before. Yes, here was the copy of the invoice, 340 francs. He had used a card to cash a check three days before that. There was the checkbook with the stub filled in. Both cards had gone back into the wallet, and the wallet into his pocket and thence to this drawer. He was absolutely certain that he had not touched them since.

He was absolutely certain that he had not carried the faience vase out into the yard.

Josie's bag was on the dresser. There was a change-purse in it, with a pocket for cards in the side of the purse. She had many more cards than Rob did—account cards for various stores at home and in Boston. Those cards were in the purse. Visa was not—the only regular credit card she had, the only one that was any use in France. Rob did not think Josie had used her Visa card at all—it had never left her bag. He had not touched it. He never did touch the contents of Josie's bag, unless she asked for something out of it when she was driving—sunglasses or a comb or a tissue.

"Darling, I thought you were going to change."

"Is somebody around here making a collection of credit cards?"

"Anybody's welcome to mine," said Step. "I'm much better without it. Invitation to extravagance. I even buy flowers with it."

Giles went up to have his bath. When he came down,

unbathed, he said, "My card isn't where I left it. I've only got Access and I know exactly where it was."

Step went up and came down. "Mine was in a sensible place," she said. "So sensible I couldn't remember it. Then I did remember. It's not there."

They went through the motions of search—pockets, kitchen drawers, the car. They knew the cards were in none of those places.

The children denied having touched any credit card. They had to be believed.

"I doubt if Thérèse knows what a credit card is for," said Josie, "but I'll ask her in the morning."

"Can you do that," said Rob, "without making it sound like an accusation?"

"I don't know."

"I'll ring American Express."

"How?"

"From the village. They'll invalidate the cards we have and give us new ones. They probably have an office in Toulouse."

Rob thought he had a list of American Express offices in Europe. Everybody who traveled had such a list. He did not have one.

The only telephone directory in the Poste was local.

The whole problem would have solved itself if they had been staying in a hotel—sufficient credit could have been arranged by telephone. Now it was impossible even to cash a check until there was another piece of plastic in Rob's hand.

"The damned things are supposed to be a convenience," said Giles. "Actually everything was simpler in the old days."

"Not if you hold on to your cards," said Rob.

Giles looked at Rob without replying. It was true that he was not a subtle man. When hc looked at you, you knew what he was thinking. That had been one of the things Rob had liked about him. Giles's look said: What have you done with all our credit cards, and do you know what you've done?

It took Josie thirty laborious seconds to infuriate Thérèse in the morning, and two hours to convince her that she was not accused of the theft of pieces of plastic. It was not clear that she was convinced. She banged saucepans in the sink with a great noise.

Followed by strange looks, Rob, with Josie, set off for the town. At the Poste they had to find out the location and number of the nearest American Express office, telephone them, arrange to have the lost card invalidated and to collect a new one. Normal life could then recommence, in some ways.

They would go to the police to confirm that there was no longer an investigation into Gwen's death, that they could leave when they wished.

They would find from the Syndicat d'Initiative a list of registered estate agents, from which they might deduce or remember those who had visited the farm. It was not important whether the farm was being sold or not, but it was important to know if those gentlemen were what they said they were.

The idea of using a public telephone to ring every estate agent in Languedoc was too wearying to contemplate.

They had to be back in time to take Thérèse home. This was a new shackle. There was no escaping it.

None of the others had wanted to come. The children had been warned of probable hours of boredom at post office and police station. Step stayed to look after Simon.

Giles gave the impression that he did not care to be driven by Rob. He even tried to dissuade Josie from going, but Josie insisted that Rob must have company.

They paid cash when they filled the tank. They had enough for that and a little over.

"What actually became of those cards?" said Josie in the car.

"Oh my God. Are you telling me I took them and hid them, in a trance or in my sleep or something?"

"I don't know. All this is making us all behave a bit oddly."

"And I flipped in the spring from overwork."

"Darling, you did."

"And I took that vase out."

"None of us can think of any other explanation."

"Did I put the bread and wine on that table? Why the hell would I do that? Did I push Gwen, throw a rock at Giles, and set fire to Etienne's truck?"

"We don't know why any of those things happened."

"Also we don't know what became of Giles's crazy sister, or my ex and her husband, or your ex and his wife. We don't know why the telephone doesn't work, and Etienne's wife won't go shopping, and Thérèse won't talk, and nobody in the village will sell anything to us.

We don't know who shouts in the yard at night."

"Yes, I think we know that."

As expected, Rob was asked to go to the nearest AmEx office to collect his card. The girl was as helpful as could be. It was something that happened all the time.

Which was the nearest office? After all there was not one in Toulouse. There was not one in any town of Languedoc, Gascony, or western Provence. The nearest, if you put a ruler to the map, was in Andorra. That would be a terrible journey, up and into the big mountains. Offices were thick on the ground on the Riviera—St. Tropez, Cannes, Nice. St. Tropez, the nearest, was nearly 300 miles by road. Or, to the west, St.-Jean-de-Luz on the Atlantic coast, almost Spain, all of 250 miles. Or they could go north to Lyon, something like 300 miles. Nothing closer? Lourdes. AmEx catered for pilgrims. Lourdes was less than 200 miles by road, going by Castelnaudary, Toulouse, Tarbes. Perhaps a cross-country way by places called Pamiers and St. Girons would be a little shorter.

That was what had to be done.

Now the telephone.

The exchange said that the telephone had been repaired, was proved to be functioning perfectly. There had been outgoing calls. Rob's French was stretched to its limits in explaining that the telephone was again out of order. He kept his temper with difficulty. It was not the fault of the girl he was talking to.

There was a list of house agents, but it was not comprehensive. Some agents had paid to figure on the list, some had preferred not to. None of the names meant anything to Josie or Rob.

A sergeant of police kept them waiting for a long time. He was a stranger to them, an officer new on the case. He waved them to silence, and studied papers in a file. It was the file on their case, Gwen's case. There was an astonishing quantity of papers; it was surprising that so much had been accumulated about so simple a matter. Rob grumbled under his breath about bureaucracy, and flies orbited the dangling lampshade. When the sergeant raised his nose from the file he treated them with strange unfriendliness. They were certainly not to leave. Charges might still be brought. Information had been provided which cast new light on the case. Other information was being sought from the British and American police, about the background of the deceased and of those with her on the occasion of the tragedy. All this was hard to come by and long in coming; the sergeant was not taciturn, but his French was difficult for Josie to follow and still more difficult for Rob.

It was Josie who exploded afterward, "How can they think any of us pushed old Gwen down the hill?"

"She didn't die and then fall. She died of falling."

"Yes, but what possible motive could any of us have?"

"That's what the British and American police are finding out for our friends."

"They might take weeks!"

"I don't think so. Everything about all of us is right out in the open. They have telephones and faxes. They cooperate all the time. The more they find out the better, and the sooner the better. Everything will confirm what we already told them—Gwen didn't have any money or an enemy in the world."

"I don't like being the subject of international police investigations. They'll know about your breakdown, my marriage and divorce, your marriage and divorce, my mother's death, Step's husband's death . . ."

"If Dorothy Schofield has been talking to them, it's a really good idea they get everything straight."

"I don't like our lives being prodded. It's like being spied on. It's humiliating. It's a sort of defilement."

"That I call an exaggeration."

Josie might have been cheered up by a good lunch in a good restaurant, but they did not have enough cash or any immediate way of getting any. They ate a cheap lunch in a cheap café, with off-duty Legionnaires drinking at the other tables.

As the minibus labored up the corkscrews of the track, a figure rose from a rock. It was Peter, in shorts and T-shirt. He waved. Rob took a hand from the wheel to wave back, and then realized that Peter was asking them to stop.

"What is it, darling?" said Josie.

"We're all hiding," said Peter.

"All? Why? What from?"

"Tan and Simon and me. Step's caught. Grandpa was caught, but I think he got away."

"What from?" asked Josie again.

"A ghastly old priest."

"Oh. I hope you were polite to him."

"We tried to be. Even Simon tried. But he absolutely

reeks of garlic. I've never smelled such breath. Indoors it almost knocks you over."

"Then he won't be bitten by a vampire . . ."

"Not if the vampire knows what's good for it. If I were you I'd turn round and go away and come back in two hours."

"No," said Rob. "If he's had the courtesy to come see us, then we must have the courtesy to see him."

"I don't think it's courtesy that made him come," said Peter.

"Duty, then."

"I s'pose a sort of duty. He looked at us as though we were criminals."

"Well, to him we are heretics," said Josie.

"It's more than that, Mum. I've known plenty of Catholics. Angelika's a Catholic. I think this old beast is snooping."

"Whatever for?"

"As though somebody's told him we have human sacrifices, or something."

"We'd better go see him and tell him we don't," said Rob.

"Well, don't say I didn't warn you about his breath," said Peter.

Peter disappeared into the hillside where, presumably, Tanja and Simon were also taking refuge. Giles had apparently sneaked off, as he did so often in Somerset. Step was battling with the priest. Perhaps they were talking Latin.

A little Renault was parked outside the yard, where Etienne's pickup had sat. The car emitted an aroma of garlic and hot engine oil.

The priest was in the uncomfortable sitting room, standing in the window with his back to the light. He was a little fat man in his fifties, with a rosebud mouth and rapidly moving eyes.

Peter was right: he had been eating a lot of garlic.

Peter was right: he was not friendly. This was not a social call, neighborly, pastoral, a gesture of welcome. It was not ecumenical or missionary. He did not shake hands. He looked from one to the others, quickly, his eyes sliding from Step's face to Josie's to Rob's and back again, as though one of them would do something dangerous if not constantly watched. He was being brave in coming here. He was visibly treading down his fright. He was seeing for himself. He spoke rapidly, aiming at points between the three of them. He was speaking to himself, making a commentary on what he saw, what conclusions he was reaching. He was not making an address or intoning a prayer, but describing them and the farm and the atmosphere so as better to understand and remember it all. That was Josie's impression. He spoke very fast. Josie understood a word here and there; minutes of his mutterings passed her completely by. He was a restless, alien, disturbing presence. He was real and three-dimensional and presumably harmless. There were dribbles of gravy on his cassock. Probably he was a real priest.

Somebody had been talking to him.

What was he making of them? What could he make of them? Josie and Rob looked normal, clean, saner than they felt. Step looked no more eccentric than many elderly people of strong will. Giles and the children looked completely normal.

They had uttered conventional greetings. After that they had scarcely said anything, any of them. They were certainly not answering questions, because as far as they knew, their visitor was not asking questions.

He seemed in a hurry to go, but he did not go. He seemed torn between a desire to go and a duty to stay. He seemed a man unable to make an end, an exit. It became excruciating to stand listening to his incomprehensible monologue.

Josie began to feel angry. But you could not, in a foreign country, chase a local priest out of the house. You were supposed to give him refreshment. The priest refused wine, tea, biscuits, fruit. He shook his head quickly, as though rejecting a bribe.

It was time to take Thérèse home. Rob pointed at his watch, exaggerating the gesture. Josie nodded vigorously. Step exclaimed at the time. Poor Thérèse! Surely this would break up the party, release them from a thraldom which was ridiculous, infuriating, deeply boring: a situation into which, Josie thought, they had been dropped only by their own good manners.

Thérèse would be ready. She would be standing by the minibus in her black shawl, holding the big empty shopping bag, in the incandescent sun of the late afternoon. She would not like being kept waiting, but she would not say anything about it, or about anything else.

Yes, yes, hurry, poor Thérèse, *Excusez-moi, mon père, il faut que la bonne retourne chez elle.*

Thérèse was not by the minibus. She was not in the yard. She was in the kitchen. She was sitting at the table. She had finished her day's work and dinner was in a casserole in the oven. She was not leaving until the priest left. It would not be respectful. It was not respectful of Rob to suggest walking out on a holy priest who had come all the way to see him. This attitude was interpretable from movements of shoulders and elbows. It looked to Rob like an impasse: one which no experience of his life had given him the social competence to deal with. He flapped his hands at Thérèse, but she sat waiting until the priest went.

Giles and the children continued in hiding. Rob was inclined to forgive the children, but he felt a growing anger with Giles. The selfish old bastard was relaxing in the benediction of solitude, leaving a man he thought was crazy to deal with these problems.

The priest's eyes meanwhile flickered between Josie and Step. He looked like a man watching a tennis match on a videotape played fast-forward. His monologue had ceased but his expression had not relaxed. He was waiting for something to happen. What sort of thing? For Giles to return? For a Black Mass to be celebrated? What did the horrid little man think he was doing?

It was astonishing that Step had waited and suffered for so long. She was not a patient personality; her irritation threshold was in some contexts even lower than her husband's. She was passionately hostile to the Church of Rome (or at least its thirteenth-century manifestation) and she was not one to bury prejudice for the sake of convention. Yet Step was taking it all on the chin as meekly as Josie herself. It was not the least of the oddities of this strange day.

Step then did, in the midst of this notion of Josie's, excuse herself from the audience. Disdaining French, she said in stately English that she required to withdraw.

The priest watched her go with flickering, jealous eyes.

Josie was rejoined by Rob, who had failed to communicate to Thérèse the merit of going home. The priest recommenced muttering, as though he now had a sufficient audience. It was becoming clear to Josie that he was crazy. She was sorry for the flock of such a shepherd. She was sorry for herself and for Rob.

Step rejoined them in the sitting-room, to Josie's astonishment. Having got clear away, the old thing might have stayed away. The stasis of the previous hour was resumed, the priest's eyes, and a single tireless fly, being the only moving things in a world which had been encased in a cube of semi-transparent plastic.

The impasse was broken by the least expected agent, by Thérèse. She burst into the room, a bomb in mourning, in a state of intense agitation.

"Encore du feu."

Fire? What does she mean, more fire? Again fire?

Thérèse was tugging at the arm of the priest. Josie ran out of the room to look for a fire in the kitchen or the wiring of the house or in the barn. Rob followed her, looking sandbagged. Step sat down suddenly.

There was no obvious fire.

Thérèse dragged the priest out of the house and into the yard. He was infected at last with her excitement. She almost pulled him to the ground in her urgency. She ran him across the yard and out to his car, which was parked exactly where Etienne's pickup had been.

The rim of the hills danced and melted as the light was refracted by the heat of the burning car.

The priest screamed.

Rob started to run for the extinguisher in the barn,

then remembered it had not been refilled.

The little car burned itself out very slowly. They watched it from below and from a safe distance, a bizarre group joined by Giles and, one by one, the children. They expected an explosion, but it seemed the fire was limited to a small part of the engine. It was half dark before Rob and the priest gingerly approached the car from either side. The metal was blistered and disfigured, more grossly than the pickup because it was a smart little car, almost new. There was a smell of rubber and ruin. The bonnet was too hot to touch until they had poured half a dozen buckets of water over it. The fire had done no damage to anything except the car.

They opened the hood and looked at the engine with the aid of the big flash. Plastic and rubber had bubbled and melted as though in a surrealist painting.

It was getting dark quickly, saffron darkening to plum over the Pyrenees. Soon a quarter moon would rise out of the Corbières.

Silent, the priest looked from face to face, staring at Peter and Tanja and Simon. He thought they had set his car on fire. In the light of the flash his thoughts were almost visible: these were wicked children from a distant, dangerous place, who had the habit of setting fire to cars. Of course he knew about Etienne's: but he had thought his car would be sacrosanct, protected by his cloth and by God.

It was a matter for the police.

Telephone? No telephone.

He would not consent to his car being towed by the minibus. Men he could trust would collect it.

Rob, feeling suddenly dead with fatigue, drove

Thérèse and the priest to the village. He dropped Thérèse at the edge of town, and the priest at a gaunt house behind the church which he took to be the presbytery.

They had all been far away from the car. Peter had been with Giles and Simon with Tanja, on the other side of the farm among the rocks. Giles had been sketching, Peter reading, Tanja and Simon playing an intermittent guessing game. Josie, Step and Rob had been with the priest in the house, and Thérèse in the kitchen until after the fire had started. It was spontaneous combustion—a fault in the wiring?—or it was a mischievous outsider.

Another of those.

"Coincidence," said Giles, "has only to be examined to be dismissed."

"Ghosts don't set light to cars," said Rob to Josie.

"I don't know what they do. I don't know anything any more."

"Yes, you do. You have to. You're my strength. All this awful year you've been my sanity and my backbone."

"I don't have either any more. This place is taking them away."

The nightcap under the stars was not a success. They were too near the burned-out car, the smell of rubber and the sense of vindictive destruction.

They were too near one another, each aware of being eyed by the other.

Rob could have slipped out of the house after talking to Thérèse, even before doing so, and put a match to an oily rag under the wiring of the car. It was objectively possible. He was sure he had not done so.

He took with him to bed a feeling that life rafts were slipping from his fingertips.

It was not a night for unaided sleep, for either Giles or Rob.

Tanja was kept awake by worry, by suspicion, by isolation, by awareness that the others were suspecting one another and herself. Of what? Of being crazy? Of being the agent of hidden enemies?

If A suspects B of having done something, does that prove that A hasn't actually done it himself? It depends if A's sane or crazy. It depends if A's *really* suspicious, or only pretending to be in order to seem innocent. That applied to everybody in the place.

The terrible old woman mouthed her accusations at the edge of Tanja's mind, Giles's crazy and vicious old sister.

Peter's father and his wife seemed more and more sinister the more Giles and Josie mentioned them. The more they *didn't* mention them, when they might reasonably, innocently, have done so.

Where were Dickie and her own mother? Why were they passing up their only source of income week after week in the high season? Was it their only source of income? What else did Dickie Hamlyn do?

Sleep eluded Tanja, as it had almost never done before. She heard with irritation the faint ticking of her quartz bedside clock. There was no other sound in the world.

The singing began. It was thin and faint, like an insect, human, inhuman, a high woman's voice intoning a chant, singing a tune which was not a tune, words which were not words. It came from the barn, the yard, from the ground below Tanja's window and from a great way off. It was a religious noise, sacred music, a psalm or prayer, nothing like any that Tanja had ever heard. It sounded ancient.

It was ancient, of course. Tanja's doubts disappeared. All that they had said was true—all that even her father had said.

She lay listening. She was not sure whether to be frightened. It was a weird unmusical music, not at all a wail, not like any bird. It must have had a meaning, a message. What was the message now? Comfort, hope? Threat, warning, despair? All those things could be heard, and none. The thin distant voice was passionate and unemotional, silver and black, hot and cold.

Would the others hear? Could they? Was the voice for them all or for her only? Was it for none of them but for the others who had lived here, who lived here? Was it all right, that she was eavesdropping on their worship? Would they mind? How could she help it?

Should she go to the window and look? There would be nothing to see. All of them had tried seeing. If there was anything to see, Tanja was scared to see it.

After the singing stopped, singing still filled the farmyard. Tanja knew she would remember it until she died.

There were movements, in the house, below. Somebody was up. Looking, listening. Nothing to see. Nothing now to hear, except in the echo chambers of the skull.

* * *

"It was a sort of incantation," said Josie.

"Why didn't somebody wake me up?" shouted Step.

Simon said he had heard singing in the night.

"Next time, we ought to try to record it," said Peter.

"Could we do that, Step?" asked Josie.

"I don't know. I didn't think of it. I don't see why not. It's a noise. We can hear it."

"Supposing it hits our brains directly, not our ears?" said Tanja.

"It sure enough hit my ears when I heard it," said Rob.

Giles glanced at him, then quickly away. Some people's evidence could be believed, some not.

They had no kind of tape recorder.

Rob had to go to the village to get Thérèse, to the town to get Etienne, to Lourdes to get a new credit card. He could maybe get a tape recorder with his nice new card.

"I think it would be wrong," said Tanja, "for us to sit around in daylight playing something like that."

"Why?" said Peter, who did not fully believe that anybody had heard anything.

"Perhaps it would be a kind of impertinence," said Josie. "As we're going to a place with good shops, let's do some good shopping."

Giles already had a list. The others made lists. Rob would certainly need his card.

A breakdown van appeared at the top of the track. The men ignored the people in the yard. They turned the van around, laboriously in the confined space, and hitched the front bumper of the priest's car to their chain. They hoisted the car's front wheels off the ground. It looked more than ever undignified, despoiled. They bumped away down the track, leaving an oil stain and a smell of burnt rubber and exhaust.

Until this operation was complete, the van blocked the exit of the yard. Thérèse and Etienne would be waiting, would eventually stop waiting, might already have stopped waiting.

Josie was most anxious, watching the time, Step least. Rob was anxious. Tanja was anxious, not because of the need of Thérèse and Etienne, but because after the previous night she was in the way of feeling anxious.

Josie said, "All that driving. I'll get Etienne, and pick up Thérèse on the way back."

"You'll never find Etienne's house," said Rob.

"Draw me a map."

Rob drew a kind of map, and Josie wrote directions for finding Etienne's house at Rob's dictation.

"I won't attempt any shopping," said Josie, "there isn't time. We'll do it in Lourdes."

Peter offered to come with Josie. She was surprised and pleased.

They got into the minibus. Josie turned the key. Nothing happened.

The bus was as dead as the telephone.

NINE

They opened the hood. Rob tried the ignition. Giles tried it. Step tried it. They were in danger of flattening the battery.

It was overchoked, perhaps? But there was no immediate, obvious smell of gasoline. The leads went from battery to distributor, from distributor to plugs. The coil, the fuses, looked present and correct. All the parts and functions that they could name to one another looked, they thought, as they always looked.

Rob took out the plugs to see if they had oiled up. The terminals were bright and dry. There was gas in the tank and it was reaching the carburetor.

"Thérèse and Etienne will have to go on waiting," said Josie.

"How are we for food?" asked Step.

"Okay for a day or two. More than that. Plenty of

cans. We can walk to the village."

"We can walk to the village. Yes. Which of us exactly do you mean by 'we'?"

"I can walk to the village."

"I guess somebody will have to do that," said Rob. "Tell Thérèse to find a friend with a car. Telephone Etienne. And find a mechanic."

They peered and prodded at the engine, but they all ran out of ideas. Rob knew nothing about cars. Like many clever men, he had a specialized brain. He was expert in some areas; others, for which he had no bent, he had left completely alone. He did not know what an alternator did, where it was, what it looked like. Giles knew very little about cars—he had always had drivers, fitters and mechanics in the army, and he continued to have them in retirement at the end of a telephone. He knew fellows who knew all about the guts of cars, and he used the knowledge without admiring it. Peter had an idea that, as a boy of his age, he ought to have been mad about cars. Folklore said so. But he had never been in the least interested in them. In these circumstances, he felt diminished by the fact. Tanja looked at him scornfully; her scorn was misplaced—she had learned a little about marine diesels from her stepfather, but she knew even less about cars than her father. Josie had never owned a car, and scarcely driven one before her marriage to Rob. Step had never, as far as anyone knew, so much as looked under a bonnet.

Simon said he knew all about cars, but he exaggerated.

Peter went to the barn, and brought out the corpse of the bicycle. Probably it had not been in full sunlight for ten years. One of the wheels was distorted into a figure of eight, and the other missing many spokes. The tires were airless, their rubber perished. A pedal was broken off and the brake cables were broken.

There was nothing on wheels in the place—no kind of trolley or handcart or pushchair, no wheelbarrow or water cart. None of them even had luggage with the inbuilt wheels of modern travelers. As things stood, anyone who left the farm must walk, and anything brought to the farm must be carried.

"Damn, we could have hitched a lift with those fellows in the breakdown van," said Giles.

"They weren't very friendly," said Josie.

"I guess the priest talked to them," said Rob.

"I wonder what he said," said Step.

"The same as Etienne said," said Simon. "That we started the fire."

"I wonder if he told the police."

The answer came almost immediately, as Rob, Josie and Peter were about to start for the village. Three gendarmes came in one of their overstated cars. The senior, who had a highly polished brown wooden face, began to speak slowly and loudly, as though to idiots. This at first sounded stupid and patronizing, but it was not stupid, because they all, even Simon, more or less understood everything he said. He spoke from notes, holding a little book in front of the marvelous buttons on his chest. The others stared at the disfigured patch of ground where the two vehicles had burned. They consulted their watches, the sun, one another. Obviously they were considering the possibility that one or both fires had been started by a ray of reflected, intensified sunlight. They knew about Etienne's pickup.

The commander concluded, reading as though in church, *"Deux voitures, en flammes, au même lieu."*

"Oui," said Rob. It was impossible to disagree that two cars had been burned on the same spot. It seemed wise to agree when possible, to show willing, to be co-operative.

"Pas hasard," said one of the younger gendarmes.

Not chance? Giles should have agreed, given his stated suspicion of coincidence. But he tried to say that, though the coincidence was remarkable, it was, as far as they knew, truly a pure coincidence. He tried to add that there might have been, might still be, a natural cause, not immediately detectable, which had caused both fires. This offering was beyond his French. He tailed away in helpless gestures.

Rob, principally addressed, found that he was understood to have admitted setting fire to the vehicles. Already too hot, hatless in the overhead sun, rattled and illogically frightened, he labored to explain that he had not intended any such admission. Something was, however, written in the notebook.

Far above and away the kites rode the thermals over the vineyards in the brilliant sky. It was a day of ruthless perfection. Tanja took Simon away into the shade of the barn. One of the policemen moved so that he could see them.

As before, as on the hillside where Gwen fell, each member of the party had to explain and to show exactly where they had all been at the moment of Thérèse's announcement of the fire.

Josie and Step had alibis provided by the priest, Giles and Peter by one another, Tanja and Simon by one another. Rob's was provided by the priest and by Thérèse, but it was not terribly good, as he had gone from room to room—it would be impossible to establish how soon after leaving the sitting room he had entered the kitchen, and vice versa.

Visibly, the police registered that Rob had twice, for unknown lengths of time, been out of anybody's sight.

Why would he set fire to cars?

The police would know by now, from Massachusetts, that Rob had had a nervous breakdown in the spring, that he was still recuperating from it, that he was on a course of prescribed drugs. They would know a lot of other things. They would have an accumulation of innocent fragments about him, about them all, which could be shuffled into patterns of malevolence or lunacy.

Every detail of both fires would be placed on file, and those files placed with that of the investigation into Gwen's death.

Pretty soon an investigating magistrate would be assigned to the case, or cases. Then one of them, or more than one, or all of them, might be charged with one or more crimes, or all of the crimes. They would really be hooked up in the French legal processes, courts, evidence, lawyers, interpreters. What would they all say, under oath, about that vase in the yard in the middle of the night?

How could you survive this kind of thing without a telephone or a car?

Did the French courts take evidence from a kid Simon's age? What would it do to Simon? What would Simon innocently do to his father, talking about the crack-up, about the way he was in April?

What would Giles say, already convinced he was mad or bad or both, prejudiced, insular, narrow-minded, deeply concerned (to give him the best of the odds) about his daughter and grandsons?

What in God's name might Step say? What fantasies might come out, and even be believed?

The gross improbability of the whole situation struck Rob, as he stood looking at the police, who stood looking at him. Was it all hallucination, the voices in the night and the watcher in the dawn and the people by day, the oddities and accidents and priests and policemen? Was he in a hospital bed, sedated in the twilight in Massachusetts? It was difficult to be sure. He felt bullied and mocked by dead engines and dead telephones and dead Cathars. Hallucinations were ganging up.

Josie and Tanja glanced at one another, sharing concern about Rob but, as always in these days, with a mutual wariness. Neither could read the mind of the other. Each was careful with the other, revealing a lot less than everything. Each, seeing the wariness, was more wary. This had once promised to become unnecessary, forgettable. Not this summer.

Sometimes you woke up after a vivid, unnerving dream, the kind that came after you had gone back into a shallow sleep after waking earlier. You lay in the middle of the events of the dream, those being for a moment the reality of the moment. It all seemed like that, even to the policeman's ballpoint. The sun was too hot.

The thought of the walk to the village grew more and more tiring. They could not wait until the evening, because they must get a mechanic for the minibus. If they went shopping, they would be weighed down when they came back. Should more of them go, to lessen the burden? But there must be enough people left here to cope with whatever came. Something was always coming. Things, people, were jumping out at them from the empty countryside.

Thérèse and Etienne would long ago have given up waiting. God knew what they were doing, thinking, saying.

No questions were directed at Giles.

Part of him was unsurprised. Nobody but a fool would suspect him of an act of motiveless vandalism, and these policemen were not altogether fools. Part was relieved. He knew—had already shown—that he was not at his mellifluous best in French, but ground to an ignominious halt at the first conditional clause. Part was resentful, even jealous. If these uniformed jacks-in-office wanted to know what was what, he was the man to ask. Giles felt he should have taken charge of things. But this was a thing he did not know how to take charge of. He was at a disadvantage. He imagined himself taking command, in mordant colloquial French, astonishing the policemen, eliciting salutes and straight backs. He flailed mentally at his helplessness to be anything but an old twit on the sidelines.

None of it seemed to be bothering Step. Her intellectual curiosity was keenly if intermittently engaged. She was wearing Giles's panama hat. To her the policemen were oddities, exotics, freaks, matter for a well-turned anecdote at home in Somerset, effortlessly capping the stories of other travelers. She might write an article about all this in the parish magazine. She might feel impatience but no threat. Women, Giles knew, had a capacity for stamina far beyond his own, shown at fêtes and flower shows, as they could drink coffee hotter and spend hours without going to the loo. They remained essentially foreign, to the point of speaking a different language.

Giles's son-in-law was being roasted, metaphorically as well as literally. Perhaps he deserved it. The police were quite right to fasten on the impossible coincidence. There were a lot more coincidences, equally impossible, that they didn't know about, might never know about.

The police were not satisfied.

There was a certain anger in their demeanor, because something was happening which they did not understand. They looked like men who thought they were being got at. They were going to make trouble, though probably not at once, and probably only for Rob Kemp.

They were paying no attention to the child Tanja. They should have been. It was no business of Giles to tell them so; in any case his French would be stretched to frame that message.

Half the day had gone.

The police went, indicating the certainty of their return.

"Oh," said Josie. "We might have got a lift to the village with them."

"It's lunchtime," said Step, emerging from her trance. "The shops would be shut."

"Well, we've got food for a day or two."

"The bus," said Rob. "We have to get the bus fixed."

"We could hire a car."

"Where? In the village?"

"No. The garage on the main road."

"They don't have hired cars there. They don't even

have a mechanic. It's just a filling station. Besides, how do I pay for a hired car?"

"With a card."

"I don't have a card."

"Get a car," said Josie, "go to Lourdes, go to American Express, pay for the car."

"Yes, darling, but if we find a car for hire they're going to want a deposit."

"Not Hertz, or any big chain."

"Where do we find a Hertz? Not in Castelnaudary. Not Carcassonne. Nowhere nearer than Narbonne or Toulouse."

"Oh," said Josie. "Without a car we can't get a card, without a card we can't get a car. How ridiculous."

"What they call a Catch–22 situation," said Rob.

"I call it rather pleasant," said Step. "No rushing about. Lovely and quiet. In the cool of the evening some of us can stroll to the village."

Josie laughed. She was not really amused. It seemed to be weeks since she had been really amused.

They did not know accurately at what time the shops shut, nor, since they had never tried it, how long it would take to walk to the village. It was necessary to get there in time to telephone a garage. They had to play safe. They could not leave it until the cool of the evening.

The sun was at its hottest in midafternoon, because since dawn it had been baking the ground, and the heat of the road underfoot rivaled that on the back of the neck. Once Rob, Josie, and Peter were down on the road off their particular hill, the land stretched absolutely flat, treeless, featureless, uninhabited, unfenced, unconscious under the tremendous weight of its ripening produce. There was no traffic on the road, no shade, no water. It was amazing that such luscious fruits grew in such arid fields, red earth as hard as the bricks that were made from it.

The kites were there. They never seemed to pounce on anything. In the end of course, they did—they must. They looked symbolic. They were symbolic. They were images of the threats above and below and around, mad sisters, ex-husbands, ex-wives, full of jealousy and greed and malice, content to wait but not to wait forever.

Fear of the known, the definable, pulsated in Josie's mind like a monstrous bladder. Only at its largest did it hide the blacker background fear of the unknown.

Perhaps because they filtered into the village, as it were, inconspicuously on foot, they did not think they were noticed. They did not see faces at windows; they were neither stared at nor obviously evaded. There was merit in not arriving in an obtrusive white oblong.

They knew where Thérèse's house was, although they had not been encouraged to go there. It was silent, empty; so were its neighbors; so was the little street which squatted on the edge of the vineyards.

Except in the event of a chance sighting, that part of the expedition was already a failure.

Should they split their force, Josie and Peter to go shopping, Rob to telephone for somebody to fix the car? They thought not. Josie was prepared to go off on her own, but she had the depressing sense that Rob and

Peter wanted to keep an eye on one another.

Peter might have been asked to keep an eye on Rob by Giles. Rob might have been asked to keep an eye on Peter by Tanja. Tan might also have wanted an eye kept on Josie herself. Anyhow none of them were going off on their own.

The telephone was the first thing.

The following hour was as frustrating as any they had spent.

Some garages listed in the book did not answer the telephone. They might easily at this time of year be shut for their annual holiday. Some of the people who answered did not understand Rob's French; they did not understand why the engine did not start, where the farm was. Some who understood were too far away or had no available mechanic.

One man was prepared to come, from a long way off, but required payment in advance in cash for his time, including the journey both ways, whether he fixed the car or not. His price was reasonable but it was beyond the cash that Rob had. He would give credit, maybe, to a local man whom he knew, but it would be crazy to give credit to a stranger who might be in Spain the next day. Rob struggled to say that he would give this man watches and cameras as security, but by the time he thought he had succeeded the man had hung up.

It was only just possible to believe that there was not a conspiracy to withhold a mechanic.

The woman in the post office said that no one in the village fixed cars. There had been a blacksmith, and after that a man who fixed bicycles. They were both dead. She did not know where people took their cars to be fixed. It was their own affair. She had no car. Her nephew sometimes took her in his car.

"We could ask the priest," said Peter.

"My God, we might have thought of that an hour ago," said Rob.

Rob had not come well out of the telephoning. He did not think Peter would think so. He had not been masterful. He had kept his temper only with an exhausting effort.

Josie saw with dismay the state to which Rob was reducing himself, his white-knuckled grip on the telephone, the trembling of the fingers which stabbed coins at the slot.

They went to the presbytery. An old woman, housekeeper or cook, said the priest was busy with the young mothers and could not be disturbed. After that he was going to the hospital to take Mass. The old woman knew exactly who they were, and that they had burned the priest's car. There was a certain triumph in her delivery of the message. She was the priest's protection against nuisance, against foreigners and car burners. He was her property. It was no less infuriating for being familiar, the lugubrious satisfaction of an unimportant person suddenly being in a position to say "No," a position of arbitrary power.

The shops and the post office were shut by the time they got back to the *place*.

The bar was open. The door was not shut in their faces. The *patron* looked at them in silence, ash dribbling from his cigarette. There were five customers in the bar, three old men and two younger. They sat in silence, looking at the newcomers.

Rob said, *"Bon soir."*

There was no response. The five customers and the patron might all have been made of plastic. The ones who were smoking smoked.

Rob asked for two beers and a *citron pressé*.

The *patron* drew two glasses of beer, pale and powerfully fizzing. He contrived to fill the glasses from the tap in the pressurized metal barrel without taking his eyes off Rob. He did not take his cigarette from his mouth. He put the full glasses on the bar, spilling a little from each. He unscrewed without looking at it the cap from a bottle, and poured yellow fluid into a narrower glass. His eyes never left Rob.

Rob thought: he thinks I'm the dangerous nut who set fire to the priest's car and Etienne's pickup. Probably murdered Gwen. Probably wrecked my own telephone and sabotaged my own car. That's what he thinks. That's what all these guys think. Probably they were talking about me when we came in. That's how come this sudden, unnatural, appalling silence.

It was even possible that the *patron* and his customers were frightened. Was that possible? Had anybody ever been frightened of him?

He thanked the *patron* with excessive heartiness. He pitched his voice to show that he was normal, sane, harmless, well-meaning. His voice fell into silence, making no ripple, causing no echo, a false noise, a madman pretending to be sane.

Rob felt rage, tension, painful self-consciousness, a wave of juvenile emotions. His hand trembled so that he spilled beer on his shirt and choked when he drank.

Peter was looking at him with an eye Rob recognized as Giles's.

Josie was looking away. The back of her head somehow revealed that the front of her head was frowning.

All right, he spilled a little beer, he choked a little because the stuff was so goddam fizzy. It happens to everybody, the sanest people, Justices of the Supreme Court, college presidents, TV anchormen.

Rob looked at the *patron*. The *patron* met his gaze steadily, wet expressionless eyes veiled, as though by a scrim, behind the smoke of the Gitane in his mouth. Rob wanted the *patron* to drop his eyes, but the *patron* did not do so. He was a free man in his own bar. He was protected by the width of the bar.

A staring match was undignified. Rob dropped his eyes. He had better things to do. He looked at the other men. They looked back at him. They were men frozen or artificial or stuffed. Rob was conscious of wet beer on his shirt front and his hand.

Rob shouted in English, "You think I'm some kind of freak, godammit?"

His hands were trembling so that he needed both of them to put his glass on the bar.

"Shut up," said Josie quietly. "Get a grip of yourself."

"I can't stand this," said Peter.

Peter put down his untouched fruit juice and went out into the *place*.

Watching him go, Josie saw that a crowd of people was looking in through the windows of the bar. Word had got about that the crazy strangers were in town, from the woman in the post office, from the priest's housekeeper. The crowd parted to let Peter through. The people fell right back so that there was no danger of touching him. That was how it looked to Josie.

Probably the glasses they were using would be sterilized, or broken and thrown away like little Indian earthenware teacups. Whatever they had might be catching. Josie shared Rob's anger, but pulled back from his embarrassing exhibition of it.

Rob was holding on to the edge of the bar, staring at his hands as though they had come as a surprise.

After mental rehearsal, Josie said in an almost level voice, *"Est-ce qu'il y a dans le village quelqu' un qui comprend les machines, les autos?"*

There was silence in the bar.

Josie looked at the *patron*. He looked away and began polishing glasses. She looked at the five seated customers. One by one they turned away, busily interested in their drinks or the sleeves of their neighbors.

Josie had guts. Steadily, politely, she said, *"C'est possible de trouver un taxi ici?"*

There was no reply. At first there was no reaction. Then one of the old men turned to look briefly at Josie before turning back to look at his shoes. In his face was simple astonishment. Of course the question was ridiculous. There could not possibly be a taxi in a remote little place like this. Nobody in the village had ever traveled in a taxi or would dream of doing so. As well ask to hire an oceangoing yacht. Josie had not made Rob look more sane but herself less so.

Where was Peter? Josie could not see him out in the *place*. Peter was all right. He could look after himself.

He could come to no harm in a public place, under the eyes of the whole village.

The *patron* scribbled something on a bit of paper, and pushed it across the bar toward Rob. Rob looked at it as though he had never seen a piece of paper before. Josie looked at it. It said "f23." Josie found two ten-franc coins and one five-franc coin. She put them on the bar. Rob looked as though he did not want to finish his drink.

The people were still looking in through the windows of the bar.

Looking anxiously at Rob, Josie saw that he was holding himself up, holding himself together, by his grip on the edge of the bar. He would seem to himself unable to let go of it, to stand unaided, to walk to the door, to go out into the *place* through that staring crowd.

It would be ghastly to have Rob falling, collapsing, losing control in front of all these people. She felt a stab of extreme impatience with Rob. It was upsetting to be stared at and treated as a leper, but it was not enough to cause a grown man to scream or buckle at the knees. There was something childish, self-indulgent, in feeling the need to hang on to a bit of wood. Josie was immediately ashamed, because Rob was sick. That did not make the immediate problem disappear. She wanted Peter's help, but Peter had run away.

Josie said softly, reasonably, "We have a long way to go. Shall we make a start?"

"They all think I'm crazy."

"They think we're all crazy. They think all foreigners are crazy."

"*You* all think I'm crazy. *You* think I'm crazy."

"I know you were sick."

"Thinking somebody's crazy is the best way to send him crazy. You know that? That's what you're trying to do to me."

"Let's go, Rob."

"I'm not going. I'm not going anywhere."

"We have to get back to the farm."

"The hell with the farm. It's full of spooks. I don't like the people there."

"We have to get back before dark."

"I'm not going out with all those people staring at me."

"There's nothing to be scared of."

"I'm not scared."

Rob's voice was scared. He had something to be scared of, which was himself, the things inside himself, the gibbering shadows, the prospect of an abject exhibition of craziness and terror. Josie wanted to tell him to grow up, to pull himself together. Ashamed of herself she might be, but she could not look at him sometimes except with her father's eyes, with Peter's eyes. Was he going to stand there all night, holding on to the bar, under the blank eyes of the customers, the silent scrutiny of the crowd outside? Was she supposed to stay there too?

She took his arm. He shook her hand away, then grabbed the bar again as though letting go for a moment had been a hare-brained risk.

"Darling, come," said Josie. "Just hold up your head and walk out of here."

None of this was invisible to the village. All of it

would be understood, even though the words were incomprehensible or unheard. They were miming their parts, words needless, the crazy man and his anxious wife. Josie could do nothing about that. She was not yet at the humiliating point of asking for help to get Rob out of the bar. She was nearing that point. It was not certain that anybody would give her any help.

"Let's get out of here," said Rob suddenly and loudly.

"Okay," said Josie.

Rob went to the door with his head down, as though intent on charging it like a bull. Josie followed him, trying not to look fluttery. Rob burst through the door and through the crowd and into the middle of the *place*, where Peter was waiting with the empty shopping basket.

Rob carried on going so fast that Josie and Peter had to trot to keep up with him.

"The way they stare," said Rob unevenly. "It makes me mad."

They plunged toward home in a sunset which was so gloriously lurid as to look corrupt.

Rob sat by himself in semi-darkness, gripping the arms of his chair. He was aware of the eyes and whispers of the others. He was aware of more eyes and whispers, scores, hundreds, indignant and contemptuous.

"We'll walk to the village again," said Josie, "and get the bus to Castelnaudary and a train to Lourdes. We'll find the American Express office and get the card and get some money and get the car fixed."

"Yes," said Giles. "Do you know when the bus goes?"

"No. It's something I ought to have thought of. But what with one thing and another . . ."

"Do you know about the train?"

"No, of course not. We'll find out when we get to Castelnaudary."

"You might have hours to wait."

"Then we'll wait for hours. We can spend a night in Lourdes if we have to, once we've got that card."

"Is . . ." began Giles. He cleared his throat. "Is Rob up to this odyssey?"

"He'll have to be. It's his credit card we're getting. I don't think anybody else can get it for him."

"I should hope not," said Step. "It's bad enough having control of one's own card, let alone somebody else's. I wonder what on earth became of those wretched things."

Giles looked as though he knew very well what had become of them.

Tanja had been directly told only that her father was not too good, that the afternoon had been tough for him. That was really all Josie said. She said it was best to leave him alone. He wanted to be alone.

Then Tanja overheard a part of a conversation between Giles and Peter. Giles said he wanted to know what really happened in the village, and Peter was only too happy to give him a version. It was the kind of old house where you often didn't hear things you were supposed to hear, and heard things you were not supposed to hear. Certainly Tanja was not supposed to hear this stuff, which showed the venom of the Brits' feelings about her father. Obviously Peter was exaggerating, sensationalizing what happened, because that was what the old man wanted to hear. Peter was the kind of smooth establishment creep who always told people what they wanted to hear. Obviously he got that from his father, because that was the only way you could freeload your way through life.

There *was* something funny in the village—Tanja had seen it, felt it. Why was there? It could only be because of things Thérèse had told the people. Why would Thérèse be mad at them? It could only be because Josie had made her mad. It was Josie's job to look after Tanja's father—that was what she took on when she married him. A fine mess she was making of that. It would be better if she got out of their lives, taking her son and her father with her.

And there had to be more to it than that. There had to be malice as well as incompetence, selfish carelessness, thoughtless egotism. There were all those things but there had to be malice too.

Tanja wanted just one ally. She found to her own surprise that she wanted her mother.

Simon wanted to swim, to go to the movies in the town, to eat various things which they did not have in the house. He was sore about the car not being fixed. He was used to a world in which you picked up a telephone and somebody came and fixed things. He was sore at being exiled from that; he was sore at being tricked out of things he needed. The adults could have done something about it if they really wanted to. He said so, loudly and often. He was querulous, fretful, rude. He was exhausting for Josie. Tanja finally lost her temper and slapped him. He made a terrific fuss. Tanja was told off, but not much.

The only person on Simon's side was Step. But she was no help to him. She was so crazy that nobody paid any attention to what she said.

Dinner was late and subdued. Simon stayed up but Rob had gone to bed. They were late because Step had done nothing about food while Josie was out. This was at Giles's command—Step was a slapdash, hit-and-miss cook, lavish with ingredients, and they might have to economize with food. They were subdued because all of them were wondering what some of the others were thinking. Some of them were wondering what would happen in the night and some what would be reported in the morning.

The evening was hot and windless. There would be a three-quarter moon.

The kitchen was in warm colors—copper, brick, ceramic, old wood, sunburnt faces. It should have been—had been—the most welcoming room in the world. Perhaps it was a refuge. It worked hard at pretending to be. But things were less and less what they seemed. They changed under your hands, perhaps shed skins and revealed themselves.

How long was it since any of them had really laughed?

That night they were in the house. Of course it was their house. Two or three, perhaps, women, children, thin distant voices, busy, domestic.

Josie wondered that the Cathars kept their children up so late.

She was bottomlessly tired after that awful afternoon, the trudge home through the breathless evening, trying to look after Rob, providing dinner for them all, getting Simon mulishly to bed, quarreling halfheartedly with Tanja, trying not to quarrel with her father. She was too tired to get out of bed. There was no point in getting out of bed. She was frightened of doing so. They were more frightening in the house than in the open, like an explosion more devastating because it goes off in a confined space.

She was surprised that the little thin voices had woken her. Like Keats, she was confused about whether she was really awake.

Rob in deep drugged sleep breathed slowly, with a kind of pitiful harshness. There was no light anywhere, nor any movement of air. The moon had risen and set. Perhaps it was nearly dawn. Time was meaningless. There must in those days have been cocks in the farmyard crowing at the first brightening of the sky. Why had the Cathars not kept their cocks, since they had kept their children and their voices, since they had kept possession of their place?

Aching with fatigue after hours of sleep, Josie thought: the crusaders thought they won but they lost, because the people are still here.

They were calling from room to room, bat-squeak voices, hungry children, too thin to be visible, cold in the heat, in the hot darkness, feeling still, moving, active, busy, frightened, angry, confident in their faith and betrayed, surviving in their despair.

Are all battlefields like this, all slaughterhouses?

Danger now, a message, an alarm. *Aide-moi!* Names again—*Ambrosin, Octavien*. A scream, pain, terror, death, relived, undying.

Josie lay in that ancient torment, listening intently to heavy silence, until the oblong of the window paled against the black of the wall.

TEN

It was as usual: Step and Josie had heard the voices in the house, and Simon said that he had. Simon said that he had understood what the voices were saying. The people were frightened because soldiers were coming and because they were already thirsty.

"I think you put that in his head," said Rob to Step.

"Possibly," said Step, "but that doesn't mean he got it wrong. I'm quite sure he got it right."

Josie thought so too.

They were running short of coffee, and there was no fresh bread. Josie rationed the coffee until they were sure of more, though her father grumbled. She toasted stale bread so that it was palatable but explosively noisy to eat. Giles's dentures had difficulty with his brittle breakfast. It was one more thing he was too old for. He wanted to go home.

"I don't want to go home," said Step. "We can stand a few temporary irritants. All my life I've been heading for somewhere, without knowing what it was. It's here. I still don't know exactly what it is."

"You'll have to leave in the end," said Peter.

"Oh yes, dear. We shall all have to leave in the end, though we may not go in the direction we expect. We'll leave the people to their home. They won't be leaving."

The wearisome journey to Lourdes by bus and train was still a necessity—the thing that had to be done before anything else was done. This was evident to them all. It was also evident that Rob was not fit for the journey so soon after the distress of the previous afternoon.

Josie fought down a renewed feeling of irritation with Rob. Giles, glancing at him but not saying anything, was making no attempt to fight down his feelings. He was not expressing them in words, but he was expressing them in every other way.

Josie saw her father glance from Rob to Tanja and back again without change of expression. None of the others saw. They were busy with their bricklike bread. Giles was lumping Tanja with Rob. Josie felt a surge of rage that her father should feel as he did, that he should show he felt as he did. It was unfair and insulting. He himself was not coming well out of their troubles. He was abject in dealing with the police, and selfishly cowardly in dealing with the priest. He was sponging on the man he was suspecting, on his own son-in-law. He had no right to feel anything except respect and gratitude.

Josie was all the angrier because she understood her father's feelings, and a part of her was ready to agree.

Rob was looking at Giles. Giles was looking at Tanja. Tanja was looking at Peter. Peter was looking at Rob. They were all pretending they were not eyeing one another, with varying degrees of success.

Simon was looking at Step, with simple and undiminished amazement. Step was looking at the ceiling.

Switch, like a squaredance. Giles was looking at Rob. Rob was looking at Peter. Peter was looking at Tanja. Tanja was looking at Giles.

This group was not a family. The only link was herself. She did not feel strong enough to hold them together.

Josie stood up suddenly, her chair making a monstrous scraping in the quiet kitchen. They all looked at her. Nobody said anything. There was nothing particular in any face. She felt like Rob in the bar. She went out quickly, unable to bear the atmosphere. She went out into the yard. The morning sun was already hot on her face and arms. To the people of the farm it had brought not comfort but despair and death. She went into the shade which had not saved them.

Simon was not reconciled to the uselessness of the car. He wanted to go on expeditions and picnics: he wanted to swim, and run up and down a different hill. But he had been told, again and again and again, that it was no good whining. Whining would not produce a mechanic to fix the wires of the engine. All it did was get on other people's nerves. Simon was agreeable to getting on other people's nerves if it was the only way of securing attention for his desires and grievances, but he could see that a little of it went a long way. Tan and Peter were both quite capable of belting him. They would get in trouble if they did, but only a little trouble, not enough to be worth it for Simon.

He was surprised to learn—from his grandfather, not from Step—that he had the same name as the leader of the crusaders they all hated. Simon de something. A pretty grand, aristocratic kind of name. For a while Simon felt important, because he was named for a man the Pope and the King of France had picked to command a crusade. But he was confused, because they all said that the guy with his name was on the wrong side. It was like being given the name Judas or Pontius Pilate or Big Bad Wolf.

When he maneuvred his armies in the barn, Simon let his namesake win some battles. He had won the battles in real life, though Step said he had lost the war. He came from a different part of France, Paris, a long way away—he was a foreigner to these people, an outsider. He wore a red cross on a tunic over his armor. That did not mean he was an ambulance man, a medical orderly, anything like that. He was a fighting man. He was killed fighting, on another crusade. That made him a hero. But here he was the villain. You could be both. People were a mixture. All the people here were a mixture—Tan, his father and mother, Peter, all of them—mixtures of strong and weak, nice and horrible. Simon guessed that he himself was a mixture, though he seemed to himself exactly the same all the way through.

He was partly a hero and partly a coward. He was a hero when he decided to make the forbidden climb up into the dovecote from the end of the barn. There was a ladder. The steps were rotten and the floor was stone, and the top of the steps was a long way up. Nobody was looking (nobody alive). Simon was pretty bored, enough to turn him into a hero.

It was a difficult climb, not just going up a ladder but more complicated than that. You were supposed to get into the dovecote from the empty storerooms below, which were completely uninteresting and smelled of emptiness, but there was no way into them except by keys or dynamite which Simon did not have. You could get directly into the dovecote, Simon thought, by the trapdoor at the top of the ladder. It was all terrifically forbidden. Simon started up the ladder, keeping his feet way to the edges of the rungs where they ought to be firmer.

He was fifteen feet from the flagstones when his foot went through a rung. He had a moment of absolute terror. He clutched at the chunky old sides of the ladder, wood older even than Step, old as the stones. He had a clear sense of a hand in the small of his back, of being saved. He hung like an insect flat against the ladder, until his feet groped for and found the next rung.

He did not dare to look down or around. He was alive, stuck like a fly to the ladder. He said aloud, softly, "*Merci,*" rolling the R like a Spaniard, the way he had picked up from the local people.

He knew exactly what had happened to him, and he knew that all the others except Step would say he was a liar. Tan would say it with rage, Peter with contempt, his mother with sadness, his grandfather with impatience, and his father like somebody repeating a lesson. Step would probably believe him, but there was no point in being believed by Step, since everybody knew she was crazy.

The question was what to do now. Simon was scared of going down, of going up, of staying where he was. They might not save him again. They had other things to think about. They were pretty busy. They had a lot of things to do, little kids to look after, meals to cook even though they were almost out of food and water. You couldn't count on them to be around all the time; it wasn't fair to them to expect it.

The least frightening option was to go on up. The rungs of the ladder looked better. Simon was nearer to the top than to the bottom. The trapdoor flapped around on its frame, no obstacle—Peter had shifted it easily with a pole. There had to be light in the dovecote—there had to be holes for the pigeons to get in and out. Simon went on up, testing every rung carefully with a foot before he put any weight on it, keeping his hands on the sides of the ladder. In a minute his head was nudging the trapdoor. Using his head, he shifted it aside. He took one hand off the ladder to heave the trapdoor out of the way. Obviously it wasn't the original trapdoor—it was a flimsy modern piece of three-ply or hardboard, something to stop a lot of dust and birds' mess coming down in the barn.

Simon heaved himself up on to the beam which formed one side of the trap. It was wood but it felt like iron, a slab almost two feet square. That was a safe place to be, if he didn't fall off. He looked round the dovecoat. It was nearly square, about three yards each way, with the main outside wall continuing for a yard above the floor on one side, twice that on the opposite side. The roof was a single slope, not peaked in the middle, chinks of sunlight showing between some of the tiles. The floor had massive joists, partly covered with planking. All of this was visible because there were a dozen slots in the wall, each the size of a brick, which showed up like headlights on a highway at night. There was a fair amount of mess, straw or hay, washing around over the joists and floorboards; Simon wondered if it was left over from the pigeons or brought there later by other birds.

When the crusaders were sitting around the hill, the people would have killed and eaten the last of the pigeons.

Simon's eyes got used to the deep shadows above and below the holes for the pigeons.

He saw first the glove, then the bottle, then a kind of big scarf or rug or rough apron. He saw the incomplete skeletons of a few birds, which he thought must be pigeons. They might have starved, or been killed by rats, or been eaten by a person. Simon looked round for this person, the remains of someone who had hidden in the dovecote from the soldiers. He did not know whether he hoped to see a skeleton in medieval clothes.

The glove was long, black, absolutely stiff. Simon could not guess what it was made of. He thought a glove as stiff as a board was a pretty useless thing.

The bottle was black too, and empty and dirty. Simon had an idea that the people in the time of the crusade did not have bottles, that bottles were invented later. Simon wondered for a moment what it took to invent a bottle, and whether the inventor had become rich and famous. The bottle seemed to mean that somebody had used the dovecote since the time of the crusade. That was likely enough. It was dry—it was a place a guy could sleep.

The rug was spread on a part of the dovecote where there were floorboards. One end was turned over to form a pad. That was a pillow. The rug was a bed.

Simon climbed off the great beam onto the joists. He crossed the dovecote carefully on the joists, on all fours, until he reached the boards and the rug. He felt the rug. It was very rough and stiff. He thought it was home-made, woven out of some kind of coarse string which no animal or even bug had ever wanted to eat. It must have been uncomfortable as a bed, but perhaps better than the bare boards. Did the man who slept here share his bedroom with a flock of pigeons? Did he eat the pigeons one by one until there were none left? Did he eat them raw? Could this rug have been lying in this same place ever since the crusade? Did the man who brought the bottle find it and use it?

Simon's groping hand encountered a metal object which he had not seen in the deep shadow in the corner. He picked it up and held it to the light of the nearest hole in the wall. It was a flattish cup with a big round handle. It was the wrong shape for drinking out of. It didn't look right for eating out of, because of the handle. It was half full of grit, dust, oddments which had dribbled into it from walls and roof, maybe from inquisitive bugs and animals, visiting birds, the processes of time. The cup was heavy. It was pretty knocked about, as though it had been used and dropped and used over a long time. Used for what? Simon wanted to ask the grown-ups, who might have an idea, but that would mean he had broken about eight strict rules.

Very far away, Simon heard his name called.

What now?

He could hide in the dovecote forever, as somebody had once tried to do. But *eventually* he would want food and drink. And the longer he was hidden the more worried they would be—the angrier they would be when he appeared.

Simon crawled over the joists to the big beam. He straddled the beam, his feet dangling, and looked down through the trapdoor. It was a long way down to the shadowed stone floor of the barn. He had already broken one rung of the ladder. He was scared at the thought of climbing down. He was scared of being seen climbing down, of what they would all say and do.

A voice spoke inside his head in the old language. The voice said it was all right to go down the ladder, that he would be safe. Simon went down, careful of the broken rung but knowing he was safe. He got to the flagstones of the barn, out of the barn into the yard, out of the yard, onto the track.

He heard his mother's voice calling him, way over the other side of the farm. He walked jauntily through the yard and through the house, the picture of confident innocence because he felt guilty about worrying his mother.

Simon drew a picture of the metal dish in the dovecote. He said it was something he had seen, maybe in a window of a store in one of the towns. He wanted to know what it was.

"A mug run over by a steamroller," said Peter.

"A wine taster," said Simon's father. "No, it's too big."

"Something used in a church," said his mother.

"A bon-bon dish," said his grandfather. "For crystallized fruit or *marrons glacés.*"

Tan made no suggestion. She was not interested.

"It's a lamp," said Step. "You floated the wick in oil."

"They would have seen the light through the holes," said Simon, puzzled. "They would have known he was up there."

None of them knew what he meant.

Simon had not properly explained how he came to be so dirty. Josie knew she ought to press the matter, get the truth out of him, but he was safe and there was too much else on her mind.

There was too much on Rob's mind. There ought to have been nothing. He was fretting. It was not doing him any good and it was not doing the rest of them any good either.

Josie remembered a campus wife she had known in another life, a stringy woman of fifty who was forever walking a springer spaniel. Her husband, professor of Oriental Studies, had an arthritic hip. She said to him at parties, "Stop limping!" She was impatient with disability. Josie tried not to be like that horrible woman.

The unanswered questions could stay unanswered, or all of them could provide any answers they wanted. The practical problems could be solved. None of it was impossible—in the ordinary way not even difficult. You could think of it as comic—a pile-up of laughable problems which would make a good story later.

Josie tried to bring a breezy humor to the business of getting Rob to Lourdes. People at the bus stop. In the bus. At the station. In the train. Local people who were traveling would talk in whispers to other people who were traveling, so that everybody would be looking at them. At least Rob would think that everybody was. Somewhere, anywhere along the line, he might get stuck. There might be a scene like that one in the bar, distressing, embarrassing, humiliating. Josie needed help for the trip. She considered them all, and concluded that it must be Tanja. It might be a terrible thing to subject the child to, but something terrible was less likely to happen if she was there.

"When?" said Tanja.

"Tomorrow; I hope. It depends on your father."

"Okay."

"It may be a very long day."

"All days are very long."

It was obvious to Peter that Tan was jumping at the chance to go to Lourdes. Why would anybody do that? A long, complicated, uncomfortable journey in this heat? Helping to look after her father on the trip? How could she help? Pick him up and carry him? Knock him out with a blackjack?

"Tan's going to Lourdes to see her mother," said Peter to his grandfather.

"You're jumping to unwarrantable conclusions."

* * *

"I understand you're seeing your mother in Lourdes," said Giles to Tanja.

Tanja looked at him with a shocked, astonished face. She blushed suddenly, deeply, painfully. She ran out of the kitchen.

Giles and Peter glanced at one another.

They both knew exactly how she felt. They had both, in their lives, been found out.

They took knapsacks with things for the night, the minimum of stuff, very likely necessary unless they got much luckier than they had recently been. Tanja's knapsack was actually a plastic bag from an airport duty-free.

Rob looked exhausted before they started. Josie felt exhausted by the thought of what they probably faced. On Tanja's small, lovely face there was no expression except, to Josie, a sense that she would look furious if she allowed herself to do so.

They set off early. It was a walk of unhappy memories. The sun was already hot.

Peter faced the day with dismay. Probably it would be the night also. Rob would not exactly speed things up, acting like a baby in front of strangers. Peter knew he had to make himself responsible for Simon. Their grandfather refused to accept any part of any such burden, saying that he had done it all once and it was somebody else's turn. Step thought nobody should accept responsibility for anybody else, the important thing being independence, self-reliance. She had a poem about being master of your fate, captain of your soul. That was just silly if it meant Simon was allowed to do what he wanted.

Peter knew from school. He was experienced. He was actually much more experience than any of the others. He knew about willful little boys, and his knowledge was up to date.

Peter was worried about Tan, too, about what she was up to with those people. He was worried by the threat to his mother and himself.

Giles had started the holiday with the complicated attitudes of tolerance. He would think as he found, giving, under the circumstances, all benefits of all doubts. It had seemed to work for a bit. But this civilized position had not survived the falling of rocks from heaven or the shortage of coffee.

Simon had got lucky, climbing the forbidden ladder into the forbidden dovecote without being found out or even much shouted at. A different personality, older, might have hesitated to crowd his luck. But Simon knew he was being looked after. Nothing terrible would be allowed to happen to him. He had been scared when Peter (or maybe Tan) had pushed him down the cliff, scared by the motorcycles, scared when the rung broke in the ladder. But he was only a small kid, and it was no disgrace to be a bit scared. He was not really scared. He was pretty tough. He had been given armor. He knew Step felt the same way. He was not sure if she had been given armor, but she certainly thought so. None of the others would understand even a little bit of any of this.

* * *

Rob stopped on the side of the road. They were halfway to the village. The sun was hot on the road and the yellow verge and on Josie's arms. Rob looked exactly as a man should not look who has been enjoying a restful convalescence in the sun.

He said, "If we had any sense we'd be staying in a hotel and none of this idiocy would have arisen."

He was blaming Josie for the fact that they had no car and no card, that they were isolated and vulnerable. Josie knew it was unmeant, illogical, a flash of resentment against the boredom and exhaustion they faced. She knew also, because it had to be accepted, what had happened to their credit cards and the vase in the yard and other things.

It was better to say nothing.

"Why don't you say something?" said Rob.

"We have to go to Lourdes," said Josie neutrally. "It doesn't help to complain."

"I'm not complaining. I'm pointing out a fact. I'm asking for recognition of the facts as they are."

"Can we please walk while you point out the facts?"

"I'm asking you to hold still and listen for a moment. Is that too much to ask?"

"Darling, we must catch that bus."

"I don't want to go on a bus. I don't want my daughter to go on a bus."

Rob sat down on the dry verge of the road.

"Rob. Please."

Twenty yards away Tanja stopped and turned. She stood watching. She did not look like a girl who could think of any way to help.

"Okay, okay," said Rob. He stood up. "Just don't

nag. Just please for Christ's sake don't nag."

This was the only part of the conversation which Tanja heard. The face she turned to Josie was crystalline with reproach, hard, hostile, faceted in the sunshine. No words came but words would come. Josie tried to find words of her own, to defend herself to Tanja, but by the time she had picked them the child had turned and was walking on along the roadside.

Peter tried reason. He abandoned reason and tried command. He abandoned command and resorted to force. The day promised to be the longest of his life.

They had an hour and three-quarters to wait for the bus. Nobody else was waiting because the local people knew when the bus went. They tried Thérèse's house and the presbytery. Both were empty, or at least locked and silent. There were faces at windows. Josie and Tanja had become hardened to faces at windows: they defied or ignored them. But the faces got to Rob. There was nothing to do in the village. It would have been stupid at that moment to buy anything. The bar was shut and the church locked. Probably nothing would have induced Rob into the bar.

They found a place where they could sit in the shade, a low wall within sight of the bus stop. Tanja prowled restlessly, her hands in the pockets of her cotton pants. Rob sat staring at the blank brick wall in front of him. He was not seeing the wall, but looking inward into a pit. Josie was frightened to say anything to either of them.

She wondered how many times they would have to

change trains between Castelnaudary and Lourdes.

After a long time, burdened women began to assemble at the bus stop. There were glances at the strangers, mutterings: a few direct, unabashed stares, olive-stone eyes then swiveling away.

Josie tried to insert a dipstick into the mood of the women. Hostility, suspicion, curiosity? Fear of the unknown? But they had all seen foreigners before—not often here, perhaps, but in Carcassonne and Narbonne and Toulouse. They must surely all have been to those places, and seen Germans taking videos of one another. The demure little group of Anglo-Americans—frigid, splintered, disunited—could not simply of its strangeness be so strange. What was it about, then, all of this? Who had been talking to these people?

Tanja was not taking anything from them. She gave back stare for stare, her underlip aggressive. She looked younger than usual.

Rob was working hard at pretending the women were not there.

Josie began to worry about whether they would get on the bus. The women waiting by the road had an awful lot of grips and baskets. They did not have quantities of live geese, ducks, chickens, but they seemed to have everything else, even to pieces of furniture.

They continued to come, younger women, children, a few men. The bus was going to be full even if it arrived empty. The people did not form a line, but it was obvious that the strangers would have been at the tail of the line if there had been one.

The bus swam into sight, chrome and glass brilliant in the sun. It stopped with a hissing of brakes and sighing of hydraulic doors. There was a kind of moderate hysteria in the crowd, conversation giving way to physical effort. The bundles of the women made entry slow. The bus was certainly going to be full.

Rob hung back. Josie touched his arm. Tanja watched them warily.

"Don't nag at me," said Rob to Josie, who had not said anything.

Josie had the sense of pulling Rob up into the bus, although they had no physical contact. Tanja hovered. The driver was impatient. It was not clear if he knew what all his passengers knew. If not already infected he was certainly shortly to become so. Josie did not think he could turn them off the bus.

Rob wanted to take another bus, to wait for one less full. But there was no other for a long time, and they still knew nothing about the times of the trains.

Tanja, without words or facial expression, was blaming Josie for Rob's problem with the bus.

They were aboard in the end, fares paid, legitimate passengers.

Josie thought that not even the most tolerant and curious student of human nature could have enjoyed that bus. It smelled of back streets—garlic, Gauloises, urine—and there was everywhere a determination to retain space won. It was difficult to find an occupied inch in which to put a foot, a hand. Areas occupied remained so, not out of need but out of pride, jealousy. Josie felt irritation with these tiny-minded people rise in her throat like bile. She played their game. Millimeter by millimeter she increased the space between her feet, the area held by her knapsack. Rob was trying to avoid contact with shoulders and elbows and hips. At his best he hated being crowded, jostled. He was a man who needed space around him. The embraces of cousins got on his nerves, and affable hosts who draped arms over his shoulders, and the New York subway and getting off an aircraft. At his best he was missing one skin. Now the skin he had could hardly hold out the world, hardly hold him together. Josie knew what was going through his mind because she could see the twitching of his face. She wanted to take his hand but she knew he did not want that. The thing to hope for was that he did not scream.

The bus was fast and pretty smooth. The roads were good. Nobody said anything. All the passengers who could were staring at them—at Rob, at Josie herself, at Tanja. Tanja stared back. Sometimes it was a good thing to have a streak of arrogance. The child must have inherited it from her mother. Anything for a bit of backbone. Rob was as stiff as a bar of metal not from strength but from passionate hatred of being where he was.

The bus decelerated sharply before hissing to a stop. This had the effect of pushing the passengers against one another. The people from the village did not like being pushed against Rob, but there was nothing they could do to prevent it.

A dozen passengers got off. Others were waiting to get on. The new passengers did not immediately climb aboard. There was a colloquy at the bottom of the steps of the bus. There were glances toward the bus from speakers and from listeners.

Josie wondered with sick anger what they were saying,

and who had told them whatever it was. There was nothing she could say or do. She hoped Rob was not taking in the conversation by the bus, or the expressionless stares of the people who climbed in.

The bus was fuller. Even for Josie it was only just bearable. Rob could not be asked to take much more of this. He had to take it.

Peter dragged Simon indoors soon after one o'clock. Grandpapa and Step were waiting for them. They had a scratch lunch, which Josie had made in the dawn and left on the kitchen table under a cloth. Giles drank most of a bottle of Minervois, the only cold thing in the world. Simon wanted apple pie with butterscotch ice cream. He said so, as he said most things, loudly and often.

The station at Castelnaudary was sunk in midday slumber. Nobody was arriving or expecting to depart. One taxi was parked by the station, its driver lingering over his lunch in the knowledge that nothing was happening.

There would be a train for Toulouse. They would change there for Tarbes, and at Tarbes for Lourdes. It was possible. People were known to have made this journey. People went to Lourdes from all over the world, though not many, perhaps, from Castelnaudary.

The clerk was efficient and helpful. He spoke no English, but he was patient. He had plenty of time in which to be patient. The clerk had not heard the received wisdom of Montferaud-St.-Antonin—nobody from the village had come to the station, nobody from the bus.

There were eighty-five minutes to wait. The downturn of Tanja's mouth blamed Josie for the wait.

Giles went gustily to sleep, which was no surprise. He stayed awake long enough to arrange rugs and pillows in the shade of the cypresses. Worrying about the others would spoil his digestion and do them no good. Peter could be trusted to look after the brat.

Before they got on the train, Josie wanted to ask Rob if he had remembered his passport. He had no other means of identification without credit cards. No office in the world would hand him a card without the evidence of a passport or something of equal authority. She had not asked the question because just now it was the sort of thing that upset him, rattled him, enraged him.

She should have asked him as they left the house. The question then would have been innocent, contained no reproach or suspicion. Anybody could forget a passport in the muddle and bustle of an early departure.

Tanja might ask him. It would be better if she did. Josie found herself angry because Tanja did not bother to check with her father that he had his passport.

The train was crowded, young people with rucksacks jamming the corridors. Some, perhaps, were returning to their studies in Toulouse; many were going all the way on to Paris. Lucky children. They could go where they wanted, unencumbered except by Walkmans and changes of socks. No one whispered about them, cast them strange glances, accused them of madness or murder. Josie remembered a time when she had been a free spirit.

Rob was visibly and vividly unhappy, standing in the corridor and swaying with the students. The passengers were neutral in the war between Rob and the world. But there were so many of them, so close, that they seemed to be attackers.

Peter had Simon under precarious control. It was pretty well a full-time job. Simon disliked the situation as much as Peter did. He was like a puppy, continuing to explore an environment which he had known intimately for weeks.

Peter was full of forebodings about what Tanja was up to. He had tried to like her and trust her for his mother's sake, but she had made it impossible.

With the best will in the world, Peter could not keep Simon under observation every second of every minute of every hour. The buildings were rambling, and the immediate area was full of rocks and scrub. It was like trying to keep tabs on a flea. Peter's attention was diverted by an insect, an unfamiliar beetle. The beetle was more placid than Simon. When Peter looked up, after no more than a few seconds, Simon had disappeared.

They were outside the farmyard, on the rough ground behind the house. Simon could have wriggled away in any of a dozen directions. He was hiding. It was a tease: it was infuriating. Peter forced himself to be alert at a time of day when it was impossible to be alert. He began to look for Simon, keeping an eye out all the time, all the way round.

Peter did not want to shout. It would be giving way to the damned kid, playing his game. Shouting might wake Grandpapa, and disturb Step in whatever she was doing. Shouting would be an admission that he had failed, that Simon had fooled him. Peter began searching for Simon, prowling, peering, listening, swearing under his breath.

They were just under an hour on the train before they had to change at Toulouse. It was a very different kind of station, noisy, sweatily busy, full of tooting trolleys and girls sitting on backpacks, men with briefcases, men with errands that caused them to bump into Rob.

Josie found out what train to get to Tarbes, and how long they had to wait.

They got coffee at a buffet on the platform. Rob's hand trembled so that coffee went all over his wrist and up the sleeve of his shirt.

Peter was beaten. He had to shout.

He shouted out, "All right! You've won! I can't find you!"

The only reply was the clicking of an insect in the khaki grass.

Peter felt a small surge of panic and a large surge of anger. The panic fed the anger and caused him to scream for Simon. The silver walls of the farmhouse gave back his screams.

Grumbling, slightly belching, Grandpapa woke up. When he took in what Peter was telling him he joined the hunt, but with an air that it was really somebody else's responsibility.

Step appeared from somewhere and joined the hunt.

They told one another that Simon was hiding—that he realized, perhaps, that his joke had gone too far, so that he was now afraid to come out.

"Come out, come out," said the echoes from the stones, and insects clicked in the grass.

"Your passport, please, Mr. Kemp?"

"Sure."

Of course it was there, in his knapsack, protected by a sturdy brown envelope.

There was a glancing, infinitesimal meeting of eyes between Josie and Tanja: thank God.

It was not a passport in the envelope. It was a piece of anonymous cardboard cut to the size of a passport; a piece of rubbish.

ELEVEN

Rob looked at the piece of cardboard with a face of blank astonishment. He delved in his knapsack, emptied it. He emptied his pockets. It was obvious that these things were useless. If the passport was not in the envelope, he did not have it. He had an imitation passport. But he went through the motions of searching just the same. Anybody would have done so.

"Somebody switched them on me," said Rob. "It's somebody's idea of a joke."

Rob had no identification of any kind. He had not carried with him any of the pieces of paper or plastic by which civilized man defines himself. He had had no need of these things. He had his passport.

The man was as helpful as could be. He looked at Rob oddly, but he telephoned to somebody in Paris.

Names, numbers, dates were quoted on the telephone.

He explained it all gently to people who already understood the situation. The security of the company and its clients forbade the issue by a local office of a card to a customer personally unknown to that office and unable to provide satisfactory identification. The company would help if it possibly could, but it would not willingly risk financing freeloaders and confidence tricksters. This was simple common sense, a basic precaution against fraud, an absolute rule. Banks all over the world had the same rule—credit companies, travel agents, dealers, stores, anybody who handed out money or money's worth required evidence of the identity of the transferee. Was that not reasonable?

"Call America, and get the head office to authorize the issue of a card," said Josie. "We'll pay for the call."

"Yes, madam. I can do so. There is no need. There is no purpose. I am already authorized to issue a card to Mr Kemp."

"This is Mr Kemp."

The clerk was silent. He was unhappy. He was not being obstructive or unreasonable.

"I left this bag on the table in the hall while we had breakfast," said Rob. "The passport was in the envelope and the envelope was in the bag. I am completely certain about that. Everyone was wandering in and out of the hall, the kitchen, going up and down stairs . . . I'm sorry," he said to the man behind the desk. "I'm sorry to have taken your time."

"I hope you find the passport, sir."

"Thank you. Thank you very much."

There was a shrill edge in Rob's voice, like machinery

without lubricant. Josie prayed that he would say no more.

Rob said, "Thank you for your concern. It is gratifying to me. It makes the whole journey worthwhile."

There was no answer to this. At least, the man behind the desk could find none. He inclined his head, with an air of wondering whether he ought to try to smile.

"C'mon, Dad," said Tanja softly.

They went out into the sun of late afternoon among pilgrims and cripples and helpers and tourists. Rob looked more in need of Our Lady of Lourdes than any of the children in wheelchairs.

Tanja was blaming Josie. Josie was blaming herself, but she was damned if she was having the child blaming her.

They did not have return tickets, because they had expected by now to have a car.

They started back toward the station to find out the times of the trains.

They searched the house and outbuildings from top to bottom. They did so haphazardly, in some panic. Giles saw that this was no good. Simon was quite artful enough to keep a jump ahead of them if they were disorganized: that is if he was hiding, which seemed the most likely. Giles organized the search on methodical lines, posting the others so that, when an area was searched, it stayed searched, sealed against the small criminal.

While Step watched the farmyard, Giles and Peter systematically quartered the ground behind, the scrub, the track and its verges. It was exhausting. They became hot and angry and frightened.

"What are you going to tell your mother?" said Giles.
Peter had been asking himself the same question.

It was another crowded train, trundling into gathering darkness, leaving the sunset behind.

Rob thought that all the people on the train were looking at him and talking about him.

Tanja retreated into a shell of sullenness.

Josie tried to feel compassionate but she was too tired.

It was Giles who stumbled over Simon—literally: he nearly fell over the boy.

It was very peculiar. It was a place already thoroughly searched. Simon had somehow got there, or been taken there. He was at the foot of one of the rocks on the rough ground behind the farm, the irregular monoliths which might once have been part of a bastion. He was not particularly hidden, but he was not obvious in the fading light unless you were on top of him. It was not possible that anybody properly searching could have missed him.

Simon was conscious but groggy. He had a lump on the back of his head.

Giles called the others. Between them they carried Simon indoors. They put him to bed, since he had had a knock on the head and might be concussed.

Simon did not know what had happened to him. He thought he knew but he was obviously wrong. Perhaps he did know and he was lying. What he said was that somebody he did not see had hit him on the head.

People did not hit small boys on the head for no reason.

They had seen no people. It was true that by the time

they started searching Simon's accident had probably already happened, and that Giles and Step were nowhere near, but still it was true that none of them had seen any strangers. Simon himself had not seen anybody. They would not have seen a stranger and forgotten. Strangers were so unusual that seeing one was an event. It had become a threat.

Simon might have thought he was telling the truth (not as when he fell down the hillside) because a person is confused after a bang on the head—memory is unreliable, the truth untellable. Simon insisted that his memory was perfectly clear, up until the moment of the bang. He did not know how he got to where his grandfather found him. He thought he must have been carried.

The state of his clothes and knees was consistent with his having crawled, but his clothes and knees were always in that state.

"A month ago," said Step, "I was frightened. I was frightened of Dorothy Schofield. Then I decided there was nothing to be frightened of. Some funny things happened and still I wasn't frightened. Now I am."

The excellent French railway system did not precisely cater for those travelers, on that day, at that hour. They had long waits at Tarbes and at Toulouse. The midday bustle had all been tidied away and put to bed. There were a few backpackers stretched out on the platform: perhaps others, gypsies, Algerians, watchful and secret.

If things had been normal, they would have booked into a hotel, telephoned the farm, hired a car to drive home in the morning. It was still difficult to accept that none of these things was possible.

"What we'll do," said Josie with a cheerfulness dredged from an empty well, "we'll call somebody collect in the morning, and get them to send a banker's draft by express."

"Yeah," said Rob. "Yeah, do that."

Rob had retreated into lassitude. Things had reached rock bottom and he did not want to think about any of it. He was a sack of dried beans, staying where he was put, exhausting to move, unresponsive.

Had he deliberately or accidentally carried a piece of cardboard all the way to Lourdes?

Tanja had also withdrawn in a different way. She had fenced herself behind thorns, like a nomad who shares his desert with lions or fools. She depended on them but she would rather not have done so. They had wasted her day as well as their own. It was not her father's fault because he was sick.

There was not much to eat at the farm. Josie had left instructions. Step scorned the instructions.

Worried about his daughter, Giles drank a lot of red wine.

Having slept early and deeply, Simon was wakeful and fretful.

Peter felt that he had to make himself responsible for them all. He knew it was too much for him.

"The American consulate," said Josie suddenly. "It's what they're for."

"What they're for," said Rob, echoing her tone as though learning a language, or being coached for a part in a play.

"We might have thought of it before. We might have thought of a lot of things before. We didn't see any need. We're not used to a situation like this. We haven't got any experience of being up against it. I suppose it's good for us. Challenge is supposed to be good for you. You're meant to show courage and . . ."

Josie tailed off. The effort was too great. It was like talking to a duvet. Rob was not taking any of it in, and Tanja was sitting apart from them under a black personal cloud, visible even in the darkness.

They were waiting at the bus station in Castelnaudary. They thought they were in time for the last bus, although there was nobody to ask. The night was dark and the town quiet. A little bit of life round the station had dribbled away when the people went home. There was not much traffic on the roads, in the streets. The clicking of insects was muffled by the day's dust, which had settled as the world became still.

Rob had said, at an hour when you could believe him lucid, that any of the group could have switched the piece of cardboard for the passport, there on the table in the hall, with all of them having breakfast or milling around. He had said that in self-defense. Objectively it might be true. It was no contribution at all, just words.

In physical terms, it was screamingly obvious what had happened to the passport.

Why?

Not an act of conscious choice. Subconscious? Why would Rob's subconscious mind, in a mess as it admittedly was, subject him and his wife and daughter to such extravagant inconvenience? Surely your subconscious worked toward self-preservation?

Was it some kind of subconscious revenge? On herself? On Tanja? Revenge for what? What had they done?

If he wanted to cry for help, why didn't he cry for help?

The word "possession" came into Josie's head, as she sat on a bench in a pool of yellow light from above.

Were there mischievous children among the Cathars? Why wouldn't there be? Boys like Simon, smocked, barefooted, hair clubbed, prankish and willful, motiveless naughtiness surviving the centuries?

It was easier to believe by the minute.

There were still forty minutes until the bus left, if it left.

The night was unusually dark, stars obscured, moon belated. They were depressed and uneasy, worried about Simon, about the others on their life-saving journey, about themselves.

Peter felt sourly that he was being blamed for Simon falling over and hitting his head on a rock. He felt a little guilty. He did not think there was any need for him to admit this. He did not want to go to bed. He did not want to be alone in the dark, because the feeling had been growing in him that he would not be alone in the dark. He had not himself heard voices, but he could no longer tell himself that the others had imagined them. There was a prickle in the small of his back. He sat exhausted at the kitchen table long after he was usually in bed.

Giles, through the bottom of his glass, saw that the whole thing was unfair. After a lifetime of honorable service he had retired, and all he wanted was to be left alone. Surely he had earned tranquillity! It was unfair that he should be rewarded by danger, discomfort, and worry.

Step went out into the yard. Giles and Peter watched her go, troubled. She herself looked more troubled than at any time since the bad days after Dorothy Schofield's visit: more troubled than by Gwen's death or the watch in the dawn or the falling rock.

A little light came out into the yard from the ground-floor windows of the house, its angle exaggerating the irregularities of the flagstones so that they resembled abstract woodcuts. The light did not reach the entrance of the yard, nor probe into the recesses of the barn. It made blacker the blackness of the shadows, so that there might have been an army there. The night was absolutely silent. Step had the yard to herself. The people were not coming, or had not come.

Giles and Peter heard her call out, "Please look after our friends."

They glanced at one another, like comrades, like contemporaries. Peter—frightened of the dark, which he had always successfully pretended not to be—felt younger than his age but also as old as Giles, because they had exchanged a glance which was partly complicity. Giles—frightened of many things to which he could put no name—felt older than his age but also as young as Peter, because they had exchanged a glance which was partly a shared, irrational, childish terror.

It was sufficiently frightening that Step was frightened.

Step's call was answered, by one voice or two. They heard the answer, Giles and Peter silent in the kitchen. Neither had heard the voice before, thin and distant, wordless, neither human nor inhuman, far away but between them as they sat.

They did not know what the answer meant. They did not know if it was truly an answer to what Step had said.

They sat motionless. Peter was too young and Giles too old to go rushing out into the yard. They were frightened to do so.

A few people gathered for the last bus, secret old people with secret packages, in the warm pools of light in the warm darkness.

Rob's shadowed face showed that he thought the people were looking at him.

It was a relief to see the people assembling there. They confirmed as probable what had seemed no more than possible, the departure of the bus toward the village.

Josie did not recognize any of the faces, but some of them recognized Rob, Tanja, herself. Of course they were from the village. They had been spending the day in town, shopping, seeing relatives, putting flowers on graves. Those people did not need to be told about the foreigners—they already knew all about them. They would tell the others—were even now visibly telling them. By the time the bus left everybody on board would know that the foreigners were murderers, arsonists, whatever they had all been invited to believe.

It was what they called a whispering campaign. It was the way they had dealt with the witches of Salem, and with Jews and Communists and anybody they envied or resented. Step blamed it all on Dorothy Schofield. Rob, with obscurer logic, blamed it on his ex-wife Anna and Josie's ex-husband Harry. Tanja, with no logic at all, blamed it on Josie. Peter blamed it on Rob, for having had a nervous breakdown. Giles denied that it existed, although he accepted that something very rum had been said to the police.

Josie herself felt simple rage, which tasted of acid, of wine gone sour, bad olives, stale bread, a summer ruined.

She foresaw with sickening clarity that, when they got back to the farm without passport or credit card, the eyes of Giles and Peter would meet. She was angry with them, too, and with Rob, and with herself for being angry.

She needed more help than she could get from any of them. The burden was becoming intolerable, as in the words of the General Confession. Feeling suddenly stupid with fatigue, she wondered dizzily if there were some reservoir of spiritual strength hoarded by the Cathars, some underground cistern into which she could lower a tube . . .

She sat on her hands in the dark, with Tanja looking at her feet and Rob looking inward at monsters.

Giles and Peter sat in silence. They exchanged a glance, as they had more and more often been doing—each increasingly becoming for the other, surprisingly enough to them both, a still point in a rocking world.

They knew they were sane.

Sane, they knew they had heard the thin incomprehensible answer to Step's call. They had the inescapable sense of a lid being lifted, and they were frightened of what moved in the pit below.

Giles was not too old, nor Peter too young, to react to hard evidence. They had seen what they had seen.

Now, for the first time, they had heard also.

Giles finished off the wine in his glass. It was impossible that his hand should not tremble. The rim of the glass knocked against his teeth. He spilled a dribble of wine on his chin. Peter looked away, with a mixture of contempt and compassion.

The lights went out.

Peter found that he was gripping the edge of the kitchen table, as he had seen Rob doing. It seemed a wise and sensible thing to do. He thought his grandfather was probably gripping the empty wineglass. It was evident that he was not doing so, or not doing so effectively: the glass exploded on the flagstones of the floor.

There was a cry from outside, in a voice unlike any voice either of them had ever heard.

Giles tried to shout, "Step!" His voice did not work. The noise he made was like that of a sick animal. Peter thought his grandfather was frightened not for Step but for himself. There was no disgrace about that.

The lights came on again.

Peter sighed, and let go of the edge of the table. Giles looked down with embarrassment at the fragments of glass on the floor, the splash of the lees of his wine.

"A hiccup," said Giles. "Happens all the time in Somerset. But it makes one wonder."

Step came in, no different from when she went out.

"Did the lights go out?"

"For a moment," said Giles.

"I thought so. I couldn't see the windows, but the black seemed blacker." To Peter she said, "It's always happening at home."

"I've just said that," said Giles.

"Sometimes it's a power cut, sometimes it's my electric kettle. It always bodes ill. It makes one wonder."

"I've just said that, too," said Giles.

"How boring you're being, then. Is Simon all right?"

"I'll go and see," said Peter.

Simon was sitting up in bed.

"You ought to be lying down," said Peter.

"I only just sat up. I couldn't stay lying down. Did you hear them?"

"Yes."

"Now do you believe us?"

"I heard a voice."

"I understood what they said."

"Rubbish. What did they say?"

"I don't know how to say it. I don't know the words."

"I bet you don't. They didn't say anything. They didn't use any words."

"They did to me."

"Lie down and shut up."

But Peter had heard. It was no longer ridiculous to him that the voices were saying something. It was ridiculous, and typical, that Simon should claim to have understood. Probably nobody in the modern world could properly understand. But when a voice was raised it was usually in order to say something.

Peter spoke more gently to Simon, telling him to lie down and to sleep. He even pretended to believe that Simon had been hit on the head.

Peter paused on the attic landing outside Simon's bedroom door. He remembered something he had read about battles, perhaps about the trenches in the First World War, perhaps something in Buchan or Sapper.

He had read that in moments of acute crisis and danger people were nicer to one another.

Did that mean that they, here and now, were in such a desperate position? Did the threat have a face or no face?

It might be terribly unimportant that Tan had seen her mother in Lourdes.

"That passport," said Rob. "I thought about it and thought about it."

He spoke with painstaking clarity, like a man who suspects he may be drunk.

"I have an absolutely distinct memory of checking it was in the envelope. I put the envelope in this bag."

"We'll find it in the morning," said Josie.

She was pretty sure Rob thought he was telling the truth. It was impossible to be quite sure.

"It's a laugh, really," said Josie. "We'll laugh about it one day. We'll dine out on it."

Tanja glanced at them and away, looking out through chinks in her barricade. Tanja had seen some of the hideous interview in the AmEx office. It was probably a good thing she had not seen all of it. Josie felt a stab of sympathy for the unfortunate official, who had been in an impossible position, who wanted to help but was powerless to do so, checkmated in any attempt by the folly of his client. It was a moment of acute humiliation. Yes, it was a good thing Tan had missed some of it. She had—what had she done?—looked at her watch and walked out. No word of farewell or excuse when she left, none of greeting or explanation when she came back. It was horrible to have the child despising her father. Her resentment of Josie was unfair but maybe natural, but to see this other, this abjectness . . .

Looked at her watch and walked out of the place. Like what? Like somebody keeping an appointment.

The bus arrived with a thudding of diesel, modern, reassuring, neutral. Its exterior was an image of the normal world. Its interior took them back to something else. Josie felt deafened by whispers. She was bottomlessly tired. She had the sense that she had carried both of them, all day, all the way, and that when they got home she would be carrying the rest of them too.

Keeping an appointment? How had they made the appointment? There might be lots of ways, messengers, a drop for letters . . . Josie knew that was the way Peter's mind had been working. That had angered and sickened her, but now she wondered if she had been angered and sickened by the wrong thing. Josie was used to uncomplicated responses even to complicated situations: we will do this; that course is right and the other wrong. Now she did not know if the situation was simple or complicated and she did not know how to react.

Tanja's face was secret. What had she got to be secret about?

Giles and Step said that they would wait for another hour. They sent Peter to bed, long after his usual time. He would not go. They said he must go, to look after Simon if the child was frightened. Peter was on these grounds obliged to go, although he knew, with self-disgust, that he was more frightened than Simon was.

Upstairs, the dangling amber-colored lights were reassuring. But they made shadows. The brighter the lights, the deeper the shadows. This was an obvious thought but not a comforting one. The lights had gone out once.

Simon had gone to sleep, but the light in his bedroom was on. Peter decided to leave it on. He left his own light on when he went to bed. Though it attracted all the insects in Languedoc, it might repel other things.

By daylight the bus journey had been long. By night it was interminable. Rob had shrunk into a small cocoon of apathetic misery, like a monkey in a cage in a traveling circus. Tanja lurked behind her defenses. The bus gradually emptied as it traveled eastward through the isolated villages among the vineyards. It was hot. There was no laughter in the bus.

When had Josie last heard laughter?

They had brought menace and treachery with them, but they had left these things behind too. As before when far from the farmhouse, Josie was frightened for those who were there. There had been strange arrivals and events, accidents, shadows. Those who were at home that night were too old or too young. She was afraid of what might be happening without herself to look after them.

Insects clicked and fretted against Peter's lampshade. There was no other sound. Peter lay awake wondering how he usually got to sleep.

Giles and Step had not yet gone to bed. Giles had opened another bottle, perhaps. They were expecting Rob and the others, back with the precious credit card.

Into the silence, two floors below Peter but loud from the yard through the open windows, exploded the ordinary stammer of the telephone.

It was late to be telephoning. Peter thought: that's Mummy ringing up, probably to say they're stuck in Toulouse.

He thought: God Almighty, that telephone hasn't worked for weeks. It *doesn't* work. We've tried and tried.

"False alarm," said Step, putting down the telephone with a funny expression.

"What?" said Giles. "Did they hang up? What did you hear?"

"Nothing. There was nothing to hear. It's dead."

"It rang!"

"A mouse made it ring. A beetle in the works."

"That's absolutely impossible."

As before, as hundreds of times before, Giles picked up the telephone, rattled the bar, listened, shouted. The telephone was curved inert plastic, responsive as a boot.

At last he said, "I don't think it could be a beetle in the works."

"Nor do I," said Step. "But it's what I prefer to believe."

The bus swam away from the stop at the edge of the village, a brilliant mobile island of modern civilization, a capsule of confidence.

Though she had hated being on the bus, Josie on the dark roadside felt a kind of nostalgia for it, homesickness for its lights and predictability. She felt lost and abandoned without it.

How could you be helpless in a civilized country in the late twentieth century? There was a whole apparatus specifically designed to help—consuls, police, the banking system, public utilities. It was funny that the whole machinery could break down for certain individuals in a certain combination of circumstances. It had not broken, merely hiccuped. In the morning they would reinsert the plug in the socket, and normal services would resume.

Had Rob hidden his passport, burned it? Would they give him a temporary one? Would that do for getting a credit card?

A dozen people had got off the bus. They had dematerialized into the darkness. Rob stood not looking about him, his knapsack at his feet. Tanja waited for somebody to do something right.

There was light where they were, other lights in the village. A great flat darkness lay between them and the farm. Warm haze, like smoke, like soup, lined the sky. To walk was to swim. Josie supposed they would see their way. She supposed they would make it. They were not yet undernourished. They were all very tired, each exhausted by the same pressures and by different ones.

Giles leaned further and further back in his chair. His mouth opened a little. He looked old and tired. He had truly meant to wait up wakefully for Josie and Rob and Tanja because he was worried about Josie going off with the two of them, like a hostage, into what was surely a camp of the enemy. And he had heard the bloodless answer to Step's appeal, and he had heard the telephone ring when the telephone could not have rung. But the day had been very long since the dawn departure of the others, their hurried breakfast and gathering of bits and pieces. That had been too early for him: the breaking, out of politeness or consideration, of a habit which had become a necessity. Standing-to at dawn was something he had left behind. He had graduated from that sort of thing. Years of early rising had earned him leisure in the mornings. And the day had been long and empty and worrying; and it was now two hours after his usual bed-time; and he had drunk a bottle and a half of wine, gradually, over six hours.

The vineyards stretched round them like a sea, flat as an inland sea, hundreds of millions of ripening grapes invisible but somehow perceptible. The road ran in their midst like the dry path opened for the Israelites through the Red Sea. There was a sense of teeming life in and under the vines, lizards and centipedes sleeplessly busy in the red dust, creatures nobody had ever seen because they stirred only by night, ancient anonymous things that had watched the Romans and the crusaders come and go, Manichaeans and martyrs and visiting Americans. There were clicks and whirrs in the darkness, the clock-work of miniature machineries, life absolutely foreign, not hostile but not friendly, neutral as the invisible moon. The little nocturnal creatures were not part of sane, daily reality; they were no comfort.

The only comfort now—the only one in this raving dream of fatigue—was the thought of getting safely home: light, the others, a drink, bed. Every problem could be faced and outfaced, but only by daylight, only after a long sleep. Each step forward felt like half a step back. The fine modern surface of the road felt to the feet like treacle. The air was dense and muggy; a skeleton would have sweated.

The illusion of absolute darkness was qualified after a little. The road was rimmed by pale verges, and the world by hills blacker than the sky.

Rob walked at a moderate pace exactly in the middle of the road. He avoided diverging, even ever so slightly, toward one side or the other, as though something hidden in the vines would reach out and grab him. What would have happened if a car had come along? There was no traffic. Rob's inscrutable present mood was not put to the test. But a man who had done the things he had done was capable of refusing to get out of the way of a car.

Josie did not know whether she was supposed to walk beside Rob. He did not look as though he wanted a companion. In a lot of places women walked behind their men. She decided that it was best to be a peasant or an Arab; she could from behind keep an eye on Rob without seeming to do so.

Tanja still distanced herself from the party. She was twenty yards behind. Her shoes made no sound. Josie had to keep glancing back to make sure she was still there. She did not know if she was looking back in the interest of Tanja's safety or of her own. Tanja would see the movement: she would see the darkness of Josie's hair becoming the paleness of her face every time she looked round, and probably she would be enraged by being checked up on. Josie was too tired to care.

She had forgotten what time they had started walking, so she did not know how long they had been walking.

She had forgotten any other way of life than this ludicrous journey half across France.

Rob trudged on in front, one of his shoes faintly squeaking as it flexed with his foot. He looked pretty defeated. It would be difficult for him, facing the others, intercepting their glances.

Josie looked back for the thousandth time. Tanja had stopped. Josie stopped also. Rob's shoe squeaked on in the darkness.

"Are you okay?" called Josie to Tanja.

"This is the turning."

"Oh. We missed it. Are you sure?"

Tanja did not reply. She turned and started along a track which Josie only now saw. She could just see also the hill on which the farm squatted, a kind of presence which was the farm itself. She thought she could see a glow from the farm's invisible lights.

"Rob!"

Rob had walked on. He was out of sight, and his squeaking shoe out of earshot. Josie muttered something she would not have said aloud, even when alone. She set off after Rob, running. She shouted as she ran. She was too tired to shout or to run.

She saw Rob ahead, a dark, hunched figure plodding along in the dark. He ignored her shouts. He did not hear them. He was sleepwalking. She had to take him physically by the arm to stop him, turn him, start him going again back toward the turning to the farm.

They were halfway up the rough track when they stumbled over Tanja, who was crouching down by the side of the road.

"I was waiting for you," said the girl unsteadily.

"Thank you," said Josie.

"Because I was scared."

"We're home."

"That's why I'm scared."

There was a thin cry from the heart of the darkness. A movement, the rolling of a stone, the crackle of dry vegetation. Another cry, different, from another place. Movements here and there, cries, close, far, from the track and the verge of the track, the rocks and scrub, cries of pain and defiance. An army was out, a population, attackers or defenders, besiegers or besieged, angry and despairing people whose voices were human and inhuman.

There was no light from the farm. There should have been light but there was none.

There came a clash of metal on metal, and a scream. A flame bloomed in the darkness and immediately died.

There was no light and no sound. The smallest insects were frightened.

They waited in the darkness, crouched. Josie had tight hold of Rob's arm, either for his sake or for her own. They waited for long silent moments, until it seemed that a sort of peace had come.

Josie stood up. "Come now," she whispered.

She pulled Rob up. He stood not tall but hunched, as though to avoid notice. She found that she herself, though she wanted to stand defiantly straight, was in a cringing, apologetic posture. Tanja stood close to her father, as though for shelter. They were frightened.

"Somebody might have left a light on," muttered Tanja.

Josie thought so too. There would have been comfort in a warm red square of window.

"We'll turn on every light in the house," said Josie.

Nervously they approached the gateless gateway of the yard. The dark bulk of the buildings obscured the thinner darkness of the sky. They moved furtively, humbly, so as not to annoy anybody, so as to avoid the risk of offense, of anger and retribution. They moved respectfully, because they were sorry for the people of the place. They went quietly and slowly, and spoke in whispers, because they were frightened.

The darkness thickened as they crept into the yard. There was masonry now on three sides, stealing air from the sky. Josie's fingers touched the flank of the dead minibus, which would have been a comfort if it had been alive, a link with the world beyond its practical usefulness; dead, it receded into a neutrality as blank as that of the lizards.

They had to grope their way across the farmyard, which was booby-trapped with chairs and tables. They whispered warnings to one another. The house should have been animated and welcoming, but it was a block of darker darkness filling one side of the yard.

What had happened to the people in the house, to Giles and Step and Josie's sons?

Josie was in the lead. She did not want to be, but she knew she had to be. It was her groping fingers that found the stone sides of the door, the door itself, the handle. The door was closed but unlocked. She turned the handle and pushed the door open. It had seemed black outside, but the interior blackness had a solid quality, as though it could be cut into cubes. Josie's fingers found the light switch by the door on the inside wall, a large old-fashioned fixture like an udder. The switch was down. The light should have been on, the lamp hanging in the hall from the ceiling in a parchment frame. She clicked the switch up and down, knowing as she did so that it was stupid, useless, that the bulb had popped.

"Light!" came Tanja's voice in a furious whisper.

"Kitchen," said Josie.

Her fingers found the table in the hall. They found the big flashlight that lived there. She clicked the switch of the flash. It was dead. The bulb was broken or the battery flat. She put it down softly. This was still no time to be making bangs, to be taking risks.

Skirting the table, Josie groped her way on toward the kitchen. The wall felt unfamiliar. Intimately as she knew it, it was strange, unexpected, baffling. She felt lost in this small familiar place. She felt little waves of panic nibbling at the beaches of her brain. Advancing inch by inch, she bumped with breast and thigh against unidentifiable things, the table again, the bottom of the stairs, things which should not have been there.

She was aware of not being alone in the darkness of the hall. Rob and Tanja were still outside in the yard, but somebody had come in with her, or was already there when she came in. Josie heard a sound of harsh and threatened breathing, and realized that it was her own.

They had been inside the house before. Why not? It was their house.

She found the wooden frame of the kitchen door. The door was open. The darkness was absolute, and, except for her breathing, the silence. She knew where the light switch was: of course she did, after these weeks. She did not know where it was. She groped for it, over the uneven surface of the wall beside the door. Switch. There! The switch was down. The light was switched on. There was no light. She clicked this switch also, up and down, knowing it was useless.

Josie stood thinking, keeping tight hold of herself, intent on being practical, leader of the party, intent on putting up a respectable show in front of people who would have high standards. Matches. What matches? They cooked on electricity, not gas, and none of them smoked. Matches played no part in their lives. Candles. They had candles. They had dined out of doors by candlelight, bombed by nameless flying things. There was a candle in a candlestick with matches beside it. Where?

Josie knew she was not alone in the kitchen.

The windowsill. Could she remember seeing the candlestick on the windowsill? The morning was too remote to remember. She was too tired to think. She heard breathing not her own. Did they breathe? If they talked they must breathe. Groping, her hand met flesh, a face.

She screamed.

There was another scream, not her scream, not an echo, not any human scream.

There were movements, bumps, sighs. The darkness was full of people. There was a scream from the yard, Tanja's scream.

A voice murmured from somewhere near the table, a voice thick with sleep, Josie's father's voice.

Step's voice said, "You're safe back, then, if you're who I think you are. They said you would be. Why have you turned all the lights off? We must have gone to sleep while we were waiting for you. Why are there so many people here?"

"I must have a light," said Josie.

"The big torch in the hall."

"It's dead."

"Like so much else. There's one on my bedside table."

Josie groped her way out into the hall, and across it to the foot of the stairs. She had the sense of pushing through people whom she never touched. There were people on the stairs, whispers, warnings. There was a cry from below. Someone was hurrying, steps audible. Cobwebby fabric brushed Josie's hand. She reached the landing and the door of her own room. There was a small torch there also, by the bed. She gasped with relief when her fingers located it. She clicked the button. Nothing.

She was suddenly certain that no flashlights in the house would work, that no matches would be found. Darkness had arrived. Would the sun rise, ever again?

There were cries, two and more voices of women, from the landing outside the bedroom, scurrying movements, footsteps, the rustle of heavy clothes, the momentary babble of a young child senseless with fright.

Josie forced herself out of the room, into the crowded landing. There was movement beside and behind her. She felt her way by the wall to the other bedroom. Groping, she found the beds and between them the table. The torch was there, with other objects unguessable to the touch. Of course the torch did not work.

It was possible that a fuse had blown which affected only the ground floor. She tried the light. There was no light.

On the landing again she was disoriented by the thick darkness, by movements and snatches of strange talk in strange high voices. She felt a surge of panic again at being lost, at the danger of falling downstairs, at not being able to find her sons.

She found at last—had even the sense of being led to—the foot of the stairs to the attics. She went carefully, her heart thudding, accompanied on the stairs.

"Peter?"

"Yes."

"Are you all right?"

"There's no light. I can't see anything."

"Is Simon there?"

"Yes. I don't know. He was awake."

Josie climbed the rest of the stairs.

"Simon?"

She groped to the door of his small room. The door was open. She found the bed. The bed was empty.

"Simon?"

TWELVE

He was hiding. He was in the cupboard or under the bed. Sudden terror was followed by rage and then by terror.

"Simon! Simon! Peter, help me find him! Tanja, help me!"

Josie felt that the bedclothes were wildly rumpled: perhaps no more so than by a child sleeping in them. Simon's slippers were under the bed and his dressing-gown on the floor. If he had got out of bed in the dark, sleepy, he would not have bothered with those things. He usually did not bother about them when he was wide awake in the morning. Was he awake? Was he sleep-walking? Could that be it? Had he crept out in the dark, among those rocks, unconscious?

Peter had been deeply asleep, in spite of himself, and he was still groggy with sleep. Giles was half stupefied with sleep and was tumbling kitchen chairs in the darkness. Tanja's voice called from the yard, frightened, confused. Peter was calling from the passage, wanting to help but wanting help himself, momentarily lost, disoriented in the darkness.

For God's sake, there must be light, there must be some way of making a flame.

All day they had been among matches, all the matchboxes and matchbooks of Languedoc and the Pyrenees, as numerous as the grapes—flashlights, batteries, bulbs, candles, spills, lighters, lanterns, torches . . .

Josie and Peter between them began to search the attic rooms, using their fingertips and their voices.

"Call softly if you call," said Josie.

"Why?"

"You mustn't wake them up suddenly."

"He's wide awake. He's here!"

"Where?"

"In Tan's room."

"It's Tan."

"Tan's in the yard. I've just heard her voice. Simon!"

Simon was not in Tan's room. Nobody was there. Somebody was there. Somebody was with them, a third, perhaps more than one.

"He's here!" said Peter angrily.

"No."

"Somebody's here."

"Yes."

Tanja and Rob were by now searching with their fingertips in the yard and barn and buildings. They were calling softly, continuously.

There was another voice upraised. Simon? Not Simon.

There were footsteps, rustles, bumps.

"Simon had a knock on the head today," said Peter to Josie.

"Oh God, why did nobody tell me?"

"There hasn't been time."

"What happened?"

"We don't know. He was groggy. We put him to bed."

"He's delirious."

"I don't think so."

"What are you doing? Is that your hand?"

"I'm over here."

"*Then who was I touching?*"

"He's not up here," said Peter shakily.

The confusion downstairs was indescribable and growing. Giles was shouting indoors, fighting battles with the rickety kitchen chairs as he tried to find matches on the shelves. Rob and Tanja were calling more softly outside the house, but also blundering inescapably into tables, ladders, old mangers and hayracks, the corpse of the minibus.

There were more voices than there were people.

Josie and Peter felt their way down the steep little stairs to the main bedroom floor. They kept close together. They would have been aware if there had been anybody else with them. They were aware that there was somebody else with them. Josie felt Peter's hand constantly on her arm or shoulder as he followed her down the stairs. She knew that it was his hand. She knew he was frightened. She found that she had become less frightened for herself but more and more so for Simon.

"Simon?" she called. "Simon?"

There was a reply that was not a reply but a scream

of the most abject misery and terror. It was like huge windows shivering to splinters, a fork of lightning petrifying where it scorched, a blaze of darkness.

There was another scream which Josie realized was her own scream, and another which was Peter's. Footsteps ran up and down.

"Simon?" sobbed Josie.

They were not Simon's footsteps.

Giles shouted incoherently from somewhere below. There was a shred of strangled laughter—laughter!—like a piece of tattered fabric in a wind. Here and there voices called and answered, voices without words, voices of miserable children.

"Simon?"

"You will not see him again."

"Who's that? Who said that?"

Step's voice came from the stairs: "Who was that talking?"

"You heard?"

"I can't believe what I heard. God in heaven, there must be matches! It sounded to me like Dorothy Schofield's voice."

"That's impossible!"

"Nothing is impossible tonight. I'm only saying how it sounded to me."

"Of course we'll see him again. It'll be daylight soon."

"In five hours."

"Not so much! It's later than that!"

"Five hours."

"We can't take five hours of this. Simon can't."

"They're looking for him outside."

"He might have gone miles!" said Josie. "Help us search this floor, Step."

"Your father needs me, I think."

It was true that Giles was knocking things over and breaking them as he tried to find matches among the glasses and dishes on the dresser.

"Simon?"

There were voices outside again, not the voices of Rob or Tanja. There was a voice in the hall and the kitchen. There were people moving amongst the furniture in the dark rooms.

"Simon?"

"It's no good calling," said Peter. "If he could hear us, he would have heard us by now."

"Oh God."

"We'll find him by daylight."

"Where? At the bottom of a cliff?"

"We must get a light. Try the light."

There was no light.

"Try the torch again."

There was no light.

Here and there, now and then, indoors and outdoors, rose the voices.

"I've lost Giles," called Step.

"I'm here!"

"I can't get to you. I'm lost. There are things in the way, people in the way . . ."

"People everywhere," whispered Peter.

"We must go outside," said Josie, trying to keep her voice normal.

"There are people outside."

"Simon must be outside."

"Yes. It may be lighter outside."

Josie had the renewed sense that there were people with them on the stairs, in the hall. Giles was still calling for Step. Step seemed to be lost, groping in the wrong part of the house.

If the sky was lighter than the ceilings of the house, the light did not fall into the yard. The buildings were blacker than the sky and the shadows blacker than the buildings.

"Simon? Simon?"

"He's not in there," said Rob from somewhere else.

"Simon, for the love of God!"

"God . . . God . . . God . . ." said an echo which was not an echo but a taunt.

"Who's that?" called Tanja. "Where are you all?"

"Here."

"Here."

"I'm here."

"Here . . . Here . . ." said the echo.

A voice whispered close behind Rob.

Peter cried out when something brushed his face.

"Simon?"

Tanja too gave a cry, at the touch of a hand on her hand.

"It's me," said Peter.

"Oh. You gave me a fright."

"You gave me one."

"Are you scared?"

"Yes."

"Listen," said Tanja, softly, urgently. "There's a thing I just noticed. There are voices, movements, people all around."

"Yes."

"But when Step's around nothing else happens."

"That's ridiculous."

"When we know where she is, there she is, and nothing else happens. Most of the time we don't know where she is. And that's when we hear all this stuff."

"No! She was with my grandfather when . . ."

"He couldn't find her. She wasn't with him."

"A voice answered her in the yard, before you came back. We heard it."

"Did you see her when the voice answered?"

"Yes. I mean . . . It wasn't her voice that answered. It wasn't her voice at all!"

"People can change their voices."

"It came from a different place!"

"She can move. She can move pretty quick."

There was a babble of hysterical laughter, mirthless, from somewhere in the darkness.

"That's her," whispered Tanja.

"Step!" called Peter. "Step!"

"Step!" shouted Giles from inside the house.

"Yes?" said Step's voice from another place. "I'm caught in a kind of maze of I don't know what."

"Simon?" called Josie in the barn. "Simon?"

Tanja whispered, "Who saw that guy watching the house in the early morning?"

"Grandpa did."

"He didn't have his glasses."

"Simon did."

"You believe that?"

"Are you saying Step *invented* him?"

"I just remembered something," whispered Tanja.

"My God, I don't know what put it in my head. When Giles's sister came she said Step was a mechanic in the army in the war. She drove cars and fixed them. She knows about cars."

"Oh," murmured Peter. The implications rushed at him. "I don't believe it."

"She was with the Free French. That means she can speak French."

"She can't!"

"Of course she can. Peter, listen. Giles took a message on the telephone that his sister hadn't gone back to Paris, that she was still around here."

"Was it him?"

"Step was in the village. She telephoned. She put on a funny voice."

"That's a complete guess."

"We're never going to be able to do better than guess. Who took the message that my stepfather's yacht was down the coast from here?"

"Was it Step?"

"Who saw your dad in Toulouse?"

"Oh. That was Step."

"Nobody else saw them. God, Peter, God. They were never here, any of them. They were never anywhere near here. Your dad's in Iceland. My mom's in Turkey. We got cards, remember? It's *impossible* my mom could be near here and not come see me."

"We thought you saw her today."

"No," said Tanja, sounding very much surprised.

"I thought . . ."

"You thought the same about your dad. That he'd make *some* kind of contact if he was anyplace near."

"Yes."

"I bet Dorothy Schofield has been back in Buenos Aires for a month."

"Children? Peter? Tan?" came Josie's voice, in which panic and despair were ringing like electric bells.

"We're here," said Peter.

There was another voice which could just imaginably be Step's keening wordlessly from somewhere.

"Step?"

The reply was not Step's voice, but perhaps it was Step's voice.

"Step?" called Giles.

There was movement in the darkness, now here, now there, and then Step's voice complaining that something had barked her on the shins.

"I suppose you're saying," whispered Peter, "that Step set fire to Etienne's truck."

"Sure."

"Why?"

"It cut us off. It isolated us completely."

"And the priest's car?"

"I don't know. It made us seem crazier. It made them more hostile. Maybe she thought it was fun to burn cars."

"You're mad. What about Gwen?"

"Gwen got a letter she wouldn't talk about or show to anybody, right?"

"It was from her doctor."

"Who said so?"

"I think . . . Step said so."

"How about if that letter was from Dorothy Schofield? They were cousins. They were close when they were kids. How about if that letter had proof of what she told Dad and me?"

"Proof that Step murdered . . ."

"That she untied a rope so her husband drowned in a river. She turned off the lights in your grandmother's house and pushed her downstairs in the dark. Listen, we heard Step's own voice just now, and we didn't hear anything else at all, not just then, no movements, no voices."

"Wait a minute. Those yobs on motorbikes, the day Gwen was killed. They went up the hill. They disappeared."

"They were guys on bikes."

"There were the ones who came here, too. They went round and round the yard."

"They were guys who came here and went round the yard. Thérèse knew them. They were just local kids."

"*Par pitié . . .*"

"Step?"

"*Hahahahaha . . .*"

"So where's Step now?" whispered Tanja.

"She's . . . Well, she was . . ."

"She was fooling around when we got back," said Tanja. "You and Giles were asleep. She was fooling around outside, hooting and moaning, running around and changing voices so it seemed like a lot of people. That was after she sabotaged the lights."

"She doesn't know anything about electricity!"

"Who says she doesn't? She broke the flashlights and hid the matches. Maybe she fixes and unfixes the telephone, uses it when she's alone in the house."

"*Why?* Why would anybody . . . ?"

"Maybe she'll tell us."

"Are you saying she's completely crazy?"

"I guess it's like Giles's sister said. She just goes by different rules, her own rules."

"Cathar rules?"

"Maybe."

Josie's voice was still miserably calling: "Simon? Simon?"

Josie's movements and Rob's could be heard in the thick darkness: other movements also.

"Step?"

"Did you get the credit card?" asked Peter suddenly.

"Step nicked Dad's passport."

"You can't possibly know that!"

"Who else did?"

"Your father—I'm sorry, Tan, but your father did some funny things."

"The bread and wine? That vase? So you all thought he was crazy, and he began to think so too. Step was right with him, remember? Here in the yard in the dark."

"Simon?" called Josie.

A thin scream hung like a wire across the darkness.

"Step?"

Peter whispered, "Why do the locals treat us like lepers? The police, Thérèse, everybody?"

"Step leaked some things. I don't know what—about Josie and my dad, about Gwen's death. It would be easy for her. She was with the Free French in the war. She was often away on her own, or here on her own. We don't know what she was doing or saying."

"That priest came already hating us . . ."

"Of course he did, the gossip he'd heard."

"Um . . . Why are you suddenly so certain about all this?"

"I don't know. I don't know if I am certain. I'm too tired to think. It's like being in a coma. You get insights in a coma."

"Do you?"

"Sure you do. That's how mystics operate."

"Um . . ."

"*Par pitié . . .*"

"Oh, shut up, Step," called Tanja. "The game's over. Where's Simon?"

"Simon," called an echo, Josie or Step or another.

"Simon? What about Simon?" came Giles's voice in the yard. He was fully awake at last; he had found his way out through the hall.

"She said we'd never see him again," said Peter to Tanja.

"Who did? Step?"

"I don't know. I thought she came upstairs. Perhaps she was upstairs already. Someone was."

"What could she have done with him?" said Tanja. Into the exhausted urgency of her voice came a wail of panic and pity.

"We'll make Step tell us," said Peter.

"Then you believe me?"

"I don't know what to believe . . . Step!"

There was an answer which was no answer, a wail higher, thinner, more desperate than that in Tanja's voice.

"Tan," called Josie, "what did you say just now?"

"Step knows where Simon is."

"Step? Where is Step?"

"Where's Step?" shouted Giles.

"*Valérien! Marius! Par pitié . . .*"

"By the end of the barn, near the gate," said Tanja to Peter.

They groped across the yard. Their eyes should have grown used to the dark, but not in this confined and echoing space, in these bottomless shadows. They clattered against chairs and terracotta pots of geraniums. It was impossible to hurry or to avoid things.

"*Hahahahaha,*" screamed a voice from behind them, from the place they had left.

"In the dawn," said Peter.

"That's too late!"

"It may be too late now."

"Oh my God, Peter!"

"What are you saying? What are you two saying?" cried Josie.

"Where is Step? We must find Step!"

There was a sound of frightened sobbing, of a young child puzzled and distressed.

"Simon?"

It was not Simon.

"Step! Step! Step!"

"Oh God, for a light."

Peter could now hear Step's voice in all the voices which were not voices. He did not know if it was only because Tan had put the idea into his head. It was amazing that the old woman could move about so quickly in the dark. She had had a lot of practice. She had been doing it all summer. Why she had done any of it was a question for later.

"For Christ's sake, Step, where are you?" shouted Giles.

"Simon?"

There was a scream from the gateway, perhaps outside. There was a brief flare of light which came and went and illuminated nothing except itself.

"Light!"

"Step has a light!"

"Was that Step?"

"What kind of light was that?"

"Step, what are you doing?"

"Step, where is Simon?"

"We must wait till dawn."

"We can't wait till dawn."

"*Par pitié . . .*"

It was a thin scream from a great distance. Step—Step?—had run away down the track toward the road.

Josie, Rob, and Tanja were by now too tired, after their calamitous day, to do anything more about anything. They were asleep on their feet, until they were too tired to stand. Giles was too old to play hide-and-seek in the dark at four in the morning. Peter continued searching and calling in silence and darkness. There were no voices or movements. Was Tan right? He was bottomlessly tired, but he forced himself to go on and on. At last he stumbled where he stood, among the rocks behind the farm, and subsided to the ground. He fell immediately asleep.

Giles, Josie, Rob, Tanja, Peter all lay sprawled in the abandoned positions of exhaustion, in a silence broken only by the feet or jaws of tiny creatures.

Josie was the first to wake, in the first of the light. She

felt heavy and helpless after the previous day, after a bare three hours' sleep.

She woke the others as she found them: Rob nearby in the yard, Tanja by the gateway, Giles in the open door of the house. Josie now felt panic for Peter as well as Simon. She found him, woken by her shouts, sitting dazedly, not remembering at once why he had gone to sleep among the rocks.

They looked disheveled and abject in the light of the brightening sky.

There was no sign of Step or of Simon.

They were groggy with lack of sleep. They were hungry. There was nothing to eat. They were thirsty. Without electricity, there was no pump to fill the tank by the house or the cistern in the attic. Both should have been full. Both were empty. Somebody had run taps until all the water was exhausted.

There was wine. Even Giles did not want to quench his thirst with wine in the dawn.

They started searching again.

They did not know if they would find Step, or Simon, or both, or neither, or in what state.

Josie sent Peter up the hazardous, unusable ladder to the dovecote. She and Rob stood at the foot of the ladder, ready to catch Peter if the whole thing crumbled.

"Oh, be careful," said Tanja.

Peter glanced at her. He saw that she did not want him to be hurt. She was scruffy and dirty and foreign and beautiful. It was something to bear in mind later.

Very carefully he climbed, with his mother below stifling squeaks of anxiety.

He had not climbed to the dovecote before—it was

nothing but a dirty and useless attic, dangerous, boring. They had all been forbidden to attempt the crazy ladder. Peter had been tempted to defy the rule, but not severely tempted. One look at the ladder and you saw the rule was sensible. Simon might have tried it. It would be safer for Simon because he was lighter.

Peter gulped when he saw the condition of the wood on which he had to put his weight.

He crawled off the top of the ladder onto the enormous beam which spanned the stone walls of the barn. The dovecote was a lump of darkness with small squares of brightness in the sides. Hanging downward from the beam, he groped for the floor and found unfloored joists. He found centuries of dirt and cobwebs. He choked in the dust he stirred with his fingertips.

The others, below, heard him choking. His mother called out.

He called, "It's dark. It's filthy. Wait a minute."

He lowered himself onto the joists, and started crawling across them toward the opposite wall where the windows were. He began to be able to see a little. He found that there were floorboards on the joists, spongy and incomplete. In the corner his fingers found some kind of rough sacking. On the sacking lay a small half-dressed body.

"Please God, please Jesus Christ," said Peter aloud.

He felt breath from the mouth. He felt heartbeats in the chest.

Simon was in far better shape than any of the others, having slept soundly for ten hours.

Josie was in a dreamlike condition, her head swimming with lack of sleep, with joyful relief, with utter confusion about what had happened and why.

Giles was indoors. He was lying down because he was too tired to stand. He had given up searching and shouting for Step. The others had accepted long before that Step was simply not there, and Giles eventually accepted it. He was aghast and completely puzzled and angry at being puzzled. He knew that somebody would have to walk to the village to report Step's disappearance, but nobody was fit to do so yet.

Rob, Tanja, and Peter had subsided together in the shade, having given up searching for Step. Tanja and Peter were showing the resilience of youth, and Rob seemed in much better shape than anybody would have expected. Possibly the strain he had been put under, the efforts he had made, had actually been good for him.

"Step gave me a hot drink," said Simon to Josie. "Sort of chocolate. She brought it up. She said it would help me sleep. I don't remember anything after that."

"Help you sleep. My God, she gave you one of Grandpa's pills. No wonder you don't remember anything."

Simon was astonished at the thought of having been given a sleeping pill. It was such a grown-up thing to have been given.

He said, "But . . . but how did I get up there? Up the ladder?"

"Somebody carried you."

"Who?"

"I think it must have been Step."

Simon looked at her as though she were crazy. She felt crazy. She felt as crazy as Step, for thinking Step could have done anything so crazy.

"You don't weigh much," she said. "Step is stronger than she looks."

"Where is Step?"

"We don't know."

Rob, Tanja, and Peter presently crossed the yard and joined them.

Rob said, "We think we understand about Step. We understand just a little. We're guessing, but we think we understand. The Cathars were real to her, right? Real, present, suffering. They were so real to her that she thought herself into a time warp. She was reliving the crusade, the siege of this place when the people were starved and then slaughtered. She was so sure about this that she pretty well convinced us. But we didn't buy the religious bit, Step's whole Manichaean thing. None of us bought that."

"I did," murmured Simon.

Not hearing him, Rob went on, "So we were the enemy, the invaders. She filled us with disinformation, and we swallowed the whole damned lot. Anna and Dickie Hamlyn, Harry and Angelika Christie, Dorothy Schofield, all thousands of miles away, none of them wishing anybody any harm. Diversionary tactics, made us look everywhere except at her. Made you all think I was crazy, bread and wine in the yard. Made me think I was crazy. Told all kinds of stories to Thérèse, Etienne, the village, the police. I'm sure the kids have this right."

"Why did she try to kill my father with a rock?" asked Josie after a pause.

"She didn't," said Tanja. "She made it look as though Dorothy Schofield hired somebody to try to kill *her*."

"Diversionary tactics? What a lot of trouble she took."

"Not really," said Tanja. "She was enjoying herself. Like when she set fire to those cars. She enjoyed that, I think."

"Where is she now?"

Where was she now? She had run away down to the road in the small hours. At least, she seemed to have done so.

"What did she have against Simon?" said Josie.

After a silence Peter said, "I once read a story about a time traveler. He went back into the past. He opened a door—just some small thing like that. Somebody saw something they wouldn't have seen otherwise. So things happened or didn't happen, and it all built up and up, and it changed the course of history."

"So?" said Josie.

"Who was in charge of that Crusade?"

"Simon de Montfort. Everybody round here knows that . . . Step was changing the course of history, by eliminating him before he began? She was saving the Cathars?"

"She was in a muddle," said Peter. "She got mixed up about when she was living and who people were."

"That's ridiculous," said Josie, as though defending Simon. "Somebody else would have led the crusade."

"No," said Rob. "Remember what Step said in Toulouse? She said it was like Hitler, one man causing a holocaust. Without Simon de Montfort, there wouldn't have been any Albigensian Crusade. I don't know if that's true, but it's what Step thinks."

Step. Where was Step?

After a little Rob said, "I don't think Giles has taken any of this in."

"How do we tell him?" said Josie. "What do we tell him?"

When Giles emerged after three hours' sleep, they told him. They did not need to tell him. He knew.

Had he, by some subconscious process, faced the evidence in his sleep? Had he, in his sleep, faced what he had known about Step for years?

Josie, Tanja, and Peter walked into the village in the late afternoon. They reported the disappearance of Step.

Step remained disappeared. Presumably she had a handful of passports and credit cards. Having rewritten history, she was anonymously relaxing and enjoying herself. Whatever crimes she had committed, she was not committing any by the fact of sitting under a tree somewhere.

Sooner or later, of course, she would be found and brought home. Her oddity would make her recognized, or she would be caught using a credit card that had been stopped. What then? Giles would have to decide, or perhaps the decision would be taken out of his hands. She would end up in a comfortable room with bars over the window, with a shelf of dog-eared books about medieval history.

Problems disappeared with Step's disappearance. Everything was mended; everything worked again. This gave support to the notion that Step had sabotaged things and kept them sabotaged.

"You see?" said Rob to Josie. "The more you think about it, the more everything is explained."

"Not quite," said Josie.

"What isn't explained?"

"I've more than once heard more than one voice."

Rob looked away. He had, too.

"Promise to write?" said Tanja. "Cross your heart?"

"I promise," said Peter. "And in ten years' time we'll get married."

Tanja blushed, which was unlike her.

"It's a deal," she said.

Simon said, as they were packing up the minibus to leave, "I must say good-bye to my friends."

"What friends, darling?"

"Why," said Simon, surprised, "Valérien, Marius, and the others. I can't write to them, you know. And they wouldn't understand if I did."

"Of course," said Josie. "Of course you must say good-bye to your friends."

Domini Taylor is the pseudonym of an internationally acclaimed writer. Previous novels of suspense by the author include MOTHER LOVE, GEMINI, TEACHER'S PET, and PRAYING MANTIS.